J. J. Connington and The Murder Room

〉〉〉 This title is part of The Murder Room, our series dedicated to making available out-of-print or hard-to-find titles by classic crime writers.

Crime fiction has always held up a mirror to society. The Victorians were fascinated by sensational murder and the emerging science of detection; now we are obsessed with the forensic detail of violent death. And no other genre has so captivated and enthralled readers.

Vast troves of classic crime writing have for a long time been unavailable to all but the most dedicated frequenters of second-hand bookshops. The advent of digital publishing means that we are now able to bring you the backlists of a huge range of titles by classic and contemporary crime writers, some of which have been out of print for decades.

From the genteel amateur private eyes of the Golden Age and the femmes fatales of pulp fiction, to the morally ambiguous hard-boiled detectives of mid twentieth-century America and their descendants who walk our twenty-first century streets, The Murder Room has it all. 〉〉〉

The Murder Room
Where Criminal Minds Meet

themurderroom.com

T0352361

J. J. Connington (1880–1947)

Alfred Walter Stewart, who wrote under the pen name J. J. Connington, was born in Glasgow, the youngest of three sons of Reverend Dr Stewart. He graduated from Glasgow University and pursued an academic career as a chemistry professor, working for the Admiralty during the First World War. Known for his ingenious and carefully worked-out puzzles and in-depth character development, he was admired by a host of his better-known contemporaries, including Dorothy L. Sayers and John Dickson Carr, who both paid tribute to his influence on their work. He married Jessie Lily Courts in 1916 and they had one daughter..

By J. J. Connington

Sir Clinton Driffield Mysteries
Murder in the Maze (1927)
Tragedy at Ravensthorpe (1927)
The Case with Nine Solutions (1928)
Mystery at Lynden Sands (1928)
Nemesis at Raynham Parva (1929)
(a.k.a. Grim Vengenace)
The Boathouse Riddle (1931)
The Sweepstake Murders (1931)
The Castleford Conundrum (1932)
The Ha-Ha Case (1934)
(a.k.a. The Brandon Case)
In Whose Dim Shadow (1935)
(a.k.a. The Tau Cross Mystery)
A Minor Operation (1937)
Murder Will Speak (1938)

Truth Comes Limping (1938)
The Twenty-One Clues (1941)
No Past is Dead (1942)
Jack-in-the-Box (1944)
Common Sense Is All You Need (1947)

Supt Ross Mysteries
The Eye in the Museum (1929)
The Two Tickets Puzzle (1930)

Novels
Death at Swaythling Court (1926)
The Dangerfield Talisman (1926)
Tom Tiddler's Island (1933)
(a.k.a. Gold Brick Island)
The Counsellor (1939)
The Four Defences (1940)

Introduction
by
Curtis Evans

During the Golden Age of the detective novel, in the 1920s and 1930s, J. J. Connington stood with fellow crime writers R. Austin Freeman, Cecil John Charles Street and Freeman Wills Crofts as the foremost practitioner in British mystery fiction of the science of pure detection. I use the word 'science' advisedly, for the man behind J. J. Connington, Alfred Walter Stewart, was an esteemed Scottish-born scientist. A 'small, unassuming, moustached polymath', Stewart was 'a strikingly effective lecturer with an excellent sense of humor, fertile imagination and fantastically retentive memory', qualities that also served him well in his fiction. He held the Chair of Chemistry at Queens University, Belfast for twenty-five years, from 1919 until his retirement in 1944.

During roughly this period, the busy Professor Stewart found time to author a remarkable apocalyptic science fiction tale, *Nordenholt's Million* (1923), a mainstream novel, *Almighty Gold* (1924), a collection of essays, *Alias J. J. Connington* (1947), and, between 1926 and 1947, twenty-four mysteries (all but one tales of detection), many of them sterling examples of the Golden Age puzzle-oriented detective novel at its considerable best. 'For those who ask first of all in a detective story for exact and mathematical accuracy in the construction of the plot', avowed a contemporary *London Daily Mail* reviewer, 'there is no author to equal the distinguished scientist who writes under the name of J. J. Connington.'[1]

Alfred Stewart's background as a man of science is reflected in his fiction, not only in the impressive puzzle plot mechanics he devised for his mysteries but in his choices of themes and depictions of characters. Along with Stanley Nordenholt of *Nordenholt's Million*, a novel about a plutocrat's pitiless efforts to preserve a ruthlessly remolded remnant of human life after a global environmental calamity, Stewart's most notable character is Chief Constable Sir Clinton Driffield, the detective in seventeen of the twenty-four Connington crime novels. Driffield is one of crime fiction's most highhanded investigators, occasionally taking on the functions of judge and jury as well as chief of police.

Absent from Stewart's fiction is the hail-fellow-well-met quality found in John Street's works or the religious ethos suffusing those of Freeman Wills Crofts, not to mention the effervescent novel-of-manners style of the British Golden Age Crime Queens Dorothy L. Sayers, Margery Allingham and Ngaio Marsh. Instead we see an often disdainful cynicism about the human animal and a marked admiration for detached supermen with superior intellects. For this reason, reading a Connington novel can be a challenging experience for modern readers inculcated in gentler social beliefs. Yet Alfred Stewart produced a classic apocalyptic science fiction tale in *Nordenholt's Million* (justly dubbed 'exciting and terrifying reading' by the *Spectator*) as well as superb detective novels boasting well-wrought puzzles, bracing characterization and an occasional leavening of dry humor. Not long after Stewart's death in 1947, the Connington novels fell entirely out of print. The recent embrace of Stewart's fiction by Orion's Murder Room imprint is a welcome event indeed, correcting as it does over sixty years of underserved neglect of an accomplished genre writer.

Born in Glasgow on 5 September 1880, Alfred Stewart had significant exposure to religion in his earlier life. His father was William Stewart, longtime Professor of Divinity and Biblical Criticism at Glasgow University, and he married Lily Coats, a daughter of the Reverend Jervis Coats and member of one of

The Boathouse Riddle

J. J. Connington

An Orion book

Copyright © The Professor A. W. Stewart Deceased Trust 1931, 2013

The right of J. J. Connington to be identified as the author of this work has been
asserted in accordance with the Copyright, Designs and Patents Act 1988.

This edition published by
The Orion Publishing Group Ltd
Orion House
5 Upper St Martin's Lane
London WC2H 9EA

An Hachette UK company
A CIP catalogue record for this book is available from the British Library

ISBN 978 1 4719 0603 9

www.orionbooks.co.uk

CONTENTS

Scotland's preeminent Baptist families. Religious sensibility is entirely absent from the Connington corpus, however. A confirmed secularist, Stewart once referred to one of his wife's brothers, the Reverend William Holms Coats (1881–1954), principal of the Scottish Baptist College, as his 'mental and spiritual antithesis', bemusedly adding: 'It's quite an education to see what one would look like if one were turned into one's mirror-image.'

Stewart's J. J. Connington pseudonym was derived from a nineteenth-century Oxford Professor of Latin and translator of Horace, indicating that Stewart's literary interests lay not in pietistic writing but rather in the pre-Christian classics ('I prefer the *Odyssey* to *Paradise Lost*,' the author once avowed). Possessing an inquisitive and expansive mind, Stewart was in fact an uncommonly well-read individual, freely ranging over a variety of literary genres. His deep immersion in French literature and supernatural horror fiction, for example, is documented in his lively correspondence with the noted horologist Rupert Thomas Gould.[2]

It thus is not surprising that in the 1920s the intellectually restless Stewart, having achieved a distinguished middle age as a highly regarded man of science, decided to apply his creative energy to a new endeavor, the writing of fiction. After several years he settled, like other gifted men and women of his generation, on the wildly popular mystery genre. Stewart was modest about his accomplishments in this particular field of light fiction, telling Rupert Gould later in life that 'I write these things [what Stewart called tec yarns] because they amuse me in parts when I am putting them together and because they are the only writings of mine that the public will look at. Also, in a minor degree, because I like to think some people get pleasure out of them.' No doubt Stewart's single most impressive literary accomplishment is *Nordenholt's Million*, yet in their time the two dozen J. J. Connington mysteries did indeed give readers in Great Britain, the United States and other countries much diversionary reading pleasure. Today these works constitute an estimable addition to British crime fiction.

After his 'prentice pastiche mystery, *Death at Swaythling Court* (1926), a rural English country-house tale set in the highly traditional village of Fernhurst Parva, Stewart published another, superior country-house affair, *The Dangerfield Talisman* (1926), a novel about the baffling theft of a precious family heirloom, an ancient, jewel-encrusted armlet. This clever, murderless tale, which likely is the one that the author told Rupert Gould he wrote in under six weeks, was praised in *The Bookman* as 'continuously exciting and interesting' and in the *New York Times Book Review* as 'ingeniously fitted together and, what is more, written with a deal of real literary charm'. Despite its virtues, however, *The Dangerfield Talisman* is not fully characteristic of mature Connington detective fiction. The author needed a memorable series sleuth, more representative of his own forceful personality.

It was the next year, 1927, that saw J. J. Connington make his break to the front of the murdermongerer's pack with a third country-house mystery, *Murder in the Maze*, wherein debuted as the author's great series detective the assertive and acerbic Sir Clinton Driffield, along with Sir Clinton's neighbor and 'Watson', the more genial (if much less astute) Squire Wendover. In this much-praised novel, Stewart's detective duo confronts some truly diabolical doings, including slayings by means of curare-tipped darts in the double-centered hedge maze at a country estate, Whistlefield. No less a fan of the genre than T. S. Eliot praised *Murder in the Maze* for its construction ('we are provided early in the story with all the clues which guide the detective') and its liveliness ('The very idea of murder in a box-hedge labyrinth does the author great credit, and he makes full use of its possibilities'). The delighted Eliot concluded that

Murder in the Maze was 'a really first-rate detective story'. For his part, the critic H. C. Harwood declared in *The Outlook* that with the publication of *Murder in the Maze* Connington demanded and deserved 'comparison with the masters'. 'Buy, borrow, or – anyhow – get hold of it', he amusingly advised. Two decades later, in his 1946 critical essay 'The Grandest Game in the World', the great locked-room detective novelist John Dickson Carr echoed Eliot's assessment of the novel's virtuoso setting, writing: 'These 1920s [. . .] thronged with sheer brains. What would be one of the best possible settings for violent death? J. J. Connington found the answer, with *Murder in the Maze*.' Certainly in retrospect *Murder in the Maze* stands as one of the finest English country-house mysteries of the 1920s, cleverly yet fairly clued, imaginatively detailed and often grimly suspenseful. As the great American true-crime writer Edmund Lester Pearson noted in his review of *Murder in the Maze* in *The Outlook*, this Connington novel had everything that one could desire in a detective story: 'A shrubbery maze, a hot day, and somebody potting at you with an air gun loaded with darts covered with a deadly South-American arrow-poison – *there* is a situation to wheedle two dollars out of anybody's pocket.'[3]

Staying with what had worked so well for him to date, Stewart the same year produced yet another country-house mystery, *Tragedy at Ravensthorpe*, an ingenious tale of murders and thefts at the ancestral home of the Chacewaters, old family friends of Sir Clinton Driffield. There is much clever matter in *Ravensthorpe*. Especially fascinating is the author's inspired integration of faerie folklore into his plot. Stewart, who had a lifelong – though skeptical – interest in paranormal phenomena, probably was inspired in this instance by the recent hubbub over the Cottingly Faeries photographs that in the early 1920s had famously duped, among other individuals, Arthur Conan Doyle.[4] As with *Murder in the Maze*, critics raved about this new Connington mystery. In the *Spectator*, for example, a reviewer hailed *Tragedy at Ravensthorpe* in the strongest terms, declaring of the novel: 'This is more than a good detective tale. Alike in plot, characterization, and literary style, it is a work of art.'

In 1928 there appeared two additional Sir Clinton Driffield detective novels, *Mystery at Lynden Sands* and *The Case with Nine Solutions*. Once again there was great praise for the latest Conningtons. H. C. Harwood, the critic who had so much admired *Murder in the Maze*, opined of *Mystery at Lynden Sands* that it 'may just fail of being the detective story of the century', while in the United States author and book reviewer Frederic F. Van de Water expressed nearly as high an opinion of *The Case with Nine Solutions*. 'This book is a thoroughbred of a distinguished lineage that runs back to "The Gold Bug" of [Edgar Allan] Poe,' he avowed. 'It represents the highest type of detective fiction.' In both of these Connington novels, Stewart moved away from his customary country-house milieu, setting *Lynden Sands* at a fashionable beach resort and *Nine Solutions* at a scientific research institute. *Nine Solutions* is of particular interest today, I think, for its relatively frank sexual subject matter and its modern urban setting among science professionals, which rather resembles the locales found in P. D. James' classic detective novels *A Mind to Murder* (1963) and *Shroud for a Nightingale* (1971).

By the end of the 1920s, J. J. Connington's critical reputation had achieved enviable heights indeed. At this time Stewart became one of the charter members of the Detection Club, an assemblage of the finest writers of British detective fiction that included, among other distinguished individuals, Agatha Christie, Dorothy L. Sayers and G. K. Chesterton. Certainly Victor Gollancz, the British publisher of the J. J. Connington mysteries, did not stint praise for the author, informing readers that 'J. J. Connington is now established as, in the opinion of many, the greatest living master of the story of pure detection. He is one of those who, discarding all the superfluities, has made of deductive fiction a genuine minor art, with its own laws and its own conventions.'

Such warm praise for J. J. Connington makes it all the more surprising that at this juncture the esteemed author tinkered with his successful formula by dispensing with his original series detective. In the fifth Clinton Driffield detective novel, *Nemesis at Raynham Parva* (1929), Alfred Walter Stewart, rather like Arthur Conan Doyle before him, seemed with a dramatic dénouement to have devised his popular series detective's permanent exit from the fictional stage (read it and see for yourself). The next two Connington detective novels, *The Eye in the Museum* (1929) and *The Two Tickets Puzzle* (1930), have a different series detective, Superintendent Ross, a rather dull dog of a policeman. While both these mysteries are competently done – the railway material in *The Two Tickets Puzzle* is particularly effective and should have appeal today – the presence of Sir Clinton Driffield (no superfluity he!) is missed.

Probably Stewart detected that the public minded the absence of the brilliant and biting Sir Clinton, for the Chief Constable – accompanied, naturally, by his friend Squire Wendover – triumphantly returned in 1931 in *The Boathouse Riddle*, another well-constructed criminous country-house affair. Later in the year came *The Sweepstake Murders*, which boasts the perennially popular tontine multiple-murder plot, in this case a rapid succession of puzzling suspicious deaths afflicting the members of a sweepstake syndicate that has just won nearly £250,000.[5] Adding piquancy to this plot is the fact that Wendover is one of the imperiled syndicate members. Altogether the novel is, as the late Jacques Barzun and his colleague Wendell Hertig Taylor put it in *A Catalogue of Crime* (1971, 1989), their magisterial survey of detective fiction, 'one of Connington's best conceptions'.

Stewart's productivity as a fiction writer slowed in the 1930s, so that, barring the year 1938, at most only one new Connington appeared annually. However, in 1932 Stewart produced one of the best Connington mysteries, *The Castleford Conundrum*. A classic country-house detective novel, Castleford introduces to readers Stewart's most delightfully unpleasant set of greedy relations and one of his most deserving murderees, Winifred Castleford. Stewart also fashions a wonderfully rich puzzle plot, full of meaty material clues for the reader's delectation. *Castleford* presented critics with no conundrum over its quality. 'In *The Castleford Conundrum* Mr Connington goes to work like an accomplished chess player. The moves in the games his detectives are called on to play are a delight to watch,' raved the reviewer for the *Sunday Times*, adding that 'the clues would have rejoiced Mr. Holmes' heart.' For its part, the *Spectator* concurred in the *Sunday Times*' assessment of the novel's masterfully constructed plot: 'Few detective stories show such sound reasoning as that by which the Chief Constable brings the crime home to the culprit.' Additionally, E. C. Bentley, much admired himself as the author of the landmark detective novel *Trent's Last Case*, took time to praise Connington's purely literary virtues, noting: 'Mr Connington has never written better, or drawn characters more full of life.'

With *Tom Tiddler's Island* in 1933 Stewart produced a different sort of Connington, a criminal-gang mystery in the rather more breathless style of such hugely popular English thriller writers as Sapper, Sax Rohmer, John Buchan and Edgar Wallace (in violation of the strict detective fiction rules of Ronald Knox, there is even a secret passage in the novel). Detailing the startling discoveries made by a newlywed couple honeymooning on a remote Scottish island, *Tom Tiddler's Island* is an atmospheric and entertaining tale, though it is not as mentally stimulating for armchair sleuths as Stewart's true detective novels. The title, incidentally, refers to an ancient British children's game, 'Tom Tiddler's Ground', in which one child tries to hold a height against other children.

After his fictional Scottish excursion into thrillerdom, Stewart returned the next year to his English country-house roots with *The Ha-Ha Case* (1934), his last masterwork in this classic mystery setting (for elucidation of non-British readers, a ha-ha is a sunken wall, placed so as to delineate property boundaries while not obstructing views). Although *The Ha-Ha Case* is not set in Scotland, Stewart drew inspiration for the novel from a notorious Scottish true crime, the 1893 Ardlamont murder case. From the facts of the Ardlamont affair Stewart drew several of the key characters in *The Ha-Ha Case*, as well as the circumstances of the novel's murder (a shooting 'accident' while hunting), though he added complications that take the tale in a new direction.[6]

In newspaper reviews both Dorothy L. Sayers and 'Francis Iles' (crime novelist Anthony Berkeley Cox) highly praised this latest mystery by 'The Clever Mr Connington', as he was now dubbed on book jackets by his new English publisher, Hodder & Stoughton. Sayers particularly noted the effective characterisation in *The Ha-Ha Case*: 'There is no need to say that Mr Connington has given us a sound and interesting plot, very carefully and ingeniously worked out. In addition, there are the three portraits of the three brothers, cleverly and rather subtly characterised, of the [governess], and of Inspector Hinton, whose admirable qualities are counteracted by that besetting sin of the man who has made his own way: a jealousy of delegating responsibility.' The reviewer for the *Times Literary Supplement* detected signs that the sardonic Sir Clinton Driffield had begun mellowing with age: 'Those who have never really liked Sir Clinton's perhaps excessively soldierly manner will be surprised to find that he makes his discovery not only by the pure light of intelligence, but partly as a reward for amiability and tact, qualities in which the Inspector [Hinton] was strikingly deficient.' This is true enough, although the classic Sir Clinton emerges a number of times in the novel, as in his subtly sarcastic recurrent backhanded praise of Inspector Hinton: 'He writes a first class report.'

Clinton Driffield returned the next year in the detective novel *In Whose Dim Shadow* (1935), a tale set in a recently erected English suburb, the denizens of which seem to have committed an impressive number of indiscretions, including sexual ones. The intriguing title of the British edition of the novel is drawn from a poem by the British historian Thomas Babington Macaulay: 'Those trees in whose dim shadow/The ghastly priest doth reign/The priest who slew the slayer/And shall himself be slain.' Stewart's puzzle plot in *In Whose Dim Shadow* is well clued and compelling, the kicker of a closing paragraph is a classic of its kind and, additionally, the author paints some excellent character portraits. I fully concur with the *Sunday Times*' assessment of the tale: 'Quiet domestic murder, full of the neatest detective points [. . .] These are not the detective's stock figures, but fully realised human beings.'[7]

Uncharacteristically for Stewart, nearly twenty months elapsed between the publication of *In Whose Dim Shadow* and his next book, *A Minor Operation* (1937). The reason for the author's delay in production was the onset in 1935–36 of the afflictions of cataracts and heart disease (Stewart ultimately succumbed to heart disease in 1947). Despite these grave health complications, Stewart in late 1936 was able to complete *A Minor Operation*, a first-rate Clinton Driffield story of murder and a most baffling disappearance. A *Times Literary Supplement* reviewer found that *A Minor Operation* treated the reader 'to exactly the right mixture of mystification and clue' and that, in addition to its impressive construction, the novel boasted 'character-drawing above the average' for a detective novel.

Alfred Stewart's final eight mysteries, which appeared between 1938 and 1947, the year of the author's death, are, on the whole, a somewhat weaker group of tales than the sixteen that appeared between 1926 and 1937, yet they are not without interest. In 1938 Stewart for the last time managed to publish two detective novels, *Truth Comes Limping* and *For Murder Will Speak* (also published as *Murder Will Speak*). The latter tale is much the superior of the two, having an interesting suburban setting and a bevy of female characters found to have motives when a contemptible philandering businessman meets with foul play. Sexual neurosis plays a major role in *For Murder Will Speak*, the ever-thorough Stewart obviously having made a study of the subject when writing the novel. The somewhat squeamish reviewer for *Scribner's Magazine* considered the subject matter of *For Murder Will Speak* 'rather unsavory at times', yet this individual conceded that the novel nevertheless made 'first-class reading for those who enjoy a good puzzle intricately worked out'. 'Judge Lynch' in the *Saturday Review* apparently had no such moral reservations about the latest Clinton Driffield murder case, avowing simply of the novel: 'They don't come any better'.

Over the next couple of years Stewart again sent Sir Clinton Driffield temporarily packing, replacing him with a new series detective, a brash radio personality named Mark Brand, in *The Counsellor* (1939) and *The Four Defences* (1940). The better of these two novels is *The Four Defences*, which Stewart based on another notorious British true-crime case, the Alfred Rouse blazing-car murder. (Rouse is believed to have fabricated his death by murdering an unknown man, placing the dead man's body in his car and setting the car on fire, in the hope that the murdered man's body would be taken for his.) Though admittedly a thinly characterised academic exercise in ratiocination, Stewart's *Four Defences* surely is also one of the most complexly plotted Golden Age detective novels and should delight devotees of classical detection. Taking the Rouse blazing-car affair as his theme, Stewart composes from it a stunning set of diabolically ingenious criminal variations. 'This is in the cold-blooded category which [. . .] excites a crossword puzzle kind of interest,' the reviewer for the *Times Literary Supplement* acutely noted of the novel. 'Nothing in the Rouse case would prepare you for these complications upon complications [. . .] What they prove is that Mr Connington has the power of penetrating into the puzzle-corner of the brain. He leaves it dazedly wondering whether in the records of actual crime there can be any dark deed to equal this in its planned convolutions.'

Sir Clinton Driffield returned to action in the remaining four detective novels in the Connington oeuvre, *The Twenty-One Clues* (1941), *No Past is Dead* (1942), *Jack-in-the-Box* (1944) and *Commonsense is All You Need* (1947), all of which were written as Stewart's heart disease steadily worsened and reflect to some extent his diminishing physical and mental energy. Although *The Twenty-One Clues* was inspired by the notorious Hall-Mills double murder case – probably the most publicised murder case in the United States in the 1920s – and the American critic and novelist Anthony Boucher commended *Jack-in-the-Box*, I believe the best of these later mysteries is *No Past Is Dead*, which Stewart partly based on a bizarre French true-crime affair, the 1891 Achet-Lepine murder case.[8] Besides providing an interesting background for the tale, the ailing author managed some virtuoso plot twists, of the sort most associated today with that ingenious Golden Age Queen of Crime, Agatha Christie.

What Stewart with characteristic bluntness referred to as 'my complete crack-up' forced his retirement from Queen's University in 1944. 'I am afraid,' Stewart wrote a friend, the chemist and forensic scientist F. Gerald Tryhorn, in August 1946, eleven months before his death, 'that I shall never be much use again. Very stupidly, I tried for a session to combine a full course of lecturing with angina pectoris; and ended up by establishing that the two are immiscible.' He added that since retiring in 1944, he had been physically 'limited to my house, since even a fifty-yard crawl brings on the usual cramps'. Stewart completed his essay collection and a final novel before he died at his study desk in his Belfast home on 1 July 1947, at the age of sixty-six. When death came to the author he was busy at work, writing.

More than six decades after Alfred Walter Stewart's death, his J. J. Connington fiction is again available to a wider audience of classic-mystery fans, rather than strictly limited to a select company of rare-book collectors with deep pockets. This is fitting for an individual who was one of the finest writers of British genre fiction between the two world wars. 'Heaven forfend that you should imagine I take myself for anything out of the common in the tec yarn stuff,' Stewart once self-deprecatingly declared in a letter to Rupert Gould. Yet, as contemporary critics recognised, as a writer of detective and science fiction Stewart indeed was something out of the common. Now more modern readers can find this out for themselves. They have much good sleuthing in store.

1. For more on Street, Crofts and particularly Stewart, see Curtis Evans, *Masters of the 'Humdrum' Mystery: Cecil John Charles Street, Freeman Wills Crofts, Alfred Walter Stewart and the British Detective Novel, 1920–1961* (Jefferson, NC: McFarland, 2012). On the academic career of Alfred Walter Stewart, see his entry in *Oxford Dictionary of National Biography* (London and New York: Oxford University Press, 2004), vol. 52, 627–628.
2. The Gould-Stewart correspondence is discussed in considerable detail in *Masters of the 'Humdrum' Mystery*. For more on the life of the fascinating Rupert Thomas Gould, see Jonathan Betts, *Time Restored: The Harrison Timekeepers and R. T. Gould, the*

Man Who Knew (Almost) Everything (London and New York: Oxford University Press, 2006) and *Longitude,* the 2000 British film adaptation of Dava Sobel's book *Longitude:The True Story of a Lone Genius Who Solved the Greatest Scientific Problem of His Time* (London: Harper Collins, 1995), which details Gould's restoration of the marine chronometers built by in the eighteenth century by the clockmaker John Harrison.

3. Potential purchasers of *Murder in the Maze* should keep in mind that $2 in 1927 is worth over $26 today.

4. In a 1920 article in *The Strand Magazine,* Arthur Conan Doyle endorsed as real prank photographs of purported fairies taken by two English girls in the garden of a house in the village of Cottingley. In the aftermath of the Great War Doyle had become a fervent believer in Spiritualism and other paranormal phenomena. Especially embarrassing to Doyle's admirers today, he also published *The Coming of the Faeries* (1922), wherein he argued that these mystical creatures genuinely existed. 'When the spirits came in, the common sense oozed out,' Stewart once wrote bluntly to his friend Rupert Gould of the creator of Sherlock Holmes. Like Gould, however, Stewart had an intense interest in the subject of the Loch Ness Monster, believing that he, his wife and daughter had sighted a large marine creature of some sort in Loch Ness in 1935. A year earlier Gould had authored *The Loch Ness Monster and Others*, and it was this book that led Stewart, after he made his 'Nessie' sighting, to initiate correspondence with Gould.

5. A tontine is a financial arrangement wherein shareowners in a common fund receive annuities that increase in value with the death of each participant, with the entire amount of the fund going to the last survivor. The impetus that the tontine provided to the deadly creative imaginations of Golden Age mystery writers should be sufficiently obvious.

6. At Ardlamont, a large country estate in Argyll, Cecil Hambrough died from a gunshot wound while hunting. Cecil's tutor, Alfred John Monson, and another man, both of whom were out hunting with Cecil, claimed that Cecil had accidentally shot himself, but Monson was arrested and tried for Cecil's murder. The verdict delivered was 'not proven', but Monson was then – and is today – considered almost certain to have been guilty of the murder. On the Ardlamont case, see William Roughead, *Classic Crimes* (1951; repr., New York: New York Review Books Classics, 2000), 378–464.

7. For the genesis of the title, see Macaulay's 'The Battle of the Lake

Regillus', from his narrative poem collection *Lays of Ancient Rome*. In this poem Macaulay alludes to the ancient cult of Diana Nemorensis, which elevated its priests through trial by combat. Study of the practices of the Diana Nemorensis cult influenced Sir James George Frazer's cultural interpretation of religion in his most renowned work, *The Golden Bough: A Study in Magic and Religion*. As with *Tom Tiddler's Island* and *The Ha-Ha Case* the title *In Whose Dim Shadow* proved too esoteric for Connington's American publishers, Little, Brown and Co., who altered it to the more prosaic *The Tau Cross Mystery*.

8. Stewart analysed the Achet-Lepine case in detail in 'The Mystery of Chantelle', one of the best essays in his 1947 collection *Alias J. J. Connington*.

CHAPTER I: THE OWNER OF SILVER GROVE

PUNCTUALITY was a virtue on which Wendover piqued himself; and it was with satisfaction that he noticed the signal drop just as he drew up his car in the little station yard. He got out of the driving seat, nodded in response to a porter's salute, and passed through the booking office on to the platform.

Wendover's world was a pleasant one. Things go smoothly for a man with kindly blue eyes, a humorous mouth under a grey moustache, and a friendly manner which can set even the shy at their ease in a moment. His small estate, the County Council, and his work as Justice of the Peace kept him sufficiently occupied without robbing him of leisure; and though quite devoid of vanity, he was pleasantly conscious of being a well-known and well-liked figure throughout the countryside.

He sauntered along the platform, examining the neat flower beds and inspecting with approval the ornamental lettering "AMBLEDOWN" which stretched across a slope of turf at the side. That was just how a country station ought to look. Nice to see the station staff taking a pride in the place, he reflected. Something at his feet attracted his attention; and, looking down, he discovered the station cat, with tail erect, rubbing itself enthusiastically against his legs. He stooped, scratched it politely under the

1

ear, and then, as a whistle warned him of the train's approach, he shooed the cat gently away from the line and moved up the platform to where he expected the first-class carriages to stop.

When the train came to a standstill, the door in front of Wendover opened, and a young man stepped out. At the sight of a girl's figure in the background, Wendover's hand went to his cap.

"I thought you would be coming down by car," he said, as she reached the platform, "so I hardly expected to be the first person to see you when you arrived. We're old-fashioned people hereabouts, so may I bid you 'Welcome home', Mrs. Keith-Westerton?"

The bride acknowledged the greeting, shyly but with evident pleasure. Her husband hastened to explain their presence.

"We'd meant to come down by road, of course. Got stuck at the last moment, though. A mudguard got a bit twisted in a slight collision, so we had to leave the car behind and take the train instead. Chauffeur's to bring it on to-morrow."

"I can drive you over to Silver Grove, if you haven't arranged for anything to meet you," Wendover suggested.

"That's all right, thanks. Very good of you, but we shall be all right. I wired from town. And, by the way, we're not going to Silver Grove. We're camping at the Dower House until we can get Silver Grove fitted up—electric light, central heating, modernising the old place a bit before we go into it."

Then, seeing Wendover's eye wandering along the train, he added:

"Meeting some one? Mustn't let us detain you, then."

Wendover, glad of his dismissal, moved off hastily in search of his guest; but a couple of steps along the platform his eye caught a figure which stood out incongruously from the rest of the passengers: an obvious French priest in cassock and buckled shoes. For an instant, Wendover's face showed surprise at this unaccustomed apparition; then, apparently, he recollected something which accounted for it.

His expression changed as he caught sight of a man in a suit of inconspicuous tweed, with a rod case in his hand; and he hurried past the priest to greet the Chief Constable of the county. Sir Clinton Driffield, seeing his host momentarily engaged on the arrival of the train, had secured a porter and collected his luggage.

"Glad to see you again, Clinton," Wendover exclaimed, as he shook hands. "Is this all your stuff?"

He turned to the porter.

"Put it in the back seat of my car, Jarvis, please."

"I'll keep the rod," Sir Clinton said, as the porter put out his hand for it. "You can put the golf clubs with the rest of the things."

They followed the porter out of the station and watched him stack the suit cases and golf clubs in the back of the car. Wendover, glancing around, noticed that luggage was being strapped to the grids of two other motors. The French priest had joined the bride and her husband; and it was evident from the way in which they were talking together that he was more than a casual acquaintance. A little apart

3

from the group, beside the second car, were two people whom Wendover took for a French maid and Keith-Westerton's man. Sir Clinton's glance ranged with apparent incuriosity over the little party, dwelt for a moment on the priest's face, and then seemed idly to examine the remaining passengers who were leaving the station in twos and threes.

"That's all?" Wendover demanded.

"Everything's in, sir."

The porter, generously tipped, closed the door. Wendover, with a friendly gesture to the Keith-Westertons, started his car and drove off through the little town.

"Nothing seriously wrong with this health of yours, Clinton?" he asked abruptly, as they left the streets behind them and came out into the open country.

The Chief Constable shook his head reassuringly.

"I haven't taken a holiday for the last two years," he explained. "Something's always seemed to come in the way at the wrong time; and, after all, I'd sooner be at work than idle—if it's the kind of work I like. But this summer I felt I was getting a bit stale; too much office work, with no amusing breaks in it, was making me a dull boy. So I called in a friendly medical and explained that I was suffering from mental indigestion due to a monotonous diet of official papers and administrative details—no food for a strong man. He saw the point at once and prescribed a couple of months' leave, to be spent in the open air by preference. Fishing, he thought, might be good for the soul. So I thought of the comforts of Talgarth Grange and the fish in your lake, naturally; and here I am.

You can take off that expression of concern; it isn't needed, really. There's nothing the matter with me, except that I feel bored stiff."

"Well, that's a relief," Wendover answered, in a tone which showed he was glad to be reassured. "Your note was a bit laconic and when you mentioned two months' leave, I was afraid there was something seriously wrong with you."

"No. A grateful county owes me a couple of summer holidays, so I'm taking payment in a lump, that's all. Lucky I've got a good man to take over the running while I'm off. By the way, what about the fishing? You've stocked the lake with Loch Leven trout, you said?"

Wendover nodded in confirmation.

"I've done hardly any fishing myself, so far. Just now, of course, the streams are all a bit low after this dry weather; but there are a few hundredweight of trout in the lake, if you can get them. By the way, that reminds me, I've put a new boathouse since you were here last. The old place was tumbling to pieces, so I've pulled it down and put up a rather nice affair instead. You'll see it as we drive along the lakeside."

Sir Clinton suppressed a smile. He remembered quite well that the shortest route from the station to Talgarth Grange lay through Talgarth village, south of the lake and half a mile away from it at the nearest approach. The northerly route, on the opposite side of the lake, ran practically by the waterside, and from it a good view of the new boathouse would be obtained. Wendover was evidently delighted with his new toy, since he was prepared to go a mile or two out of his way in order to show it off to his guest.

The Chief Constable pulled out his case and lighted a cigarette.

"And what's the news of the great metropolis?" he asked lazily. "Parish pump still in working order, I hope? Guides, Scouts, Cubs, and Rangers meet as usual? Church Organ Fund struggling grimly towards solvency? Flower Show well over and Bazaars looming menacingly on the horizon? How nice and restful it all sounds! You're a lucky man, Squire."

"My gardener got two Firsts and a Second at the Flower Show," Wendover retorted almost seriously.

He liked the old nickname "Squire" which Sir Clinton used. It fitted him aptly enough, he knew, and the old-fashioned ring of it appealed to him. Though by no means behind the times, he had a faint, half-regretful liking for things which reminded him of older days; and, quite unconsciously, his manners suggested a leisurely courtesy dating from an earlier epoch.

"Good man, that gardener of yours," Sir Clinton said approvingly. "If you don't mind, I want to ask him about one or two things of mine. My fellow's quite good, but your head man knows just what's what."

He shifted slightly in his seat to bring his shoulders to just the right inclination for comfort.

"I'm going to enjoy myself, Squire. I feel it in my bones. Now that I've cut free from my office, I begin to believe that a holiday was what I really did need. Think of going out in the dew in the morning and fishing strenuously for hours. Think of coming home, radiant with triumph, carrying a couple of superior-sized minnows by a bit of grass strung through their gills, just to show that there's been no waste of time. And all the pleasant tales, of an evening, about the big 'uns that just got away."

Wendover smiled at the picture. Sir Clinton's picture hardly did justice to his skill with a rod.

"And meanwhile, I suppose, crime will be having it all its own way while you go about with a pickle bottle, netting tittlebats?"

"My first rise!" Sir Clinton said with a smile. "I thought I could tempt you, Squire. We had a pair of white gloves at the Assizes this time, and of course I wanted to boast about it. Serious crime in the County is down to nil. Just as well you J. P.'s are unpaid; we've left you nothing to do."

"H'm!" said Wendover chaffingly. "There's a serious crime wave blowing up over this part of the country, but my colleagues and I are nipping it in the bud, free of charge. Yesterday I fined a poor devil five bob for aggravated chimney-on-fire; and he had to pay costs as well."

"The iron hand, eh? Well, a J. P. who can nip a wave in the bud ought to be capable of anything; so I suppose we can sleep quietly in our beds. Let's change the subject before you smother yourself in compliments. I had a rather rum fellow passenger in my compartment coming down."

"That French priest, you mean?" Wendover interrupted.

"That French priest, as you say," Sir Clinton went

on indolently. "I fell into talk with him on the way; thought perhaps he might feel in need of assistance. Not a bit of it. He'd never been in this country before; but he talks English with very few slips, wherever he picked it up. A clever cove; very alert, I found him, when I could get him to talk. But if I were choosing a confessor, I don't know that he'd be quite the man for my money."

"What makes you say that?" Wendover demanded, with more interest in his tone than Sir Clinton had expected.

"He struck me as being rather likely to be on the hard side," the Chief Constable answered. "I couldn't quite imagine him taking a lax view of things. In fact, I got the impression that if we turned the clock back a few hundred years he'd make an excellent inquisitor. The kind of man one feels would go any length to stamp out sin, and think himself justified in doing it. A sort of cold fanatic."

"Oh, indeed?" said Wendover, with little enthusiasm in his tone.

Sir Clinton glanced at his host's face.

"I gathered that he's like myself at present—on a sort of holiday and spending it hereabouts, attached to some local family or other—that young couple you spoke to on the platform, evidently. Who are they? I didn't know you had any Catholic magnates round about this district."

"You know Silver Grove, don't you, Clinton?"

"The house a mile or so away from yours, at the other end of the lake? Their ground marches with yours on the west side, doesn't it? Yes?"

8

Sir Clinton recognised that now he was "for it", and entirely through his own doing. It was Wendover's pride that he took a keen interest in his own country-side; he liked to know who was who, not from any desire for mere gossip, but simply because, as he put it, "a man ought to take some decent interest in his neighbours." He had, neatly docketed in his memory, a vast amount of information of this sort; and when he was questioned about any one, he drew rather lavishly on his stores, so that the putter of an idle question was apt to be swamped by a flood of information which he had never desired to elicit. Sir Clinton, knowing the symptoms of old, resigned himself to his fate.

"That's the place," Wendover confirmed. "Well, Silver Grove has been in the Keith-Westerton family for generations. They're among the oldest families in the district. But the place has been shut up for ages. Young Keith-Westerton had a long minority. His mother died when he was born; and his father died too, when the boy was a mere child—1906 or 1907, if I'm not mistaken. Round about then, at any rate. So the estate was put into the hands of an agent—a good man—and the boy himself was brought up by a couple of maiden aunts."

"Why didn't they live here, seeing that the estate belonged to them?" Sir Clinton inquired.

"Oh, they lived up in the North somewhere. They had a small place of their own and there was no point in leaving it. The boy didn't miss anything on that account; and one could hardly expect them to dig themselves up by the roots just for the sake of living down here in somebody else's house, could one? I knew them only slightly, but I can remember them vividly; for they impressed themselves, somehow, just by their total lack of any desire to impress one. Dear old ladies, you know, but about half a century behind the times, even on their first birthdays, and without the slightest inclination to catch up after that. Silver hair and bonnets, and white hands, and soft, diffident voices. When I knew them, they dressed always in black and white. I expect in their young days they may have worn white and black in summer time; but I couldn't imagine them varying from these two schemes even when they were in their twenties. I know they wore bonnets to their dying day, and I've often wondered how they managed to get that brand of headgear as time went on—had them specially made, I suppose. Survivals, that's what they were; and yet, you know, rather nice survivals."

"They must have had character, evidently, if they stuck to bonnets as late as that. It sounds hardly credible."

"Fact, all the same," Wendover assured him. "Well, as you can guess, two old ladies of that type didn't know much about the world; but that didn't prevent them having very clear views about it. They thought it was a dreadful place, full of all sorts of temptations and so forth. They doted on the boy, you understand; and naturally, with these notions of theirs, they wanted to shield him from contamination as long as they possibly could. They bathed the cub in that atmosphere of theirs: quiet manners, soft voices, sub-dued tones; and it must have sunk in to some extent just because they themselves were such nice old things in their faded way. Their worst expression of disapproval, I remember, took the form of saying that something or other 'wasn't quite nice'; and even that was uttered in a faintly apologetic tone, as though things of that sort shouldn't really be mentioned at all. You can guess how many things never *were* mentioned at all. Nothing ever rippled that backwater."

"He must have found it a change when he went to school," Sir Clinton suggested.

"School! He never went to school," Wendover continued. "These two old ladies had a perfect dread of the influence a Public School might have on the boy. I expect they'd read 'Tom Brown's Schooldays' and got their ideas out of that. Public Schools were sinks of vice; though I'm sure, if you'd asked them, you'd have found they hadn't the foggiest idea of what they meant by vice. Flashman, I take it, was their idea of vice incarnate.

"No! No Public School for Colin! Instead of that, they engaged a private tutor for the boy. I saw him once—just the sort of tutor one would expect two old ladies to pick out—a rather namby-pamby cove on the whole, quite in agreement with all the old ladies' ideas. The only thing I liked about him was that he taught the cub to box fairly decently. I suspect he must have done that on the quiet; for I'm quite certain the two aunts would have said, gently but definitely, that it 'wasn't quite nice' if they'd got wind of it."

"His young friends must have found him unsophisticated."

"He hadn't any young friends. The old ladies didn't encourage great, rough, noisy boys to come about the premises. One never knew what sort of corrupting influence might be among them. He and this tutor fellow were great friends, and he didn't miss youngsters much."

"The Army training must have waked him up, surely."

"He was only eighteen when the War ended—never was in even a cadet battalion. The old ladies lasted through the War and for a year or two longer. They must have been about eighty by that time. They were only 'Aunts' by courtesy, really; I think great-aunts would be nearer the truth. Anyhow, they lived just long enough to see Colin come of age; and then, I suppose, they said '*Nunc dimittis*' or an equivalent, for they died shortly after that, within a week or two of each other. Colin came into their money as well as Silver Grove. I forget exactly how much it amounted to; but I remember when I saw the wills in the *Times* I thought he'd got more to play with than might be good for a boy brought up on that plan."

Sir Clinton, knowing that Wendover himself was a rich man, could guess that young Keith-Westerton must have inherited a very considerable sum.

"And when he got out of leading strings . . . ?" he asked.

"Well, you remember what the post-war boom was like, when everybody seemed to have plenty of cash to spend and thought there was more coming in after the first lot was done. And you remember, I expect,

12

what a godsend the general social mix-up was for the class that you're supposed to keep an eye on. Every goose laying golden eggs and getting robbed of 'em double-quick, by fair means or foul. That was the time when people began to get a bit of their own back, after the repressions of the War. And young Keith-Westerton had been repressed, too, and for longer than the four years of the War."

"So the old ladies' training hadn't really got home?"

"Well, for a youngster to plunge straight into that kind of world, with his pockets stuffed with cash and no one to look after him . . . I don't think any training would have done much good unless the cub had it in him to profit by it. And it seems young Keith-Westerton's training hadn't become second nature by any means. Once he got his claws on the dollars and tasted pleasure, he fairly went the pace. So I gathered, at any rate. He'd no friends of his own age to tell him he was making an ass of himself when he went too far; and of course it's a waste of breath for older people to step in. He got in with some pretty queer fish, I'm told, and they skinned him efficiently, as long as he gave them the chance."

"I seem to have heard this sort of tale before," Sir Clinton protested. "He wasn't saved by the love of a pure woman, or anything of that sort, was he? I'll believe it, if you insist; but I'd really rather not make the effort."

"Calm yourself," said Wendover. "I won't strain your credulity to that extent; for, as a matter of fact, I don't know what waked him up in the end. Something did, apparently, and pretty sharply too, I'm inclined to think. Probably something happened to open his eyes, and he saw what a fool he'd been making of himself. Anyhow, he seems to have chucked over his gang of parasites, male and female as the Lord created them, and he settled down to a less rackety life."

"Sudden attack of common sense, perhaps."

"Short and sharp, then, I should judge," Wendover qualified. "For I shouldn't give young Keith-Westerton a prize in a brain competition. He's just an impulsive young fool, to my mind, though he may be well-meaning enough. I hope so, at any rate. There'll be more than himself in the soup next time, if he gets into trouble."

Sir Clinton, watching the faint cloud on his host's face, had little difficulty in seeing his drift. Wendover, though a confirmed bachelor, had a soft side where a pretty girl was concerned; and it was evident that he was now thinking of the bride whom he had welcomed at the station. Young Keith-Westerton might get into a hole without Wendover troubling himself much; but trouble for Keith-Westerton nowadays meant trouble for his wife as well, and at even the prospect of that, Wendover's sympathy was excited.

"You mean his wife? The tall, dark, girl with a good figure—carries herself well. A sort of exotic touch about her somewhere. Is she a Creole, by any chance?"

"No. A Creole's a half-breed, isn't it? Or is it? It's a word I can never remember the exact meaning of, somehow. I had a notion it meant a half-breed."

"A Creole, Squire, is a descendant of settlers in places like the West Indies—or Mauritius, I believe. Creoles may be either white Creoles or t'other kind," Sir Clinton explained, with the air of quoting from a dictionary.

"Well, she's a West Indian, so you hit the mark; but she's pure white. There's Spanish blood in the family, I gather. Young Keith-Westerton bubbled over with her genealogy once to me—a long chain of descent from señors, grandees, hidalgos, and magnificos—and a most impressive array it sounded. He was evidently anxious to let me hear all about it— at that stage, you know, when a youngster thinks his girl must be as interesting to every one else as she is to himself. I don't want to give you the notion that he's snobbish and set up with marrying into an old family. After all, the Keith-Westertons are as old as a good many of the Spanish families."

"And the Wendovers are a bit better than any damned foreigners, eh, Squire?" insinuated Sir Clinton slyly.

"Of course," Wendover retorted with equanimity.

"Seen any of the grandees? I saw you'd met the girl before."

"I've only seen 'em in the distance. Three months or so ago, I ran across young Keith-Westerton in the village, quite by accident, one day, along with the girl. They were engaged, it seems, and he'd brought the whole damn family down in tow with him—father, mother, sister, and the girl herself. They were staying at the Talgarth Arms to inspect Silver Grove and the ancestral acres. It seems they're going to settle down here now; and reopen Silver Grove, after all these years. I think that's a sound scheme, you know; I like to see a man look after his own property instead of leaving it all to an agent: after all, one's tenants have some claim on one, I think."

Sir Clinton nodded his agreement. Wendover's ideas might verge on the feudal in some respects, but he believed in looking to the good of the people on his estate.

"Silver Grove will take a bit of modernising, I should think, if it hasn't been used for a quarter of a century."

"A fairly big job," Wendover agreed. "Of course, they can't live in it while the alterations are being made, so they're going to settle down for a while at the Dower House at my end of their grounds."

"With my amiable friend the Abbé Goron to keep them company? Where does he fit into the picture? Were the old Keith-Westertons Royalists and Jacobites and Papists?"

"No. Covenanters on one side and Cromwell's men in the English branch of the family. It's this girl that young Keith-Westerton's married; she's a Papist. I might have guessed as much from the list of dons, hidalgos and alguazils in her pedigree."

"Alguazil, I take it, is ironical; or perhaps a compliment to my profession? From your worried look, I gather that you'd rather young Keith-Westerton had stuck to his own sect when he went out seeking for a wife?"

Wendover evidently felt strongly on the matter. "Well, I never liked these mixed marriages; that's a fact. And if I were a Catholic, I'd feel just the same about it, I'm sure. It may work all right with the right people; and I hope these two will run well in double harness. But all the same, on principle I'm against anything of the sort. I'm not going to try to justify my ideas on grounds of reason, any more than I'd try to justify my dislike for anchovy sauce. I know I don't like it, and that's all that there is to it."

"H'm!" said Sir Clinton thoughtfully. "If there's any trouble over that question, I don't know that I'd care to be in your young friend's shoes. I've seen one or two of that type of girl before; and although they're quite all right, still . . ."

"Still what?" snapped Wendover, who hated implications.

"Still . . . My impression is that if you scratched young Mrs. Keith-Westerton, you might find her pretty unforgiving once you got below the surface."

"Then don't scratch her," Wendover retorted crossly. "I sha'n't."

Sir Clinton, knowing the readiness with which his friend would spring to the defence of a pretty girl, thought it prudent to change the subject.

"You're going north of the lake?" he asked. "Why not have gone through Talgarth village? That's a mile or two shorter, isn't it?"

"I wanted to let you have a look at that new boat-house of mine. There it is, just across the lake—yonder."

The new boathouse was much more commodious than Sir Clinton had expected: a big red-roofed building with a light balcony overlooking the lake.

"I'll show you it later on," Wendover said, as a belt of trees shut off the view. "It's really built on piles over the lake. In the summer, the boats lie in shelter under the building itself; one doesn't need to pull them up out of the water, and they're always dry even after a shower, that way. It saves the bother of shifting cushions under cover and all that sort of thing. And, another thing, nobody can get at them without a key. You've no notion of the damned cheek some people have, Clinton. The last boathouse was easy enough to get into; and one infernal scoundrel of a poacher—Cley's his name—had the nerve to take out one of my own boats at night when he wanted to net my trout. What do you think of that for sheer insolence?"

"Where was your keeper all that time?"

"Ill in bed, poor devil. No blame of his. No evidence, of course, except a boat sticky with fish scales in the morning. But there was no doubt who did it; only one sweep in the neighbourhood would have the nerve to try that on."

"An enterprising fellow, Mr. Cley, evidently. What sort of person is he?"

"Oh, one of these jaunty devils—Jack's as good as his master and a damned sight better, you know: the sort of thing all this cheap education's producing, I suppose. Very popular with silly girls—got one or two of them into trouble. Altogether a regular bad hat. I wish we were back in the old days of Botany Bay when you could get rid of people of that sort at one fell swoop; catch 'em with a rabbit in their pocket and give 'em a free passage to the Antipodes. I don't like his influence about the place."

"Can't you turn him out? You needn't have him as a tenant if you don't want him."

"He lives on Keith-Westerton's ground—just up there behind that rise. There's a whole family of them, two other brothers of much the same kidney, and they all live together in one cottage. Very convenient when you want an alibi sworn."

"I'll stir up my local minions, if you like," Sir Clinton suggested.

"It'll take more than your minions to catch Master Cley," said Wendover in a despondent tone, as he turned the car into the avenue which led to Talgarth Grange.

CHAPTER II: THE DEATH OF THE GAMEKEEPER

LONG ago, Wendover had been attacked by what his friends unkindly termed "that telephone-extension craze." At Talgarth Grange, a plug had been planted in every room which could, by any stretch of imagination, be supposed to require telephonic connection; and, for a time, the instrument accompanied Wendover about the house with the fidelity of Mary's lamb.

Gradually, he and the telephone grew less inseparable, until at last only a single plug was in regular use. Every night, when going to bed, he picked up the machine, carried it upstairs, and solemnly plugged its connection into the socket in his bedroom. No one had ever disturbed him with a night call. The ceremony had degenerated into the purest formality. But it had established itself as an integral part of the evening routine; and Wendover had grown so accustomed to it that a break-away would have caused him disquiet. "You never know, you know," was his slightly confused defence when chaffed on the subject. "Somebody might want to ring me up."

And now, at long last, he was awakened in the dawn by the trill of the telephone bell. Somebody did want to ring him up. In fact, to judge from the vehemence of the bell hammer, someone meant to ring him up as thoroughly as possible.

Wendover sleepily stretched out his hand for the receiver at his side. The message over the wire roused him even more effectively than the bell had done. After a breathless reply, he leaped out of bed; disconnected the instrument; and hurried, telephone in hand, along the hall and into his guest's room.

"I say, Clinton, wake up! Wake up, will you? Your people from Talgarth have just 'phoned to say a man's been shot dead and they want to speak to you. Here, I'll plug in the 'phone and you can talk to them yourself; they asked for you."

Long before Wendover's fumbling hands had got the telephone connected, the Chief Constable was alert, as though he had been awake for hours. Taking the instrument from Wendover, he gave his name and listened with an impassive face to a communication over the wire.

"Very well," he said at last in reply; and then he replaced the receiver on its bracket.

Wendover, unable to extract any definite meaning from Sir Clinton's three syllables, could not restrain himself even for a moment.

"What's it all about, Clinton? Who is it?"

"Horncastle's the name they gave," the Chief Constable replied, as he began to dress himself.

"Horncastle? That'll be one of young Keith-Westerton's keepers. Poor devil, what a pity!"

Sir Clinton seemed faintly surprised by Wendover's emotion.

"Strange attitude, this, for an amateur criminologist, even in pyjamas, Squire. I've never seen you blench at a death or two, in pursuit of your hobby. You saw four of them at Lynden Sands and never turned a hair, so far as I remember."

"Yes, but that was different. I didn't know any of the people. This is a bad business. Why, I was speaking to the poor beggar not three days ago. I knew him quite well."

"I didn't," Sir Clinton put in brutally. "So I can approach the affair as it ought to be approached—without sentiment and without bias. I say that lest you should expect me to suspect your poaching pal, Cley, merely because he gave information that he'd found the body."

"Cley?" Wendover exclaimed, and his tone was heavy with suspicion.

"It's not a criminal offence to find a dead body," Sir Clinton pointed out. "I've done it myself and escaped without a stain on my character. You'd better wait for details before swooping to conclusions. All that I've heard, so far, would fit quite well with a shooting accident."

"Then why did they ring you up?"

"Because Severn, the Inspector here, hasn't handled a case of this sort before; and he's not quite sure of his ground. Since I happened to be on the spot, he asked me as a favour to give him my advice. It may be necessary to detain Cley, or it may not. Severn wasn't too proud to consult me about it. That's all. And now, if you're thinking of coming with me, I think you'd better put on something warmer than these pyjamas. It's a bit chilly just after sunrise."

While Wendover was hurriedly dressing himself, the Chief Constable went down to the garage and brought a four-seater around to the front door. It was, as he had said, a chilly morning, even though by this time the sun was well above the horizon. There was not a breath of wind; some white clouds hung high in the blue; and on the lawn the dewdrops sparkled like a host of tiny gems.

"Severn and a constable are cycling up. They'll meet us on the road," Sir Clinton explained, when Wendover joined him. "Your friend Cley and another constable will follow on foot."

"Where did it happen?" Wendover demanded, as the car moved off.

"Just off the Ambledown-Stanningleigh road, down by the lakeside, at Friar's Point, I gather."

"You can see it from the boathouse, on the other side of the lake. It's young Keith-Westerton's ground. Cley was most likely taking up night lines when the keeper caught him."

"Set your tie straight, Squire," Sir Clinton advised, with a touch of asperity in his tone. "I suppose it must have got disturbed in that last leap of yours to an unjustifiable conclusion. How they ever put you on the Bench, if you go on like this, is a mystery to me. A bit too much like Lewis Carroll's dog:

> " 'I'll be judge, I'll be jury,'
> Said cunning old Fury.
> 'I'll try the whole cause
> And condemn you to death.'

"Let's hear what happened, before we start theorising as to *how* it happened."

Wendover suppressed a sharp retort. After all, the Chief Constable was a tired man, and tired people are apt to be impatient. Besides, there was no denying that Sir Clinton was perfectly justified in his criticism.

On the road opposite Friar's Point, they came upon the Inspector and the constable standing beside their cycles. Sir Clinton stepped out of the car, nodded to his subordinates, and then, without speaking, surveyed the lie of the land. A slope covered with thick grass descended from the road towards the lake and terminated at a pine spinney which covered the Point itself and concealed the shingle at the waterside. To the left of the spinney, the red roof of the boathouse could be seen across the lake. Wendover, descending in his turn from the car, gazed at the scene. The familiar background, the green slope, the fine tracery of the firs against the sky, the iron mirror of the unruffled lake, seemed an incongruous setting for a tragedy.

His eye was caught by a movement of Sir Clinton. Turning from the landscape, the Chief Constable looked up at the sky as though estimating the position of the sun; then, kneeling down, he seemed to be feeling for a moment or two among the grass by the roadside. Rising to his feet again, he pulled out his handkerchief and dried his hand. Then, seeming reassured, he turned to the officials beside him.

"That will be all right, Inspector," he said, as though to explain his proceedings. "Now, before your

24

witness turns up, perhaps you'll give us your story. You didn't tell me much over the 'phone, so probably we'd better start afresh."

"First of all, sir, I'd like to thank you for coming. I'm just afraid I may have brought you out on a wild-goose chase," Severn admitted nervously. "But one or two things make me a bit suspicious that there's more in it than just an accident; and I don't want to go either too far or not far enough in the matter of this man Cley. That was why I ventured to ask for your advice, sir, though I know I oughtn't to have troubled you, especially when you're on leave."

He hesitated for a moment; then, with a glance at Sir Clinton's face, he added:

"Inspector Armadale's an old friend of mine, sir; and it was what he's told me about the help you've given him in some of his cases that made me venture to ring you up and ask you."

"I don't mind," Sir Clinton said, in a tone which brightened the Inspector's rather worried face. "Now, give us the plain facts first of all—and only the facts."

"This is Constable Eccles," the Inspector explained. "You'd rather have him tell his own part of the thing himself, wouldn't you, sir, since he was the first to hear about the business?"

Eccles, evidently delighted at being allowed to bring himself directly to the notice of the Chief Constable, pulled out his notebook and, at a gesture of permission from Sir Clinton, launched into his tale.

"This morning, sir, according to orders, I was

patrolling this road and coming along in this direction from the Ambledown side when at twenty minutes to five about a couple of hundred yards from here, just round that bend you see there"—he pointed towards Ambledown—"a man came up to meet me and I recognised him as Bob Cley—Robert Cley, I should say, sir."

Constable Eccles, having terminated this masterpiece of the aperiodic style, took a much-needed breath and continued his tale:

"I saw at once that he wasn't quite himself, sir. He seemed to be struck all of a heap, to put it that way, as though he'd had a bad shock of some sort, but he didn't avoid me at all and came straight to meet me."

"That was at twenty minutes to five—half an hour before sunrise," Sir Clinton interjected. "You saw all this clearly?"

"I could see him well enough when he came up to me, sir. As soon as he recognised me, he said, 'Hullo! That you, Eccles? I want you,' just like that, in a kind of shaky voice. So I said, 'Well, what is it?' Then he said, 'Horncastle's got his touch. He must've slipped an' his gun's gone off an' blown his head in. He's down there at the shore. I've just seen his body an' I was on the road to give warnin'.' So I said, 'Is he badly hurt? Are you sure?' And he laughed, a queer sort of laugh, like as if he was a bit in hysterics —had lost his nerve slightly, I should say, sir—and he said, 'He's dead, I tell ye. His skull's blown in. You'll never see anything deader.' So then I said, 'Come along with me and show me where he is.'

And at that he said, 'I'll see you damned first. I want to see no more of him. Go yourself, if you like. He's lying on the shingle at Friar's Point. It looks to me as if he'd slipped on the bank an' dropped his gun an' it went off an' shot him dead. You go if you want to. I'll wait for you here.' "

Constable Eccles lifted his eyes from his notebook and scanned Sir Clinton's face doubtfully.

"I wasn't just sure what to do next, sir," he went on. "I didn't want to let Cley slip away, for one thing; and for another, I didn't want to go trampling over the ground in a poor light and perhaps making a mess of things; and for a third, I felt I ought to make sure that poor Horncastle really was past help, for Cley might've been mistaken, for all I knew. I was perplexed over what to do, but then it occurred to me that if I walked straight down to the lakeside and along the shingle to Friar's Point, I wasn't likely to disturb anything much in the way of traces, so I got out of Cley just exactly where Horncastle's body was lying and then I did as I said, leaving Cley sitting by the roadside and telling him to wait there till I got back."

"Very good," Sir Clinton commented, to the evident relief of the constable.

"When I got to the body, sir, it was light enough to see pretty well, and I used my flashlight so I saw quite clearly that Cley had made no mistake when he said Horncastle was dead. I took care to disturb nothing and I only touched the body to feel whether it was cold or not."

"A second good mark," Sir Clinton commended.

"I don't see that you could have done better than you did. Good work. Now go on."

Evidently reassured by Sir Clinton's tone, Eccles continued his narrative.

"The body, sir, was distinctly cold, one could tell at once that he'd been dead for a while. It was lying . . ."

"Don't bother about that. I'll see it for myself in a minute or two. Just tell us what you did."

"I left it exactly as it was, sir, and came back along the shingle, the way I'd gone, so as to make no traces on any soft ground around about the body. There was a heavy thundershower yesterday afternoon and the ground's soft enough to take impressions, perhaps."

"Perhaps," Sir Clinton echoed, in a doubtful tone, which suggested that he had no great hopes.

"Then I told Cley he'd have to come with me and repeat his story to Inspector Severn at once, before he forgot anything. He made no open objection and he and I went down through Mr. Wendover's grounds and I knocked up the Inspector."

"That's all perfectly clear," Sir Clinton said with satisfaction. "Now, Inspector, have you anything to add to this?"

"The constable came to my house at 5:10 A.M." Severn explained. "He told me what he's just told you and then I brought Cley in and questioned him. His story tallied completely with what the constable had told me, so far as that went; and in addition, he told me how he came to discover Horncastle's body. If you don't mind my suggesting it, sir, I'd like you to question him yourself when he turns up—he may be here any minute now—and I'll be able to check whether what he says to you agrees with what he said to me. It'll save time and save you the trouble of hearing the same tale twice."

The Chief Constable nodded his agreement with this.

"On the face of it," he pointed out, "the thing looks like an accident. What makes you think it's anything else?"

The Inspector evidently felt that he was on thin ice. He had to justify disturbing the Chief Constable and he knew that he had really very little definite evidence.

"The fact is, sir, that there's been bad feeling between Cley and Horncastle for a long while. That's not evidence, I know; but it's notorious in the place all the same. Both of 'em were keen on the girls—sort of local Don Juans—and there's been a lot of trouble over one of 'em getting into the other's road in that field, from time to time. That's in addition to the fact that one was a notorious poacher and the other a gamekeeper. Cley and the keeper both said quite openly that the other one would get his touch sometime or other; and Cley's got a temper that might have gone off any day and landed him deeper than he meant to go at the start. I dare say that sounds a bit feeble, sir; but there's been enough in it to make me feel . . . well, not very sure about the whole business. They were both dangerous, and that's a fact. Horncastle had a black temper too. In fact, he had a row with Mr. Keith-Westerton just the other day and was under notice. When you get two tempers like that coming up against each other, and one man's found shot dead with the other in the neighbourhood of the body. . . . Well, sir, it suggests a good deal to my mind; and I don't want to let Cley slip through my fingers. On the other hand, I don't want to detain him unless there's a chance of bringing something home definitely."

The Inspector evidently saw that he had failed to make out a case for having disturbed his superior. Sir Clinton, however, seemed to understand the position.

"So you thought you'd like to have an impartial opinion on the point?" he suggested. "H'm! I don't mind."

He turned to the constable.

"You didn't hear any shot while you were coming along the road? No? And Horncastle had been dead for some time, you thought, when you came to examine him. Then Cley obviously wasn't coming red-handed from the crime when you met him. Either his tale's true or else he must have murdered Horncastle earlier in the night and spent the intervening time somewhere or other."

"Here's the constable bringing Cley, sir," Severn said, with a gesture to draw Sir Clinton's attention to the two approaching figures. "Will you question him yourself? I've got all I can out of him already."

The Chief Constable nodded and turned to examine the poacher as he came up to the group. A tall, powerful man of about thirty, Cley would probably have made a good impression in normal circumstances; but now his coarsely handsome face bore an expression of sullenness and uneasiness which gave him something of a hang-dog look.

"Tell the Chief Constable what you know about this business," ordered Severn curtly.

Cley, evidently taken aback to find himself confronted by so high an official, stared sulkily at Sir Clinton for a moment or two before opening his mouth.

"If you think yer goin' to trip me up by askin' me to tell it all over again," he said grudgingly, "yer makin' a mistake, as ye'll see. I've told ye nothin' but what was the plain truth; but if ye want it again, then this was the way of it. I got up this mornin' about an hour afore dawn for to do a bit o' business I had on hand."

"You didn't look at your watch, I suppose?" Sir Clinton asked.

Cley gave him a glance charged with suspicion.

"I don't need no watch for to tell me the time; I can guess it, near enough for my business. It was about an hour before dawn. I made some tea to warm me up, seein' it was a chilly mornin'. Mebbe one o' my brothers'll remember hearin' me rattlin' the kettle an' stirrin' up the fire."

He glanced defiantly at Severn and stung the Inspector into a retort.

"They'll remember it if you remind them, I'll bet."

Sir Clinton checked his subordinate with a look.

"Go on," he said.

"After I'd had my tea, I went out for a walk."

"A moonlight stroll, eh?" interjected the Chief Constable, with no irony in his tone.

"No, there warn't no moon then. I just went out for a stroll, as you say; an' by chance I happened for to walk down to the lake, here."

"You could find your way all right, I suppose? You knew where you were going?"

"Seein' as I was born within half a mile o' here, I did know my way."

"Then where did you cross the road to get to the lakeside?"

Cley considered for a moment.

"It'd be a matter o' a hundred yards—no, say fifty yards—along the road from here, towards the Grange, as near as I can remember. There's a bank of ferns there, an' I got off the road just on the near side o' them. I can show ye the place easy enough."

"And then?"

"Then I walked over the grass down to the waterside where the shingle is, an' I turned this way along the shingle till I came to Friar's Point."

"You heard nothing unusual during this stroll of yours?"

"Nothin' that I'd call unusual. The night's full o' sounds, o' course, but there warn't any sound as caught my attention in pertic'lar, if that's what you mean; nothin' of that sort. Just the ord'nary night noises. I was walkin' quietly along, when all of a sudden I near stumbled over him, just saved myself from trampin' on him in the dimness, 'cause I wasn't payin' much attention to what was under my feet."

"Tell me exactly what happened then," Sir Clinton said, as Cley paused in his narrative.

"I thought as how it was likely a tramp havin' a doss; or else some drunken swine sleepin' off his dose, more like, for he was half on the bank and half on the shingle an' no tramp would sleep that way, 'less he was off his chump. So I was for leavin' him alone, and then somethin' about him made me think—I dunno why, but there was somethin'—an' I thought I'd have a look at him. Now I come to think about it, I remember I didn't hear any breathin', so it's like enough that that was what pulled me up. My hearin's pretty good. Anyway, I out with my matches an' struck a light, an' with the first flash I made out 'twas Horncastle, by the look o' his clothes. That match just flared an' went out, so I stooped down an' struck some more. Ugh! It was plain enough Horncastle's got his touch; I've never seen anythin' like that. I saw his gun beside him, that old-fashioned thing he always used to carry with him. Thinks I, 'He's been steppin' up on to the bank an' slipped an' shot himself, just as I expected he would, some day, with that slovenly way he had with guns.' An' then I thought of goin' for to give the alarm, an' it came to my mind as how Eccles here patrols this trip o' the road, so I left Horncastle an' I cut up on to the road again."

"You didn't touch the body or the gun?"

"No, I did not. I've sense enough for that."

"And what happened after that?"

"I got off the grass over yonder, about where you see that big stone"—he pointed to a spot about thirty yards along the road towards Ambledown—"an' then I felt queer. I wasn't sick, but I was mighty near it; an' I sat down on that stone for a while till I felt better; an' then I set off towards Ambledown, expectin' to fall in with Eccles or else meanin' to rouse up some people at a house further along the road. It was just about dawn when I come on Eccles; I know that, an' he can vouch for it too, 'cause he looked at his watch."

He glanced sullenly from face to face in the group as he stopped speaking, but nowhere did he detect a friendly expression. Sir Clinton, though not hostile, seemed purely businesslike. The police were obviously suspicious; and Wendover's features plainly betrayed his dislike for the poacher.

"That's just the plain truth of it," Cley said, with a faint touch of hopelessness in his tone. "Ye needn't think I had any hand in it, for I hadn't. I never laid a finger on him."

Sir Clinton disregarded this completely.

"I may have a question or two to ask you, later on," he said. "In the meantime, you and the constable can take a stroll up the road. You're fond of strolls, I gather. Take him around that bend, out of sight," he added to the constable, "and bring him back again if we whistle for you."

Cley, his sullenness tinged now with a very apparent fear, moved off in company with his watchdog.

"And now, Inspector," Sir Clinton suggested, "I think we may take a look around for ourselves."

CHAPTER III: THE PEARLS

WENDOVER, his mind concentrated upon Friar's Point, where the body lay, was surprised when Sir Clinton led the way along the road towards the Grange instead of going down to the waterside. Then it occurred to him that a detour was advisable, lest they should obliterate earlier tracks.

"Did Cley's second story tally with the one he told you before, Inspector?" Sir Clinton demanded, as they walked along.

"Practically," the Inspector admitted. "He gave me more details about the look of the body when he examined it, but so far as his own movements were concerned, he didn't change anything in repeating the thing, sir."

"And you?" the Chief Constable inquired, turning to Eccles.

"What he told me, sir, wasn't just word for word what he told you; but so far as his own movements were concerned, it was the same story both times. He was a bit strung up when I saw him first, and the way he told it was different—calling on God and all that sort of thing, sir—but it came to much the same thing really."

"We can check some of it, at any rate," Sir Clinton said in an indifferent tone. "The dew won't evaporate for a while, and so long as it lies, his tracks should be clear enough on the grass."

He halted where a large clump of ferns grew on the bank by the roadside, examined the turf carefully before stepping on it, and then climbed to the top of the low ridge.

"Part of his tale's accurate," he reported, after scanning the tract between the road and the lake. "There's a fairly plain trail with the dew brushed off the grass. Just go along the road for about ten yards, Inspector, please. . . . A bit farther. . . . There. Stop! . . . Would you mind having a look at the bank just in front of you?"

"There's a mark here that might have been made by a boot slipping and scraping the turf as some one clambered up the bank," Severn reported, after a careful examination.

Sir Clinton came down from his post of observation, inspected the place indicated by Severn, and marked the spot by placing two or three stones in the ditch immediately below. This done, he drew from his pocket a large packet of notepaper.

"I raided your writing room while you were dressing," he said to Wendover, with something suspiciously like a grin. "Your expensive deckle-edged notepaper with the artistic azure tinting is hardly likely to be common hereabouts, which makes it very suitable for this sort of work. Where's that rainwater pool I noticed?"

The thundershower of the previous afternoon had left its traces in the ditch beneath the fern clump. Sir Clinton stooped and immersed the notepaper in the water until the sheets were limp and saturated.

"Less chance of it blowing about, in that state, if the wind does happen to rise," he pointed out, as he tore the paper into fair-sized fragments. "And now, I think, we might go on the trail. Will you follow me, one at a time, and keep directly in my tracks, all of you? We mustn't go trampling all over the place."

Following Sir Clinton, Wendover reached the top of the bank. Before him, on the gentle slope down to the lake, he could see the plain track along which the dew had been brushed from the grass. Here and there, along it, the tall blades had been bent forward by the foot of the walker. Evidently Cley had spoken the truth when he described that part of his route.

Sir Clinton, keeping well to one side of the trail, scattered his fragments of notepaper along Cley's actual track until it ended on the shingle which fringed the lake. Here the party halted for a moment.

"Beyond this," Sir Clinton pointed out, "Cley seems to have walked for part of the time on the turf—you can see the track if you look carefully—but when he came to rough ground he got down on to the shingle. In the main, his tale's correct. Now we'd better take to the shingle ourselves. No use leaving tracks if we can help it."

Fifty paces brought them behind the screen of the firs which extended outward from Friar's Point, so that they lost sight of the highroad; and a few steps farther on, they came to the fatal spot. Horncastle's body lay half on the bank and half on the shingle, as though he had slipped while mounting the low ridge and had slid downward in his fall. He lay face downward, his chest on the grass, his arms asprawl; and the gun, gripped in his right hand by the barrel, had its muzzle directed towards the ghastly wound above his ear.

Sir Clinton, after a cursory survey, turned to gauge the altitude of the rising sun.

"The first thing is to check Cley's tale before that dew gets any thinner," he pointed out. "We can come back here any time and go into things thoroughly. And we needn't waste time in hunting for tracks in the pine spinney just now; it'll be easier to go through it and pick up his trail on the wet grass beyond."

He led them along the shingle for thirty or forty yards and then through the shallow arcade of the pines to where the grass grew, beyond the shadow of the spinney.

"H'm! Here's a clear trail going in the right direction," he reported, as the others came up. "There's no need for all of us to tramp along it. Will you take this paper and mark the line, Inspector? We can watch you from here and see where it takes you."

He accompanied Severn to the edge of the trail, glanced at the grass, and then turned back to rejoin the rest of the party.

"It looks as though Cley's story were all right. Whoever made that track was going in the same direction as the Inspector."

Severn's expedition was a very short one. The trail crossed the slope and reached the highroad just at the point where lay the big stone on which the poacher said he had seated himself.

"That may prove part of Cley's story to be true,"

Wendover argued, as they waited for Severn's return, "but it doesn't necessarily mean he didn't shoot Horncastle."

"Quite correct," Sir Clinton admitted at once. "But we needn't waste time in inferences just now, with the sun rising higher and the dew getting thinner every minute. We've got another trail to look for— the one that Horncastle made in coming here."

"Perhaps he came along the shingle," Wendover objected.

"Perhaps he did," Sir Clinton acquiesced. "But personally I'd walk on grass rather than shingle any day, if I had the choice, more especially if I were a keeper who wanted to move quietly instead of advertising his presence to all and sundry. At any rate, it's worth the trouble of hunting, even if we find nothing."

While Severn was returning, the Chief Constable strolled along the outskirts of the spinney in the direction of the Grange, scanning the grass as he went. In a few minutes he beckoned to the remainder of the party. Wendover, as he came up, saw a third trail before him, fainter to his eye than the others, but still clear enough.

"Oh, that's Horncastle's trail, is it?" he said, in a rather disappointed tone. "So you were right, after all. He must have come down almost straight from the road, apparently."

"If Horncastle took the trouble to walk backwards from the road to the beach, then it may be his trail, certainly," Sir Clinton retorted. "Go and look at the way the grass is disturbed, Squire. That trail was made by some one going up from the spinney towards the road."

This irony was reserved for Wendover's ear. When the two officials came up, Sir Clinton dropped persiflage.

"Here's an extra track leading up from the spinney to the road," he pointed out. "Cley may have made it or he may not. If he did, then there must be a second downward track of his somewhere. And we've still got to find the keeper's track if we can. What I want you to notice about this track is that it's a shade fainter than the tracks which correspond to Cley's story. Now we'll follow up this trail first of all."

Halfway between the shore and the road, the track dipped into a little cup in the ground, and on the floor of this was a small pool of standing water, evidently a relic of the heavy thundershower of the previous afternoon. The trail lay straight through this and became clear again upon the further side. Sir Clinton cautiously approached the side of the pool and examined the bottom.

"The water's lying on the grass," he said over his shoulder to the waiting group. "There aren't any footprints, since there's no mud that I can see. Still, with luck, it's a gift from the gods. I'm sorry, Constable, but I want to try an experiment and you're the victim. Come down here."

Rather mystified, Eccles gingerly descended the slope of the cup. Sir Clinton took his arm and placed him in position.

"I'll have to blindfold you, I think," he explained.

"The other fellow came along in the dark, and blind-folding is the nearest we can get to that."

Taking out his handkerchief, he bandaged Eccles' eyes.

"You can see nothing? Right, then. Now I'm going to give you a turn or two around and I'll leave you facing the road. Go straight ahead. I'll see you come to no harm."

Eccles walked forward as directed; and, to his obvious disgust, trudged straight into the pool of standing water. From the expression of his mouth, it was clear that he thought poorly of this sort of experiment. But any idea of a practical joke was swept from his mind by the seriousness of Sir Clinton's face as he removed the bandage.

"Feet soaked? Clean over the boot tops? Just unlace 'em and let's see the exact extent of the damage."

Eccles, puzzled by this strange method of obtaining evidence, sat down and took off his boots. Sir Clinton examined them and then felt the constable's socks.

"Completely soaked. I'm sorry, but you'll see the point in a minute or two. It had to be done. Now we'll follow up the trail till it reaches the road."

This took a very short time, and when they reached the highway, Sir Clinton asked the Inspector to summon the other constable whom they had left in charge of Cley. When the poacher and his guardian arrived, Sir Clinton told Cley to take off his boots. The poacher at first demurred, but gave in after some argument. Sir Clinton picked up one of the boots, heavy with steel boot protectors, and felt the inside.

"The outside's wet with walking through the grass, of course," he said to the others, "but the inside's fairly dry. Just feel his socks, will you, Inspector, over the instep."

"Practically dry too," Severn reported.

Eccles, who now saw the point of Sir Clinton's experiment, could not repress a grin at the sight of Cley's obvious bewilderment at the turn of events.

"You can put your boots on again, my man," said Sir Clinton. "That's all I wanted. And after that, the constable here will go home with you and check that story about your early morning tea. If I were you," he added drily, "I'd keep my mouth shut while he's questioning your relations. That advice is in your own interest."

Cley seemed unable to settle in his own mind whether this was encouraging or not; but a glance at the Chief Constable's face assured him that he would gain nothing by further protestations. As he bent down to lace his boots, Sir Clinton spoke again:

"Give me your box of matches."

Cley, evidently taken aback, handed over a cardboard box, about two inches in length, marked with the name of a Norwegian firm and bearing the legend: SAFETY MATCH. When the poacher and his watchdog had gone off down the road, Sir Clinton turned to his companions.

"We haven't seen Horncastle's own track yet; and we ought to find that, even if it's only for the sake of completeness. The easiest way will be to walk from lakeside to lakeside around the spinney's edge, between it and the high road. That arc is bound to cut Horncastle's trail if he walked over the grass into the spinney. Just wait here. I'll have a look around."

Starting from the shore of the lake on the Grange side of Friar's Point, he carried out his scheme; and just before he reached the shingle on the far side of the Point, they saw him halt and then begin to follow a fresh trail inward towards the border of the spinney. Having completed his task, he called to them to come down to the beach.

"Apparently that was Horncastle's track that I struck over there," he explained, as they rejoined him. "I saw two marks of a nailed boot on a patch of mud, with a nail pattern corresponding to the arrangement of the heavy nails on the boots of the body. So far as I can see, there's no other trail across the grass."

Severn opened his notebook and drew a rough diagram.

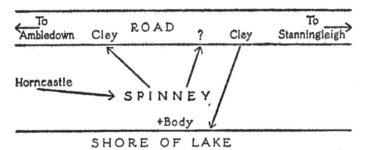

"That's it, more or less, isn't it, sir?" he asked, showing it to Sir Clinton, who nodded in confirmation.

"Um . . ." the Inspector mused aloud. "Horncastle came here and didn't go away; that's correct.

Cley came and went; that fits his story. The third man went away; but there's no sign of his incoming trail. He must have come along the shingle, I suppose."

"Suppose we examine Horncastle's body, now," Sir Clinton suggested. "There's no need to leave it here longer than is necessary. Once the news gets out, we shall have a crowd around us, if we don't hurry."

When they reached the body again, however, Sir Clinton's first action was to kneel down and examine the smooth surface of the clay where the bank had been abraded. Severn, peering over his superior's shoulder, could not help wondering what the Chief Constable found to interest him on that almost polished surface which showed no trace of scores or scratches. Sir Clinton did not enlighten him, however; for as soon as he had completed his examination of the clay, he rose to his feet and began to study Horncastle's corpse.

Wendover, coming up on the other side, found himself shuddering at the spectacle of the ghastly wound inflicted by the gun.

"It looks as if he'd come down with a smash and the gun had gone off and blown his head in, poor devil," he commented. "You can see the charge has spread a bit and torn the turf slightly just below the place where the main bulk hit him. That proves the gun was fired along the ground, clearly enough. It's the old hammered double-barrel he always used."

Sir Clinton seemed to be thinking hard as Wendover spoke; but for a few seconds he said nothing.

"We'd better take things in their order, Inspector," he suggested at last. "The police surgeon ought to be here very shortly, so we'd better leave the body itself alone till he comes. Let's start with the gun."

He bent over it for a moment, pegged in some matches along the line of the barrel, and scrutinised the dead man's hand which still loosely clasped the weapon.

"The second hammer's at full cock," he pointed out indifferently. "Just measure how far his hand is from the muzzle, Inspector, please, and make a note of it."

"Six and a half inches from the muzzle to his thumb, sir," Severn reported.

Sir Clinton nodded. Then, taking the dead man's wrist, he shook it slightly.

"He's got hardly any grip on the barrel," he reported. "Make a note of that too. It might be important. *Rigor mortis* hasn't set in yet, you'll notice, at least not to any marked extent. Now we'll have a look at the gun."

He gently disengaged it from the dead man's hand, taking care to hold it in such a way as to leave no fingerprints on vital points.

"Got your insufflator with you?" he demanded. "'There's no wind, and we may as well be sure about things before we go any further. Just powder it, please. You won't find much, I expect."

Severn obediently tried the experiment.

"Why, there's nothing here!" he exclaimed in astonishment, as he completed the distribution of the powder on the surface of the weapon. "That's dashed rum. He must have handled that gun pretty freely and left finger marks all over it; and yet there's nothing here but . . . Somebody's been rubbing the thing—cleaned the whole affair . . . H'm! I didn't give Cley credit for being as sharp as that."

"I never expected you'd get much," Sir Clinton explained. "See that bit of broken grass sticking to the lock? That was on the top side of the gun as it lay on the turf, so it didn't come there by accident during the recoil. I guessed from that that you wouldn't find much. Somebody's cleaned the gun after the discharge; and I'm inclined to bet that if you hunt around here a bit, you'll find the tuft of grass he used in wiping off the finger marks."

Wendover, more convinced than ever that the poacher was the culprit, searched zealously; but the Inspector was the lucky man.

"Here it is, sir," he announced, as he held it up.

His expression showed that his respect for Sir Clinton's acuteness had risen considerably.

"We needn't trouble to be careful in handling the gun now," the Chief Constable said, picking it up as he spoke. "Let's just be sure about things. . . . Yes, that's all right. There's an exploded cartridge in the right barrel and a live one in the left. It looks as though he'd been shot with his own gun, all right."

"And while he was lying on the ground," Wendover put in, returning to his earlier point. "But Horncastle was a big hefty beggar. That's what puzzles me, Clinton. If he was shot like this, by Cley, why didn't he struggle? He was about a match for Cley, and I can't see Cley holding him face down on the grass and shooting him with his own gun."

"Neither can I, Squire. But here's the surgeon coming, I believe. He'll perhaps be able to give us a hint or two."

The police surgeon proved to be a businesslike person, who wasted little time in talk.

"Not much need for me to come here," he said, rather crossly, as though annoyed at having been dragged from bed before the normal hour. "Cause of death's clear enough—gunshot wound in the head. The rest's a matter of an autopsy, which can be done in the proper place."

As he was beginning his examination of the body, Sir Clinton arrested him for a moment.

"The two things I'm interested in, Doctor, are what hour of the night he died, and whether you can find any signs of a bruise on the point of his jaw. And when you do your P.M., would you mind examining the back of the skull to see if there are any traces of a blow there?"

The surgeon seemed slightly surprised.

"Eh? Bruise on the jaw? All right. Inspector, give me a hand, will you, to turn him over."

When the body was face upwards, he examined the chin.

"Yes, there's a bruise on the skin just at the point of the jaw. What of it? He must have come down on his face when he fell. Nothing in that."

Sir Clinton has been scrutinising the turf at the edge of the pool of blood in which the corpse's head had been lying.

"Just come here, Doctor," he suggested. "Feel the softness of that grass and the earth underneath. Do you think you'd get that kind of bruise from it? And is the bruise large enough to fit your notion?"

Hardly concealing his vexation at being caught napping, the surgeon had to admit that his explanation would not fit.

"H'm! No, I suppose you're right. Bruise looks as if it had been made with a small hard object. A stone perhaps? No, no stones on the turf hereabout. H'm!"

"And the approximate time of the man's death?" Sir Clinton inquired.

"Tell you in a minute or two. Got to take the temperature before I can make a guess at it."

While the surgeon busied himself with this work, Sir Clinton seemed preoccupied. With downcast eyes, he wandered aimlessly to and fro about the shingle, as though he could not bring himself to leave the immediate neighbourhood of the body. The doctor completed his test, examined his watch, and made a mental calculation.

"Death occurred somewhere about midnight, most likely," he declared at last. "Rigor's developed at the head and neck but hasn't reached the chest yet. That confirms the temperature evidence. Round about midnight's as near as I'd care to put it."

Sir Clinton nodded, as though his thoughts were elsewhere, and drew out a pocket diary. Wendover was somewhat puzzled to note that the page which the Chief Constable consulted was one headed: "Moon's Phases." Pulling out his own diary and turning to the corresponding data, he discovered that the moon was thirteen days old and that it had southed at about half-past ten on the previous night; but this suggested nothing important to his mind. Meanwhile the doctor had packed his bag and, with a rather surly farewell, had gone off to his car.

The Chief Constable suddenly awoke from his reflections and turned to Eccles.

"Was it cloudy, last night?" he demanded. "Heavy clouds?"

Eccles thought for a time before replying.

"Well, sir, it wasn't what you'd call just exactly a cloudy night," he answered at last. "What I mean to say is, there was mostly a clear sky and one or two bright stars shining, as well as the moon 'd let 'em, and the moon itself was bright most of the time; but now and again, every half hour or so, a big cloud would drift up."

"And cover the moon, perhaps?"

"Sometimes that did happen, sir, and things got fairly dim then, as you can understand. I remember that clearly enough. That was just the kind of night it was."

"The moon had set before Cley got hold of you?"

"Oh, yes, sir. Long before that."

"That's just what I wanted to know," Sir Clinton said, in a tone which conveyed to Eccles the idea that he had been of considerable assistance. "Now just look here, Inspector. This seems rather interesting."

He led them to a point on the shingle about ten feet from the body. Wendover, following the Chief Constable's finger, saw a spent match lying between two stones. Sir Clinton fished it out carefully and held it up for them to examine.

"It's burned down a bit, but it's obviously a Norwegian match with a square cross-section—exactly like the ones that Cley had in his box. So at any rate that part of his story is true enough. He lighted matches to look at the body. This match is quite dry, so it must have been thrown down after the dew fell last night."

He moved a few steps, stooped down, and pointed to a second spent match on the stones.

"See that? Now when I pick it up you'll see something different."

"It's a round-stemmed match—a Swan vesta by the look of it," Wendover exclaimed.

"Exactly," Sir Clinton confirmed. "And, like the other, it's quite fresh."

"So there must have been a second person lighting matches beside the body?" Wendover said, rather disconcerted.

"Wait a bit," the Inspector broke in. "I'd like to have this clear, sir. If you believe Cley's story, he came here after the moon had set, so he had to light matches to see anything clearly. That's all right. But if the death took place at about midnight, then the moon was shining its best. . . . Oh, I see now why you were asking these questions about clouds. You mean this match must have been struck in a cloudy interval, when the moon wasn't giving enough light?"

"It's quite probable, but not certain."

The Inspector pondered for a moment.

"Whoever struck this match was the man who left the fourth trail, then, sir?"

"Quite likely."

"What could he be doing here at that time of night?" Wendover demanded.

"Committing a murder, for one thing," Sir Clinton retorted. "He may have had other objects in view as well, of course."

"You seem very sure it's a murder case," Wendover said in a critical tone. "At first sight, I thought Cley might have killed Horncastle; but it might just as well have been a pure accident. I don't see that an extra trail and a Swan vesta make so much difference as all that. Look at the way the keeper slipped and fell. The second barrel of his gun was at full cock even after the affair, so likely the first hammer was cocked too. When he slipped on the bank and came down with a smash, his gun went off and shot him."

"And then he got up and cleaned his fingerprints off his gun? He must have been an amazingly tidy fellow."

Wendover flushed with vexation at having forgotten this glaring piece of evidence.

"Perhaps you'll describe your supposed murderer," he suggested ironically, to cover his mistake. "We might recognise him."

"I don't much care for following in the footsteps of Sherlock," Sir Clinton said mildly. "But if you insist on it, I'll do my best. The murderer belongs, probably, to the middle class or higher up on the social scale. He's a person of fair physique at any rate. I should guess that he's got some knowledge of boxing. His boots and socks were thoroughly soaked last night. And I should think he has his wits about him, on most occasions. Does that help much?"

Severn saved Wendover from the necessity of a reply.

"I'd like to know just how you've worked that out, sir," he interjected. "Some of it I can follow, but not all of it."

"It's obviously a murder and not an accident," Sir Clinton pointed out. "If it had been an accident, then Horncastle slipped on the bank and knocked his gun in his fall, so that it went off and shot him. But on that basis, the scrape on the bank here must have been made by Horncastle's boot. It wasn't. Horncastle's boot has a pattern of heavy nails on the sole. They would leave grooves on the surface of the clay when they slipped in making a scrape. There aren't any grooves on the surface of that scrape. Ergo, that scrape wasn't made by Horncastle slipping as he got up the bank; it was made by a second person who wanted to suggest the slipping idea and to make it seem self-evident that the affair was accidental. Only one kind of person would fake evidence of that sort—a murderer trying to cover up his crime."

"Then that clears Cley, sir," the Inspector pointed out. "His boots . . ."

"Have boot protectors on the soles which would leave marks? Exactly. Cley didn't commit the murder."

"Well, what about this fellow being middle class?" Wendover demanded. "How do you prove that?"

"You can get foreign safety matches for ninepence a dozen boxes," Sir Clinton reminded him. "That's the brand used by Cley and the working class generally. It's only a plutocrat like yourself who thinks of buying Swan vestas at three-halfpence a box. But I'll admit that isn't absolutely sound evidence. It's more to the point that this scrape was made with a smooth-soled boot, the kind of boot you find on town pavements. The country people round here wear sole leather with nails or boot protectors, seeing that they do their walking on rough roads. So a smooth boot sole points to a middle-class type of wearer. Neither bit of evidence in itself means much; but put the two together and you can't help thinking the man must have been a cut above a ploughboy."

"I don't need the wet feet business explained," Severn confided, rather sheepishly. "That business of making Eccles walk through the pool yonder makes that quite clear. But you say this murderer was a man of, fair physique. A man of fair physique couldn't have held Horncastle down with one hand while he used his other hand on the gun. Horncastle was a tough 'un, sir. It would have taken a pocket Hercules to manage a job like that."

"A jujutsu expert might have managed it, all the same, I think," Sir Clinton suggested. "But as a matter of fact, I don't imagine that jujutsu came into the business. I said he was probably something of a boxer."

"I see what you mean!" Wendover exclaimed. "You're thinking of that bruise on the keeper's jaw? You mean the murderer knocked him out and then fixed him up while he was unconscious and could make no struggle? Is that it?"

"Something of the sort," Sir Clinton admitted. "It's

quite certain that Horncastle put up no sort of struggle. There are no marks to show anything like that. Obviously Horncastle must have been unconscious when he was shot. The knock-out on the angle of the jaw would keep him quiet for a short time; but it's quite on the cards that he was knocked out down there on the shingle, and that when he fell he got concussion through falling back on to the stones. That would keep him quiet for quite long enough for the murderer to do his work."

"Oh, so that's why you asked the surgeon to examine the back of the head for a bruise?"

"Naturally one wants to know what happened."

The Inspector had been thinking hard during this exchange.

"Then I take it, sir," he said at length, "that your idea of the business is something of this sort. Horncastle met the murderer on the shingle, and they had a quarrel about something. The murderer hit Horncastle on the point of the jaw and knocked him out; and most likely Horncastle fell backwards, limp, and came down bang on a stone with the back of his head and got concussion of the brain with the blow. That put him to sleep and left the murderer a free hand. He carried Horncastle up to the bank—that's where your 'fair physique' comes in, since Horncastle was a fairly heavy man. By that time there was a cloud over the moon and the murderer had to strike matches to see what he was doing. He blew Horncastle's head in with his own gun and then he went off by the track you found, and he landed up on the high road over yonder."

"After faking the scrape on the bank with his own boot," Sir Clinton amended. "It was that touch that made me fairly certain he had his wits about him. A neat idea, though it didn't work out quite as well as he expected. And, by the way, you'd better make a note of another point, Inspector. Suppose you slip while you're carrying something in your hand. You grip hard on the thing you're carrying, usually. It's instinctive to tighten your hold. Now if Horncastle was holding his gun by the barrel and had slipped normally, he'd have gripped his gun tight. In suicide cases, it's usual to find the weapon tightly grasped; all the more so in this case, if it had been an accident. But you saw for yourself that there was no grip on the gun at all. Horncastle's hand was quite loose on it. From the look of things, I expect the murderer arranged it so as to look as though the recoil had carried the gun through Horncastle's hand, so that he was left gripping it near the muzzle. I think I was right in saying he had his wits about him. But it didn't convince me."

"He must have had his wits about him to think of cleaning his own finger marks off the gun," Wendover admitted.

"Well, he was between the devil and the deep sea, there," Sir Clinton pointed out. "If he left his fingerprints, then he ran a big risk; but if he cleaned them off, he left something that wouldn't fit in with the accident theory at any price."

"What do you think was the motive, sir?" the Inspector asked hopefully.

"You can't think of the motive? We're in the

same boat, then, for neither can I. Had Horncastle
any disagreements with people likely to be wearing
town boots?"

"Well, sir," the Inspector was obviously embarrassed, "Mr. Keith-Westerton had just discharged
him the other day, and Horncastle made a song about
it, from all I've heard. But that's neither here nor
there."

"Then where is it?" Sir Clinton inquired quiz-
zically. "It's your business to hunt up anything that
may be connected with this affair, Inspector, quite
regardless of social standing or things of that sort.
Remember that."

The Inspector digested this rebuke without remark. Sir Clinton, having reminded his subordinate
of his responsibility, turned the talk at once.

"I think we'd better be thorough while we're at it.
There may be some more matches lying about down
there and we may as well pick up what we can. Two
or three samples will be more convincing than a single
specimen."

He moved off and began to search diligently among
the shingle. As the others were following his example,
he suddenly stooped and picked something out of a
cranny between two stones.

"Here's a pretty thing," he said, holding out a
tiny object on the palm of his hand.

The Inspector was the first to reach his side.

"A pearl from a necklace?" he said, after a glance
at the object. "One of these Woolworth things, I expect. A lot of the girls around here are wearing
them."

"I'm afraid you're wrong, Inspector. This isn't one of the fish-scale and ammonia productions. I don't know enough about pearls to put an exact price on it, but it's a good pearl and a necklace of them would be worth a few hundreds at least."

He bent down again and picked a second pearl from among the pebbles. Severn joined in the search and two more pearls were discovered.

"You'd better turn some one on to make a thorough search round about here," Sir Clinton suggested to the Inspector. "There may be a few more lying among these stones. We've got enough for our present purposes."

He examined the pearls on the palm of his hand for a few moments, as though trying to estimate their value.

"Things like these are hardly likely to go missing without somebody making a stir about it," he said to Severn. "You haven't had any burglary hereabouts lately?"

"No, sir," the Inspector said. "At least, none's been reported to us as yet. But if the things were stolen last night, there's hardly been time for the news to come in."

CHAPTER IV: THE BOATHOUSE

"WE may need an accurate map of these trails, if it ever comes to a trial," Sir Clinton pointed out, as he handed the pearls to the Inspector for safe keeping. "You'd better get one made as soon as possible, in case the wind rises and disturbs these papers."

"I'll do that myself, sir," Severn assured him. Then, seeing Sir Clinton look rather doubtful, he added, "I was an instructor in map reading and field sketching during the War, sir. I've had plenty of practice in traversing; and with a six-inch ordnance map, there's nothing in it. I've got a good prismatic compass at home."

The Chief Constable nodded his approval of the proposal.

"With cross bearings from the map, it won't take long," he admitted. "But you'll be fairly busy with other sides of the case, I expect."

The mention of the trails brought Wendover's mind back to an obvious fact in connection with them.

"The murderer left a track *away* from Horncastle's body, but we haven't found his incoming trail yet. He must have got here somehow."

"By land, or sea, or in the air, as the prayer book says," Sir Clinton suggested gravely. "I think we can leave the air out of it. No aeroplane could have landed here without crashing; and the chance of a helicopter being in the neighbourhood seems small."

"Since there's no trail on the grass," Wendover pursued, unperturbed by Sir Clinton's irony, "the murderer must have come along the shingle, where he would leave no track."

"He might have come across the lake in a boat," Sir Clinton pointed out.

Wendover shook his head.

"The only boats are in my boathouse over yonder, and that's under lock and key."

"And you have the key, if I remember?"

"Yes, here, on my chain."

Wendover dived into his trouser pocket and fished out a bunch of keys from which he selected a Yale key and held it up.

"But if I'm not mistaken," Sir Clinton reminded him, "you used to lend keys of the boathouse to a lot of people round about here, so that they could use your boats when they felt inclined."

Wendover could not repress a smile. It was not often that the Chief Constable fell into his trap.

"That's quite true," he admitted. "But as a matter of fact, those keys are useless now. There's been an epidemic of small thefts hereabouts of late, and as the keys of the boathouse had been handed around rather freely, I was afraid they might have got into wrong hands, so I changed the lock a few weeks ago. The old keys are no good. And as nearly everybody is away from home just now, I didn't trouble to issue the fresh set to my neighbours."

"Then how did it happen that three or four days ago I saw the Keith-Westertons take a boat out?

They didn't come to the Grange to ask for your key, I noticed at the time."

"Oh, I gave them a key each," Wendover explained, in a rather nettled tone. "Mrs. Keith-Westerton sometimes goes up in the afternoon to sit on the balcony above the lake. I don't suppose you're going to attach any importance to that? What I meant was that no irresponsible person could have a key of the boathouse in his possession."

"I'd just like to be clear about this, Mr. Wendover," the Inspector put in. "There's nothing in it; but still we have to be sure of our ground, you understand. You've got a key; Mr. Keith-Westerton's got a key; and Mrs. Keith-Westerton's got a third key? And you haven't lent any other keys? Where do you keep the rest of your duplicates? Could any one get access to them?"

"Not unless they picked my pocket of my safe key," Wendover answered rather crustily. "All the remainder of the duplicates I keep in my safe, and no one can get into that without my key. It's on my chain here—see! And I haven't lent any one a new key except those two that I gave to the Keith-Westertons. It's out of the question that the murderer could have used one of my boats. He must have come along the shingle."

Something in Sir Clinton's attitude seemed to give the Inspector a bias against Wendover's opinion. He considered for a moment or two before speaking.

"I'm not doubting for a moment what you say, Mr. Wendover," he said reluctantly, "but you know I'll be asked all sorts of questions if it comes to a trial, and I think I'd like to be on firm ground on this point. There's just the chance that some one may have used a boat and, with your permission, I'd like to have a look at your boathouse, so as to be able to say that I've left no stone unturned. One never knows what a prosecuting barrister may want to use, and if we get the murderer, his counsel's dead certain to ask if we examined the boat question thoroughly. If I don't look into it, it leaves an opening for him to suggest that an alternative route was available to the murderer and to throw doubt into the jury's mind about the rest of the evidence on the strength of it."

"Oh, well, you can poke about the boathouse to your heart's content," Wendover agreed, without enthusiasm. "You'll find nothing there, I'm sure. My key and the Keith-Westertons' keys are the only ones that will open the door."

Sir Clinton, having let the Inspector act as his cat's-paw, intervened with a suggestion.

"If the murderer came along the shingle, it'll take a long time to find his tracks at the far end, probably. He may have walked on the beach the whole way around the lake, for all one can tell. The dew would be off the grass long before we could cover the ground. Since the Inspector wants to look over the boathouse, let's go there first; and if there's nothing there, then we know the murderer must have come by the lakeside. That's the quickest way of dealing with the thing."

He glanced at Horncastle's body.

"The constable had better wait here till he's relieved. We can stop at the Grange, and you can telephone to make your arrangements about removing the body, Inspector. You've made all the measurements you need, I think? I saw you jotting them down in your notebook. Anything more? Well, then, we'd better go up to the car."

A few minutes took them to the Grange, where Severn got in touch with the police station and gave his orders; then once more they got into the car and drove to the boathouse.

It was a two-storeyed erection. The upper floor projected over the lake, while part of the space below this formed a dock for the pleasure boats. As the ground sloped steeply up from the water at this point, the only entrance was a door on the side remote from the lake, and this gave access to the upper-storey rooms.

Sir Clinton stepped out of the car and went up to the door.

"A bar handle, unfortunately," he pointed out to the Inspector, "so that's one chance less of getting fingerprints if we need them. A man grips a bar with his palm and not with his finger tips. And the milled head of a Yale handle on the inside won't give much help either. Just a moment, though."

He walked in turn to the various windows which could be reached from the ground and examined the fastenings.

"All fast," he reported. "If any one got into the place they must have gone through the door. Now I think we'll look inside."

Wendover, with an ill grace, produced his key and

opened the door. The Inspector stood aside to let Sir Clinton enter first.

"You've never been in here before, Inspector?" the Chief Constable asked, as he led the way. "Well, this door on the right leads into a cloakroom, you see?" He threw open the door as he spoke. "This spiral stair on the left of the front door leads down to the lower flat; and the door on the left, beyond the stair, opens into a sort of store and workshop. That door straight in front of us leads into a lounge, with a balcony beyond which overhangs the lake. Suppose we start with the workshop and work around, room by room."

Wendover, hardly able to conceal his contempt for what he regarded as a pure waste of time, followed his visitors into the little room. He noticed, with a certain malicious delight, that Severn seemed rather taken aback by Sir Clinton's desire for thoroughness. Evidently the Inspector saw little chance of picking up clues in that locality. Wendover had an innate fondness for order and neatness in his arrangements; and this room was always kept spick and span. Every tool had its special hook or rack to which it was restored as soon as it had been used; nails and screws were kept in tiers of drawers, each of which had a sample clipped outside to facilitate a search; and the power lathe might have been exhibited in a shop window, so well was it kept.

Wendover's eye passed approvingly over his little arsenal, reviewing the hammers, saws, chisels, gimlets, spokeshaves, planes, and try-squares, rank above rank, on the wall. Suddenly, as his glance ranged from row to row, it was arrested by an empty clip. Something was out of place. With a slight gesture of vexation, he turned to the carpenter's bench, expecting to find the missing article there. But the tool was on neither the bench nor the work table.

"Something gone astray?" demanded Sir Clinton, who had been watching Wendover as he reviewed his implements.

"Only a small turnscrew. It must be lying about somewhere, but I don't see it."

"What size is it? Eight or nine inches long? Can you see a screwdriver of that size anywhere, Inspector? We'll have a look around for it."

Wendover wished to brush the matter aside, but Sir Clinton persisted in searching, much to the Inspector's disgust. Severn hadn't come there to look for screwdrivers, he reflected in mute protest. Clues were what he wanted to be after; and he could not understand why the Chief Constable should be wasting his time on trivialities. It seemed futile to spend precious minutes in hunting for a mere mislaid turnscrew.

Wendover, when he saw the thoroughness with which Sir Clinton set about the search, was better able to gauge the ultimate object of it. Sir Clinton knew his host's fondness for orderly arrangement. If the tool had gone astray, then evidently its owner had not been the last to use it. Some one else must have found a need for it, and failed to return it to its proper clip after the work was done. Mrs. Keith-Westerton would be most unlikely to need a screwdriver. Young Keith-Westerton might have used it.

Or else some unauthorised person. . . . But an un-authorised person was exactly what they were look-ing for. And a screwdriver would take fingerprints nicely. Wendover, though still sceptical of any con-nection between his boathouse and the murder of the keeper, was nevertheless drawn to take part in the search by a curiosity which spurred him on despite his incredulity.

It took a very short time to ransack so orderly a place, and before long Sir Clinton was satisfied that the missing tool was not there. He seemed, if any-thing, pleased with this negative result, and still more so when a search of the cloakroom failed to bring the screwdriver to light.

"We can keep our eyes open for it as we go through the rest of the place," he said, as he opened the door of the lounge.

If the Inspector hoped to find any obvious traces of an intruder in that apartment, he must have been disappointed. Some comfortable cane chairs stood in a random arrangement about the room; a couple of tables, with ash trays and matchboxes, occupied the centre of the expanse of planked floor; a third table with an old-fashioned table grand model gramophone was placed in a corner; while the whole side of the room opposite the door was glazed and gave access through a French window to the balcony which over-hung the lake. The blinds on all the windows were down.

Sir Clinton stepped over and examined the ash trays, in which some cigarette stubs had been left.

"Proceeding à la Sherlock," he said, with an expressionless face, "I find that these stubs were once State Express cigarettes. You smoke Abdullahs, Wendover. You know my methods. You didn't smoke these, so somebody else did. I presume it was Keith-Westerton?"

"Yes, I remember he smokes State Express."

"Nice and tidy you keep this lounge," Sir Clinton commented, glancing around it approvingly. "You must spend quite a while each week in sweeping and dusting it, not to speak of washing up and cleaning the ash trays. When do you do it?"

"What are you talking about?" said Wendover indignantly. "I don't clean up this place. One of the maids looks after it, of course."

"And you give her a key when she comes up?"

"Naturally, I give her my key."

"Ah, then there *is* a chance of an unauthorised person getting hold of a key, after all?"

"The maid's perfectly reliable," Wendover protested.

"I don't say she isn't. Still, there it is. Your key has been in other hands."

Sir Clinton, having reminded Wendover of this, seemed averse to further discussion of the point. He and the Inspector began to search the lounge, a fairly easy task, owing to the bareness of furnishing.

"No screwdriver here, sir," Severn reported, after a tour of the place.

Sir Clinton made a gesture of agreement, but as he did so he stepped forward and scrutinised the plaiting of one of the chairs. Taking a penknife from his pocket he used it to extract something which had apparently sunk into a little hollow among the canes.

"What's that?" Wendover demanded.

"Another pearl," the Chief Constable answered, holding the tiny object out for their inspection. "I think we can take it that the murderer must have been here sometime—that is, if he was the person who dropped the other specimens beside Horncastle's body."

"I suppose he must," Wendover admitted, with a slightly crestfallen air. "And that probably means that he did take one of my boats across to Friar's Point."

"And then the boat kindly brought itself back again to this side, all alone?" Sir Clinton inquired. "Well, we can inspect this accomplished skiff in a minute or two."

He turned to the Inspector.

"What do you make of this distribution of these pearls?"

Severn seemed for a moment unable to catch the drift of the question. Then his face brightened.

"I think I see what you mean, sir. He must have had them loose in his pocket when he came here. He sat down in that chair, I suppose, and somehow or other one of the pearls slipped out of his pocket and lodged in that cranny among the canes. Then he went over and murdered Horncastle; and while he was stooping over the body, lifting it from the shingle up to the bank, some more of the pearls dropped out."

"It's possible," Sir Clinton admitted. "A millionaire might carry valuable pearls about with him, loose in his pocket and ready to drop out. Still, I'd think again, if I were you. But the pearls can stand over for the present. It's the screwdriver that's worrying me just now. You've looked everywhere on this flat."

"Even inside the gramophone, sir."

"What do you want with a gramophone up here?" Sir Clinton inquired idly, turning to Wendover. "I see you've got a pile of records as well."

"It's an old one I had in the house, before I put in wireless," Wendover explained. "Some youngsters who were staying with me a month or two ago brought it up here to play fox trots. The floor's good enough for dancing, and a couple of the girls were keen enough to dance anywhere."

The gramophone seemed to draw Sir Clinton. He crossed the room, opened the lid, and glanced at the turntable.

"You looked in here, Inspector?"

"Yes, sir. No screwdriver there, nor anything else except needles."

"It's what isn't here that worries me," Sir Clinton said, leaving the lid of the instrument up. "Did you happen to notice that there's no nickel point in the middle of the turntable?"

Severn stepped over and examined the instrument. His face fell as he did so. The turntable axle was missing.

"No, sir. I didn't spot that. I was looking for something apart from the gramophone, and I expect I saw the turntable in position and missed the other thing; didn't think of examining it carefully enough, evidently."

Sir Clinton made no reply. He examined the heads

of the nickelled screws which held the board below the turntable in position; tried his fountain pen vertically on one of those nearest the hinges of the lid, as though measuring the free space above the screw; and finally, closing the lid, he lifted the whole instrument off the table and put it down again.

"So that was it?" he said musingly. "You're not likely to see your screwdriver again, I should think," he added, turning to Wendover. "Better buy a new one."

He opened the doors in front of the gramophone and peered inside for a moment.

"You'll need to buy a new motor and a new horn too, if you ever want this thing to work again. Both of them are gone. But perhaps you authorised somebody to take them?"

"No, I didn't," Wendover declared. "If they're gone, then it's been done in the last day or two, for I remember hearing the gramophone two days ago when the Keith-Westertons were up here in the afternoon. They played one record, for I heard it over the water when I was out in a boat."

Then the grotesqueness of the situation seemed to strike him.

"What the devil would any one want to steal the motor of a gramophone for?" he demanded. "You can't murder a man with a thing of that sort; and besides, Horncastle wasn't killed by any fantastic method of that kind. That was just plain shooting. I don't see what the gramophone's got to do with it at all. What do you make of it, Clinton? Do you really suppose a murderer went about burdened with a heavy bit of machinery like that? What could he do with it?"

"It's a bit early yet to say," Sir Clinton answered in a colourless voice. "Still, I shouldn't be surprised if we come across your motor before we're done with this case. It opens up a lot of interesting speculations. I shouldn't wonder . . . if Horncastle turns out to be a mere pawn in the game. However, there's nothing to be gained by standing here chattering. Suppose we have a look at the balcony now, and then go downstairs and see what's to be seen there."

The balcony yielded nothing of the slightest interest; and Sir Clinton led the way to the stairhead. The lowest turn of the iron spiral brought them out on a sloping platform which occupied half the length of the boathouse and which ended in a sort of dock walled in on both sides and closed, on the water front, by a large door through which the boats could pass.

"A bit gloomy in here, with the door shut," Sir Clinton remarked. "I don't want to switch on the electric light. You'll have to test all the switches for finger prints, Inspector, so we mustn't leave our own on top. We'll open the door instead."

The door was controlled by a running-chain arrangement from the platform; and Sir Clinton, taking precautions not to obliterate any finger marks, swung the leaves apart and admitted the full flood of the morning daylight.

"No chance of any one making his way in here by water," the Chief Constable pointed out to Severn. "The door, you see, goes right down below water level; and if any one tried to dive under it, he'd come across a few strands of barbed wire."

The tiny dock was obviously safe from intrusion. Walled in on both sides, roofed over by the upper storey of the boathouse and protected by its door, it could be entered only by way of the spiral stair if the water-gate was closed. Four boats were moored at the edge of the landing stage, very spick-and-span with gay cushions in the stern seats. At the back of the platform were oar racks; and in one corner lay a small outboard motor, suitable for clamping to a rowing-boat's stern.

"Oars all present and correct," Sir Clinton said, running his eye along the racks. "Now we'll have a look at the boats."

As they walked down the platform, Wendover's glance caught something which gave him a rather unpleasant shock. On the cushions in the stern of one boat lay a lady's vanity bag which he felt sure he recognised. The Inspector's eye lighted on it almost at the same instant.

"Hullo! What's this?" he exclaimed jubilantly, as he hurried forward to secure it.

"Don't handle it carelessly," Sir Clinton cautioned him. "We may need to look for fingerprints."

Severn stepped into the boat, lifted his prey, and came back on to the platform again. Gingerly he opened the bag and glanced inside.

"Here's a handkerchief," he reported, drawing it out as he spoke. "Initials in the corner, 'D. K. W.'"

"You needn't guess," Sir Clinton remarked, studying Wendover's face as he spoke. "It's Mrs. Keith-

Westerton's bag. I've seen it in her hand once or twice lately."

Wendover hastened to remove any false impressions which, he feared, Severn might have received.

"Mrs. Keith-Westerton was out on the lake yesterday afternoon," he explained, as though dismissing an irrelevant matter. "She must have left her bag in the boat by an oversight."

"Obviously," Sir Clinton agreed, in a dry tone. "She left it behind, or it wouldn't be here now."

Wendover had an uncomfortable feeling that Sir Clinton had repeated the truism without lending any support to the implication in the original version; and a glance at Severn's face showed him that the Inspector had noted his superior's reservation.

"Just try these anchor chains, Inspector," Sir Clinton suggested. "Give 'em a good tug and see if they're firm."

Each boat had a tiny anchor in the bow, lying on some fathoms of light mooring chain. Severn tried each in turn.

"They're all right, sir," he reported. "The rings let into the wood are as solid as you could wish. I couldn't stir 'em if I put my whole weight into it."

Wendover could make nothing of this and he was not sorry to see that Severn was no wiser, as his face showed.

"Now, I think we'll have the floor boards up in that boat," Sir Clinton continued, without pausing to explain his ideas about the anchor chains. "Careful, Inspector, when you're lifting them. We don't want to lose anything overboard."

Severn obediently lifted the floor boards of the boat in which he had found the vanity bag; then, getting down on his knees, he began a careful examination of the inner side of the skiff's hull. Suddenly he picked up something and turned round with an air in which triumph and surprise were mingled.

"It's another of these pearls, sir—and there's another one still, down there. . . . I've got it. That's two more of them."

He bent again to his task and finally fished out one more pearl.

"All three of them in the after part of the boat, I think?" Sir Clinton asked, as Severn stepped back on to the platform

"Yes, sir, between the stroke's seat and the stern seat, roughly," the Inspector confirmed. "They might have dropped from the pocket of some one sitting on either seat, well enough."

"Ladies don't have pockets nowadays," Wendover commented acidly.

"Nor do men usually wear pearl necklaces nowadays," Sir Clinton pointed out. "Curious, these vagaries of fashion."

He knew perfectly well how Wendover was feeling. The Squire always had a soft spot for a pretty girl; he wouldn't like to see her dragged into a business of this sort, even indirectly. And, besides, Wendover had more than a little of class consciousness. Mrs. Keith-Westerton—or at least her husband—belonged to Wendover's own caste; and so in this case the personal was reinforced by the social appeal. The Chief Constable's own business, however, was to get to the bottom of the affair, no matter who might be mixed up in it. He could hardly refrain from probing the business merely because of Wendover's predilections in favour of his friends. He began to wish that the Inspector had left him alone. Things were growing awkward, evidently.

"I want you to think for a moment," he said, turning to Wendover, and speaking in a serious tone. "Can you think of anything missing here: spare chain, wireless accumulators, an anchor, anything of that sort?"

Wendover thought hard for a few moments, then shook his head.

"No, there's nothing been stolen, if that's what you mean. That screwdriver's the only thing I miss."

"Well, it isn't here," Sir Clinton said. "I've kept my eyes open down here; and you keep the place so tidy that I'd no difficulty there. Just take the floor boards up in the other boats, Inspector, please. We may as well be thorough."

But Severn's search of the other skiffs revealed nothing of the slightest importance. While he was busy, Sir Clinton occupied himself with an inspection of the landing stage and the water in the dock. He found nothing, however, except a number of spent Swan vestas, some on the platform, others floating in the water.

"Nothing much in that," he decided aloud. "We've all been smoking here, and most likely we've pitched our spent matches about. I know I contributed one or two myself, yesterday, when I had a boat out."

Severn stepped out of the boat which he had been searching.

"Is there anything more to do here, sir?" he inquired.

"Not at this moment," Sir Clinton decided. "We'll close that water gate and then go upstairs."

When they reached the lounge, the Chief Constable turned to the Inspector.

"I don't expect to get much from fingerprints; but you'd better see what can be done. The electric switches, that water-gate affair, the oar handles, and possibly the chairs and the gramophone: try the lot. It'll probably be time wasted, for I think we're up against somebody who'll have had the sense to wear gloves, if fingerprints were likely to incriminate him —or her, as the case may be."

"Then I suppose I'd better go down to Headquarters and get arrangements made, sir?"

"No," said Sir Clinton, to the obvious surprise of the Inspector. "You're going to wait here on the premises until you're relieved. No one is to get into the boathouse till further orders. That's absolutely essential. Nobody of any sort, you understand, except myself and Mr. Wendover, if he comes with me. I'm going back to the Grange now. I'll telephone for a man to take your place. And, Inspector, see that you put two men here to-night, with the same orders. One man alone might go to sleep; and I want no risks of that sort."

At Sir Clinton's first sentence, Severn's face fell. It was clear that he had been counting on breakfast as the next item on his programme. Wendover's ready sympathy was aroused.

"I'm hungry myself," he said, with a smile. "All right, Inspector, I'll send you something to eat as soon as we get back home. That'll save time. You can stoke up while you're waiting for your relief. Like tea in your Thermos? Or coffee? We can't have you starving on the premises."

"And as soon as your relief turns up, come down to the Grange," Sir Clinton added. "You've a busy morning before you yet."

Severn thanked Wendover for his thoughtfulness and accompanied them to the door. As they reached the threshold, the Inspector's eye was caught by a tall figure, in the familiar uniform of the Salvation Army, coming up the rough woodland road which led to the boathouse from Talgarth village. The man caught sight of them at the same instant and quickened his steps.

"Is Mr. Keith-Westerton here?" he demanded, as he came up to the group.

"Severn shook his head.

"Mrs. Keith-Westerton, then?" the Salvationist persisted.

"No, she's not here. What makes you think she would be?"

The Salvationist paid no attention to the question.

"Is there any one in that boathouse?" he persevered.

"No. There's nobody here except ourselves."

As a landowner, Wendover inclined to be easygoing. He put up no notices to trespassers and he allowed people to come and go upon his ground without restriction. At the same time, he expected them, as a matter of courtesy, to ask his permission if they happened to run across him personally; and subconsciously he resented the behaviour of the Salvationist. The fellow ought to have explained his presence, first of all, instead of catechising his betters. Besides, what had a Salvationist to do with the Keith-Westertons, people in Wendover's own class?

"What's your business?" he demanded abruptly.

For a moment the Salvationist seemed taken aback. Then a gleam of fanaticism kindled in his pale blue eyes.

"I'm an insurance agent," he explained.

Sir Clinton suppressed a smile as he watched his host blunder into the trap.

"Oh, indeed," Wendover commented coldly. "I don't think you'll make a success of it if you thrust yourself on people before they've had breakfast. You'll hardly find them in the best mood for business at this hour of the morning. Your employers would hardly thank you for your zeal, I should imagine. What company do you represent?"

"Our concern's the biggest thing in fire insurance, the very biggest thing that's in the market to-day," the Salvationist explained eagerly. "I give you my word for that. Put yourself on our books, and we can offer you safety, certainty, and an easy mind. We're prepared to undertake any risk, the bigger the better. And we do what no other concern can do. Note that carefully. We've no graduated premiums; everybody insures with us at a flat rate premium that's within the reach of the poorest man in the land. Just mark that and think over it well. And we've bonuses, too, bonuses that make all our competitors look silly. That's a plain fact; there's no disputing it. We're beyond competition. We charge a premium that any one can pay; we've got a security that can't be equalled; and our bonus payments are liberal beyond belief, almost. And here's a copy of our prospectus. . . ."

He produced a small volume from his pocket and held it out to Wendover, who was slightly offended on discovering that it was a Bible.

"Every promise in it will stand examination," the Salvationist went on. "It's a sound business proposition. Look, now! You pay a premium every year to insure your furniture against the risk of a fire in your house; and you think that's money well spent, don't you? Of course you do. Well, then, why not pay our premium and insure something that's worth a good deal more to you than a few chattels? Why not take advantage of our offer and insure your soul against the risk of eternal fire? We're not trying to make money out of you. The only premium we ask is a repentant heart, down on the counter. Pay that over, and you've no need to fear hell fire. You're covered by our guarantee. And we'll throw in all the joys of heaven as a bonus. Think it over. It's a sound proposition, none sounder. You can't get as good terms anywhere else."

In religious affairs, Wendover was something of a Laodicean, but the Salvationist touched him on the raw by the calm assumption that the Squire was already to be reckoned as among the damned. What annoyed him still more was the bad taste of the harangue. Religion, by the Wendover standard, was something respectable and not a thing to be handled in the manner of a pushing commercial traveller. A reminiscence of the late Doctor Mahaffy came to his mind and saved him from an angry retort.

"You're wasting your time," he said, with a twinkle in his eye. "It's not a matter I discuss with strangers; but since you treat me as an intimate friend, I don't mind telling you that I'm saved—though it was a deuced narrow squeak."

"I'm used to scoffers," the Salvationist retorted. "I was one myself, before I saw light. You're an ignorant and self-righteous man, just as I was. I'll pray for you."

Sir Clinton, seeing Wendover's face redden under this, broke in swiftly.

"May I ask your name, Mr.——?"

"Sawtry," the Salvationist supplied. "Save-your-soul Sawtry, they call me, usually. I've been the instrument in bringing many a soul to safety."

"Thanks, Mr. Sawtry. Would you mind telling me why you came here at this hour of the morning looking for Mr. Keith-Westerton? This isn't his boathouse. Surely you'd find him at home instead of down here."

"He's not at his house," Sawtry answered, with a gleam of triumph. "That's why I came here. They said he'd probably gone to the lake for a bathe before breakfast."

"He's not here," Sir Clinton assured him. "You

must have wanted him very urgently, surely, if you couldn't wait till he'd had his breakfast?"

"I wanted to see him on private business," Sawtry replied, with a sudden ebb in his flow of eloquence.

"You asked for Mrs. Keith-Westerton also," Sir Clinton reminded him.

"I've got some private business with her too."

"This is Inspector Severn," Sir Clinton informed him. "He may want to ask you a question or two."

"Then I sha'n't answer," Sawtry said bluntly. "I know a thing or two about the law; you can't get over me with bluff. You've no power to question me about my private affairs. So you can stuff that in your pipe and smoke it to pass the time. That's my answer to you, Mr. Inspector. Some of the smartest men in the C. I. D. have tried to get ahead of me in their time. They didn't manage it, so it's not likely that you'll better their work. And now I'll wish you good morning. You've no right to detain me."

He turned abruptly on his heel and walked off down the road by which he had come. Sir Clinton gazed after him thoughtfully.

"What he says is true enough," he commented, after a pause. "But I'd give something to know what's behind all that. He's been under suspicion, at one time. He must be a bit impulsive or he'd have kept his thumb on that, instead of blurting it out. What did you make of him, Inspector?"

"Well, sir, he talks like a gentleman—I mean his accent's all right. If you took him out of that uniform and put him in plain clothes he'd look upper class, I think."

"I was wondering what his line was before the Salvation Army made him see the error of his ways. With that manner and his glibness, he'd do well at the confidence trick. I wonder if he's a genuine convert."

CHAPTER V: THE KEITH-WESTERTON IMBROGLIO

"Now let's settle the next moves," Sir Clinton suggested, when Severn had rejoined them at the Grange after breakfast. "We've found nothing useful in the way of fingerprints on that bag, so we may as well use it in another way. We'll go to the Dower House, ostensibly to return lost property. I'm the finder; you're the police, Inspector; and Mr. Wendover will come along as a friend of the family, if he wants to. You'll do the questioning. We must find out what the Keith-Westertons were doing last night—and this morning as well. It may lead to nothing; but it's the obvious first step. You'd better question the servants as well when you're about it."

Accompanied by Wendover, the two officials drove down to the Dower House. The Squire's mind was a battle ground of emotions. He hated the idea of meddling in the private affairs of his neighbours, since he had not the slightest belief that Mrs. Keith-Westerton's bag had any connection with the Horncastle murder. On the other hand, he could not suppress a natural curiosity to see the full development of the case, even in its blind alleys; and in addition, he hoped that he might be able to put a spoke in the Inspector's wheel if he grew too blunt in his inquiries.

"Exert a moderating influence," was the form in which he phrased this idea in his own mind.

Severn's ring was answered by an obviously agitated maid.

"I don't think Mr. Keith-Westerton's in just now," she explained in answer to the Inspector's inquiry. "He went out on the chauffeur's motor bike before breakfast."

"Mrs. Keith-Westerton will do as well, if she's at home."

"Mrs. Keith-Westerton isn't at home, sir."

"Then we'll come in and wait for a while," Severn proposed, after a glance at Sir Clinton.

"It's no good waiting for Mrs. Keith-Westerton; she's gone from home; and I don't know when Mr. Keith-Westerton will be back."

"We'll wait for a short time, anyhow," Severn decided, in a tone which took no denial.

Rather reluctantly, the maid showed them into the smoking room and left them. Wendover, feeling in a false position, walked over to the window which overlooked the drive. Sir Clinton and the Inspector, having no ties of bread and salt to hamper their feelings, made themselves more at home.

"Rather untidy, burning papers in an empty grate and leaving the ashes," Sir Clinton commented, as he drew the Inspector's attention to the fireplace.

Before Severn could say anything, Wendover stepped back from the window with a sharp movement, as though to avoid being seen from without. They heard the whirr of a motorcycle on the drive. In a few minutes, young Keith-Westerton entered the room and favoured his visitors with a glance in which Wendover seemed to detect a mingling of suspicion and apprehension.

"Well, what d'you want at this ungodly hour?" he demanded angrily of the Inspector. Then, seeing Wendover and Sir Clinton he moderated his voice. "Sorry. I haven't had breakfast yet."

"This bag has been found," said the Inspector, producing it as he spoke. "I believe it belongs to Mrs. Keith-Westerton, so I've brought it around to make sure."

Wendover, watching Keith-Westerton's face, was encouraged by the immediate change in its expression. Obvious relief was written large on it as soon as the Inspector had spoken.

"Oh, yes. That's her bag. See her initials on it? Thanks for bringing it around. Very good of you."

He took the bag from the Inspector and stood in an attitude which suggested dismissal in the plainest fashion. Severn was obviously undecided as to his next step; and Sir Clinton gave him no help. As the pause became awkward, the Inspector made up his mind.

"There's something more valuable than the bag, but I'm not quite sure about it. Has Mrs. Keith-Westerton a pearl necklace among her jewels, by any chance?"

"Yes, she has. What about it?"

"Would you mind seeing if it's all safe?"

"I expect it is. She was wearing it at dinner last night. D' you think we've been burgled?"

Wendover, studying Keith-Westerton's expression

closely, saw something like bewilderment replace the earlier relief.

"I'd like you to see if it's there, all right," Severn persisted politely. "We've had some information received that makes me ask that."

"Oh, all right. If you make a point of it. But I'm sure . . . " he hesitated for a moment and then went on. "I'm not sure I can tell you anything certain. I'll go and look."

In a few minutes he returned with an empty necklace case in his hand.

"It doesn't seem to be here," he said, as though in some perplexity. "It's generally kept in this and not along with the other things in her jewel case. And it's not with the other things, either, for I've searched."

"Were the pearls in it anything like these?" Severn asked, as he drew some tiny objects from his pocket and laid them on a table. "I don't expect you to identify them, of course. Your jeweler could do that for us, later on, perhaps."

As Keith-Westerton bent over the table, Wendover could see a deepening of his perplexed expression.

"They're very like them. That's as far as I can go."

"Perhaps Mrs. Keith-Westerton could be certain?" Severn suggested.

"She's not here at present."

"When did she leave?" Severn demanded.

Keith-Westerton seemed taken aback.

"What the hell's that to you?" he retorted angrily.

Severn's face lighted up at the tone.

"I shouldn't lose your temper, sir, if I were you,"

he said decidedly. "We're in very deep water in this business, and it would be better if we take it quietly."

At the words "deep water", Wendover saw Keith-Westerton's look change to one of apprehension, like that which he had worn when he first came into the room. There was no denying that he looked like a man who momentarily expects trouble to break on him. Severn, watching also, evidently decided that now was the time to show his hand.

"Your keeper, Horncastle, was found shot dead this morning—murdered, we have reason to believe."

If the Inspector hoped to get evidence from Keith-Westerton's face at this point, he must have been embarrassed by the obvious confusion of emotions which struggled for expression. It was clear that Keith-Westerton was taken aback by the statement; and yet Wendover, searching for something else, could not help feeling that a faint relief underlay the main feeling. Then the perplexed look returned to the eyes and deepened, as though the young man could not see his line of action clear before him.

"Horncastle shot?" he said, with obvious mistrust in his tone. "And you say it's murder? How d' you know that? It doesn't sound likely. Who'd murder him?"

Severn, scanning Keith-Westerton's face, apparently made up his mind to put all his cards on the table.

"This is a very awkward business," he said, with a certain reluctance. "The fact is, I've got to ask you some questions. You mayn't like them; but I've got to ask them and you'd be well advised to answer them frankly. When did you see Mrs. Keith-Westerton last?"

This blunt question seemed to throw Keith-Westerton into complete confusion.

"What's my wife got to do with it?" he demanded, after a moment or two. "Leave her out of it, d' you hear? What right have you to drag her name into a case of this kind, eh?"

"Now this sort of talk does no good, Mr. Keith-Westerton," Severn pointed out coldly. "You've as good as identified these pearls as belonging to Mrs. Keith-Westerton. Very well, then. These pearls, or some of them, at least, were picked up alongside Horncastle's dead body. I don't know how they came there. I don't suggest anything. But you can see for yourself that questions are bound to be asked."

Wendover could see that this evidence came as a thunderbolt on Keith-Westerton. He looked suddenly like a sick man, and almost mechanically he moved over to a chair and sat down, as though he felt unable to stand. Wendover's eye was caught by a slight rhythmic quiver of his knee, which betrayed that he was strung up to a high pitch of nervousness and had lost some muscular control. At last, moistening his lips, Keith-Westerton spoke in a high-pitched voice.

"There's nothing in it. There's nothing in it," he said, as though trying to raise his courage by repetition.

"Then the truth's the best thing," Severn suggested dryly. "When did you see Mrs. Keith-Westerton last?"

Instead of answering immediately, Keith-Westerton quite obviously turned the question over in his mind.

"Last night," he replied reluctantly after a few seconds.

"At what hour last night?"

Again Keith-Westerton evidently paused to consider the query carefully.

"Just after dinner."

"You said good-bye to her then, I suppose, since she was going away?"

This time Keith-Westerton's reluctance was even more apparent than before.

"No," he said, at last, "I didn't see her before she went."

"She left unexpectedly, then?" Severn demanded sharply. "Did you know that she was going away last night?"

"I didn't know beforehand."

"Where has she gone?"

Wendover, watching Keith-Westerton's face, had no difficulty in deciding that the answer to this, when it came, would be a falsehood, either direct or indirect.

"I can't tell you."

The Inspector's face darkened at this evasion.

"You'll gain nothing by this, Mr. Keith-Westerton," he said with asperity. "Either you know where she is or you don't. Which is it?"

"She's somewhere where you won't find her, anyhow," Keith-Westerton snapped out. "What right have you to badger me about my wife's affairs, eh? It's a free country, isn't it?"

"Up to a point, it is," Severn agreed, in a more

courteous tone. "You refuse to answer that question? Well, I can't force you. I think you're making a bad mistake, that's all. Now I've got to ask you about your own movements last night."

Keith-Westerton shrugged his shoulders impatiently; but Wendover could see that he was relieved at this turn in the inquiry.

"You and Mrs. Keith-Westerton had dinner together, I suppose?"

Keith-Westerton contented himself with a nod of assent.

"Had you any disagreement during the day? Did anything happen which might have made her go away from home suddenly?"

Keith-Westerton's face betrayed something of the thoughts in his mind. "How much should I give away?" seemed written plainly in his expression; and his eyes hinted at a swift rejection of one idea after another.

"We hadn't the slightest disagreement," he replied at last, dragging out his sentence as though even at the last moment he might wish to reconsider his course. "There was nothing in the very slightest that you could call a disagreement, up to the moment when I left her."

"You left her? Where did you leave her?"

"In her sitting room next door—where we usually go after dinner."

"I see," said Severn. "You left her there. And that would be about—what time?"

"A few minutes after nine," Keith-Westerton answered at once.

"Oh, within a few minutes—say five minutes?"

"Immediately after nine," Keith-Westerton said definitely. "I'd been keeping my eye on the clock."

"And you went out, I take it? Did you change before you went out?"

"No, I put on a light coat over my dinner jacket. I changed into outdoor shoes. I was going out for a walk."

"I see. You didn't say good night when you went out, or good-bye, or anything of that sort? No? Now, Mr. Keith-Westerton, what sort of walk did you take?"

It needed no expert in physiognomy to see that this question gave Keith-Westerton trouble. He considered for some seconds before replying, lamely:

"It was a fine night. I walked about a good deal."

"On the main roads?"

"Mostly. Once I crossed a field, but there was a heavy dew. After that I kept to the road or to paths."

"I see. And you got home again—when?"

"I don't know, really," Keith-Westerton answered hesitatingly. "Round about one o'clock in the morning, I should think."

"Must have been a long walk you took, surely. Where did you go?"

"Just round about. I can't remember exactly where I went. I was in a brown study, most of the time. Busy thinking about some business and didn't notice where I was going."

"I see," Severn commented discouragingly. "Well, you must be able to remember what direction you started in and what road you came back by, surely."

Keith-Westerton obviously resented this.

"I turned along the road towards the Grange to start with, and I came back the same way finally. I really can't remember where I got to. I was just walking aimlessly, trying to think something out."

"H'm!" Severn mused aloud. "Can't you remember anything more than that? No? Well, what happened when you came in?"

"I took off my shoes. . . . Then, I think I came in here for a moment or two. . . . And almost at once I went up to my wife's room."

"And found she wasn't there? Did you search for her?"

"No, I went to my own room."

"I see."

Severn's tone indicated very clearly that whatever he saw, it was not an explanation of Keith-Westerton's behaviour.

"You have a key to Mr. Wendover's boathouse, haven't you?"

This question evidently perturbed Keith-Westerton profoundly. For some reason, Severn's inquiry seemed to touch him unexpectedly on a raw spot.

"Yes, I have," he admitted.

"And Mrs. Keith-Westerton had a key also?"

"Yes."

"Now, tell me," Severn spoke very suavely, "did you visit the boathouse in the course of your walk?"

It was obvious that this question gave Keith-Westerton more trouble than any of the others.

"No use humming and hawing about it," Severn said sternly. "Either you did or you didn't. Which is it?"

"I didn't," Keith-Westerton said sullenly, but without convincing any of the trio that he was speaking the truth.

"Oh, well . . ." Severn seemed as though he wished to give his victim a chance of reconsidering his statement; but as Keith-Westerton remained silent, he went on. "You row a boat, don't you? I mean, you're in practice?"

"Well enough," was the reply, in a tone which showed that the bearing of the question escaped Keith-Westerton.

"Can Mrs. Keith-Westerton row?"

"She's learning. She rows not badly, considering how little practice she's had."

"When were you out on the lake last?"

"Yesterday afternoon."

"Mrs. Keith-Westerton with you?"

"Yes."

It was evident that no thought was needed by Keith-Westerton before answering these questions. Severn now switched his inquiries to a fresh line.

"Mrs. Keith-Westerton didn't take her jewels with her when she went away?"

"No, I told you that they're upstairs in her jewel case."

"She must have taken something with her, surely —clothes, a suit case, or something."

"I don't know. Probably her maid could say."

This was what Severn had been angling for.

"I'll see the maid then, by-and-by, H'm! Mrs. Keith-Westerton would hardly walk out on the roads carrying a suit case. She must have had some conveyance?"

"I wasn't here to see," Keith-Westerton said, as though he were scoring a point.

A momentary reflection, however, seemed to suggest a fresh idea to him; and he bit his lip as though he had made a mistake.

"Did she take your car?"

"I wasn't here to see."

"Then I'll have to ask your chauffeur about that," Severn replied, keeping his eyes on Keith-Westerton's face.

"If you want to," was the answer, given in a tone which indicated that this suggestion was anything but palatable.

"About when did Mrs. Keith-Westerton leave the house?"

"I wasn't here to see."

"You're not trying to help us much, Mr. Keith-Westerton," Severn pointed out seriously. "Remember, this is a bad business. A man's been murdered. . . ."

"Well, what the devil's that got to do with me?" Keith-Westerton demanded callously. "One would think, by the way you've been poking your nose into my affairs, that you thought I'd murdered him. Are you charging me with that? Let's have the cards on the table."

"I'm not charging you with murdering him. I don't know who shot him," Severn explained suavely. "But I've got to clear up the matter of these pearls; and I must say plainly that I don't think you're doing any one much good by this sort of thing, Mr. Keith-Westerton. We know a good deal more than you think."

Wendover caught a twinkle in Sir Clinton's eye as Severn produced this well-worn cliché. It seemed to have its effect, however, for Keith-Westerton looked distinctly uneasy when he heard it.

"You don't want to add anything to what you've told us already?" the Inspector asked.

Keith-Westerton shook his head.

"Then I think I'd better see your servants," Severn suggested. "I'd rather that you weren't here when I question them."

"I don't mind," Keith-Westerton replied, with an attempt at indifference which was far from successful. "If you ring the bell, you can get any one you want."

"Just a moment, Mr. Keith-Westerton," Sir Clinton interposed. "Can you give us the name of the jeweller from whom this necklace of Mrs. Keith-Westerton's was bought, if it was bought recently?"

"Instow and Gower, Bond Street."

"Thanks. By the way, have you been using a screwdriver at the boathouse recently?"

"No, I haven't. I'd no earthly reason for using a screwdriver there. I told you I hadn't been near the boathouse."

"You were there yesterday afternoon, weren't you?" Sir Clinton reminded him. "Well, it's not of much importance. And now, I think, the Inspector had better interview your staff."

Keith-Westerton rose and, with a suspicious glance at his unwanted guests, walked to the door.

As soon as he was out of the way, Sir Clinton stepped over to the empty grate and bent down.

"Just look here for a moment, Inspector."

Severn, coming to his side, found him examining the ashes of a sheet of paper. Beside them was a crumpled and unburnt envelope which the Chief Constable gingerly fished out and smoothed delicately. Wendover, with an internal grumble about "Russian methods", glanced over Sir Clinton's shoulder and read on the envelope the single word "COLIN" in a large feminine hand.

Sir Clinton, putting the envelope down, returned to the examination of the ash fragments.

"Nothing much to be made of those," he said regretfully. "The pieces are too small. But I think, if you look carefully, you'll see one word on that bit. The ink shows up very faintly as grey on the black of the ash, and if you get the light in the proper quarter, you'll be able to read it."

Severn went down on his knees and moved about until he came into the right line.

"I see a capital G," he reported slowly. "Then there's a letter missing. And after that I can see RON. And just in front of the G I think I can see something that might be an E at the end of the word before."

"The Abbé Goron?" Wendover exclaimed. "Is that it?"

"Not so loud," Sir Clinton cautioned. "It may be either 'Pére Goron' or 'Abbé Goron'; they come to much the same thing, so far as we're concerned. Goron is the word; that's the main point. It seems as though you'd have to look up my friend the priest, Inspector, and see if he knows anything helpful. You'll find him a tougher nut than young Keith-Westerton, though, if I'm not mistaken."

"You think that priest's mixed up in the business?" Wendover demanded, all his latent distrust aroused. "What makes you think that?"

Sir Clinton put the question aside without offence.

"I'll talk about it afterwards as much as you like; but just now we ought to be interviewing these people before they have time to compare notes. Once the police come in, every one starts chattering, you know; and if we don't hurry, they'll have fogged each other's recollections completely. Just ring the bell, please, Inspector."

CHAPTER VI: THE TELEPHONE CALL

THE girl who had opened the door to them answered the Inspector's ring; and now she seemed even more flustered than before.

"I'm Inspector Severn and I want to ask you some questions," Severn said baldly. "How many of you are there on the staff here?"

"There's me—I'm house-parlourmaid—and there's Mrs. Featherstone, she's the cook; and there's Sandeau, Mrs. Keith-Westerton's maid; and there's Hyde, the chauffeur; and there's Ferrers, he's Mr. Keith-Westerton's gentleman's gentleman, but he's partly butler too, till we move over into Silver Grove; and then there's Disley, she's a sort of scullery maid and helps generally; and that's all that's here now."

Severn had pulled out his notebook and jotted down this list, an action which seemed to disturb the girl still further.

"You needn't get flurried," said Sir Clinton kindly. "All we want is a little information which can't do you any harm. Just answer Inspector Severn's questions as well as you can. He won't eat you."

The Chief Constable's smile reassured the maid slightly. Sir Clinton evidently thought it better to put the next question himself, as she seemed terrified of the Inspector.

"You waited at table last night, I suppose? I'm asking that just to test your memory. You did? Was any one else there?"

"Ferrers, sir."

"No guests, I suppose? Just Mr. and Mrs. Keith-Westerton?"

"Just the two of them, sir."

"Did you see anything out of the common during dinner?"

"Well, sir, Mr. Keith-Westerton didn't seem in his usual spirits, perhaps; he wasn't so cheery as he usually is, I thought, a bit moody, as if he was thinking about something different from what he was talking about. I did notice that, I must say, and I just wondered if . . ."

She pulled up sharply.

"You needn't be afraid to tell us anything you remember," Sir Clinton reassured her. "You just wondered if . . ."

"Well, I just wondered, sir, if that telephone message had anything to do with it. That was all."

"Let's keep to what happened at dinner, for the present. Mr. Keith-Westerton wasn't moody because of any disagreement with Mrs. Keith-Westerton, I suppose?"

"Oh, no, sir; no, indeed. I wouldn't like you to think that. He was every bit as nice to her as he usually is. She was in very good spirits, I remember that quite well, and it wasn't a case of putting a good face on things or anything of that sort, I'm quite sure. They talked quite a lot at dinner, about this and that, and he just seemed a bit absent-minded, once or twice. It was so unusual with him that I happened to notice it, though it was really nothing."

"Now about this telephone message you mentioned. What was that?"

"That was about a quarter past seven, sir. I answered the phone, and I heard a lady's voice asking for Mr. Keith-Westerton. He was upstairs; I heard him whistling; he usually whistles about the house, it's a habit of his; so I went and gave him the message. And now I think of it, he said something about it at dinner to Mrs. Keith-Westerton. A friend had rung him up, he said, and he'd have to go out for a short time after dinner."

Sir Clinton evidently wished to put no further questions, so Severn took his turn.

"After dinner, what did you do?"

"I went out for a walk; Mrs. Keith-Westerton gave me permission."

"Alone?"

"No. I went out with Hyde."

"The chauffeur? And when did you get back?"

"About ten o'clock, I think. Yes, it would be about then."

"And after that?"

"I went to bed."

Severn finished his jottings.

"Now I'll read this over to you and you can sign it."

The maid, evidently startled by this formality, glanced at Sir Clinton as though to ask if this was usual; but when he had reassured her, she made no difficulties over her signature.

"Now, that's all we need from you at present," Sir Clinton explained. "But . . . don't tell any one what questions you were asked, you understand? No use running into trouble." He let this sink in, and then added, "Let's see. Mrs. Featherstone is the next person we want to see. Ask her to come here, please."

Mrs. Featherstone proved to be a rather stolid matron from whom Severn extracted nothing whatever that seemed to bear on the case. She had gone to bed early. On being pressed, she confessed that, having feared that she had caught a chill, she had taken "something hot" before retiring, and this had sent her to sleep almost immediately.

"Who brushes the shoes in this house?" Sir Clinton inquired, when Severn had given the cook up in despair.

"Disley, sir."

"Well, I should like to see Disley. And, by the way, if you have a couple of deep soup plates among your crockery, I should like to see them. Disley can bring them. Mr. Keith-Westerton won't object."

Severn stared at his superior when he made this request, but Sir Clinton vouchsafed no explanation at the moment. They had not long to wait before a small maid bustled into the room with the two plates in her hand.

"Please, sir, Mrs. Featherstone wants to know if these'll do, sir."

Sir Clinton gravely took them from her, examined them with a solemn air, and put them down on a table.

"These will do excellently. You're Sarah Disley, aren't you? And you clean the shoes?"

"Yessir."

"Did you clean Mr. Keith-Westerton's shoes this morning—I mean the ones he wore last night when he was out after dinner?"

"No sir. When Mr. Ferrers brought them to me, sir, they were soaked through, sir, so I couldn't clean them till they were dried, sir."

"I'd like to see them for a moment. Can you bring them? And remember. You're not to repeat anything that's been said to you, except about the soup plates."

Sarah Disley was obviously delighted with this caution. It apparently gave her a feeling of importance. Wendover, amidst his preoccupations, found time to smile. Perky little creature! She evidently was seeing herself as a minor star in some film drama.

In a couple of minutes she returned with the shoes. Sir Clinton took them from her, walked over to the window and turned his back so that she could not see what he was doing. Severn joined him. When they came back again, Wendover saw, from the Inspector's expression, that something definite had been found. He put out his hand and, as Sir Clinton passed him the shoes, his fingers encountered the humid inside surface. No man ever got his footgear so wet as that by merely walking for a short time through dewy grass.

Sir Clinton turned to the scullery maid again.

"And what did you do with yourself last night?"

The girl's sharp young eyes opened a little at the inquiry. She was obviously quite at sea as to the meaning of this incursion of the police and she could not quite make out the drift of the question.

"Me, sir? After dinner I washed the dishes. And then I did some sewing for a while. And then I went up to bed, sir."

"When was that; can you remember?"

"About ten o'clock, sir. I always go to bed then; I need a lot of sleep, sir."

"And you sleep sound? You don't wake up in the middle of the night?"

"No, never, sir. The alarm wakes me in the morning, sir."

"By the way, what's the name of the house-parlourmaid?"

"Holland, sir. Ida Holland."

"Then that's all I want to ask you. Send Mrs. Keith-Westerton's maid here."

When Louise Sandeau presented herself, Wendover mentally compared her with the house-parlourmaid. Holland had behaved like a normally sedate girl who had been flustered by unexpected happenings. The lady's maid, on the other hand, struck him as an alert, high-strung type, holding her excitability in check behind a superficial coolness. Holland was the prettier girl of the two, but the Frenchwoman had more strength of character in her expression.

"She'd grow on you more than the other one," Wendover commented to himself. "But there's more of the glad eye about her than I care about," he added, on further inspection.

Sir Clinton left the Inspector to handle this fresh witness; and Severn began his inquiries by asking the maid's name and how long she had been in Mrs. Keith-Westerton's service. In her replies, Wendover noted, her English was fluent, almost correct, though her accent betrayed her at once as a foreigner.

"I have been with Madame Keith-Westerton for quite a long time—some years before she was married."

"Was she wearing a pearl necklace at dinner last night?"

"Yes, she wore it."

"She's gone away on the spur of the moment, it seems. Did she say anything to you, last night, which throws any light on that?"

The maid considered for a moment, then shook her head.

"No, no. She said nothing about that to me."

"Was she worried in any way when she was dressing for dinner last night? Did she seem not in her usual spirits?"

"No, indeed. She was just the same as she always is."

"She gave you no instructions to pack a suit case, or anything like that?"

"Oh, no, nothing like that. I had not an idea that she was going away."

"Have you any idea of what she did take with her?"

"She changed her dress before she went away, and she took some necessaries in her suit case—enough for a week-end visit, perhaps. But she took no evening dress with her."

"You can write out a list of what she did take, by and by, so far as you can make it out. Can you describe the dress she must have worn when she went away, the one she would travel in, if she took more than one?"

The maid described a travelling costume in some detail.

"The other dress which is missing is an afternoon one," she explained. "She would not travel in it, I should suppose. The other things I shall write down for you," she added, with a faint touch of archness in her manner.

"Did you see her after she went down to dinner?" Severn demanded.

"No, not at all. She does not expect me to be in attendance on her when she retires at night, so I am free in the evening."

"H'm! Well, after you were free, what did you do last night?"

"I?" the maid exclaimed, with an air of surprise. "I went for a walk. Perhaps I should say that I am fiancée to the valet of Mr. Keith-Westerton. We went out together, naturally."

"When did you leave the house?"

"It would be about half-past eight," the maid replied, without any hesitation. "We walked up through the woods behind the house, here, and then along the shore of the lake."

"Did you go near Mr. Wendover's boathouse?"

"Oh, no. We could not go there. Besides, there was some one in the boathouse last night. I saw the lights illuminated."

"About what time was that?" Severn demanded.

The maid considered for a few moments.

"I cannot say precisely," she admitted. "I was not

looking at my watch, you can figure to yourself"—she gave Severn a coy look—"but it was perhaps half-past nine . . . or possibly a little before then . . . that I saw the lights switched on. We had turned back again by that time. After that, we sat down. The lights remained on for a long time . . . perhaps an hour."

Severn reflected for a moment before putting his next query.

"Did . . . Do you know a man Horncastle, one of Mr. Westerton's keepers?"

"Yes, indeed! He has given me trouble, that one. He tried to—what do you call it?—pick me up, more than once; and it gave me great trouble with my fiancé, who is jealous of any man.'"

Wendover had little difficulty in surmising that quite probably Ferrers' jealousy had, in this case, a fairly substantial basis. Louise Sandeau, with her glad eye, was hardly the sort who would discourage attentions, no matter how casually they were offered. And, in a flash, Wendover linked this with the murder. Cooler reflection, however, persuaded him that he was on the wrong track. If there was no more in it than this, the motive was too slight to be worth considering. If Ferrers had been one of those foreigners who can be strung up to any pitch by jealousy, then there might be something in it. But an Englishman of that class would never turn a casual flirtation into a murder drama.

"When did you see Horncastle last?" Severn demanded.

The maid reflected for a moment or two.

"It was last week—last Wednesday," she replied. "I had to be very severe with him then. He was much too enterprising."

Her manner suggested that in her case this was quite to be expected; obviously she did not underrate her own attractions. Severn, apparently to her disappointment, dropped this line of inquiry.

"When did you get home last night?"

The maid shrugged her shoulders suggestively.

"I really cannot tell. When one is with one's fiancé, time flies, does it not? One pays no attention to the clock. But I imagine that it would be near midnight when I arrived here."

"He came with you?"

Louise laughed with a musical trill.

"No, he did not. Imagine now, he is a slave to tobacco. And I, I do not like smoky kisses, no, indeed. When he is with me, he does not smoke. But he must smoke before going to bed, it seems—one last pipe. So I say to him always, 'Say good night, now, *mon chou*, and then you can smoke that pipe you long for.' And he stays out, while I come in. That is better than quarrelling, is it not?   A much pleasanter arrangement."

Severn nodded. Then a thought seemed to strike him.

"Mrs. Keith-Westerton had gone before you came in?"

"That I do not know," the maid replied at once. "I went straight to bed. Naturally I did not come into this part of the house at all."

Severn appeared to have come to the end of his

inquiries. Sir Clinton seemed to feel that he should say something.

"Mrs. Keith-Westerton paints pictures, doesn't she? Has she taken her paint box with her, do you know?"

This inquiry obviously puzzled the maid.

"I did not think of that," she confessed at once. "Shall I go and look?"

"If you can find it, I should like to look at it," Sir Clinton said in a casual tone. "That's all you want to ask, Inspector?"

Severn nodded; and the maid accepted her dismissal with a final flash of her rather fine eyes.

"You might ask your fiancé to come here," Sir Clinton said, as she was leaving the room.

Wendover had already seen Ferrers at the railway station on the day when the Keith-Westertons arrived home from their honeymoon. Now, under the sedate mask of the well-trained man-servant, he thought he detected something abnormal; and the man's first words gave a clue to its nature. Ferrers turned at once to the Inspector.

"What right have you to badger Miss Sandeau with a lot of questions?" he demanded.

Sir Clinton, evidently fearing that Severn might be drawn into a retort, intervened swiftly.

"You can take it that Miss Sandeau was treated perfectly politely by the Inspector," he said, in a tone which seemed to smooth away Ferrers' grievance. "We have, unfortunately, to ask all of you some questions."

Ferrers made a silent acknowledgment of this and

then turned to Severn as though awaiting his inquiries.

"Did you see Mr. Keith-Westerton before dinner last night?" the Inspector began.

"Yes. Two or three times a week he asks me to spar with him, just to keep in practice. I had the gloves on with him for a quarter of an hour or so. That was about six o'clock or so."

"Are you any good at it?"

Ferrers' mouth twisted in a faint smile.

"I'm not good enough to stand up to him if he really meant business," he admitted wryly. "He knows far more about it than I do."

"That was round about six o'clock," Severn proceeded. "Did you notice anything about him that struck you? Was he just as usual in his manner?"

Ferrers reflected carefully before answering.

"I should say that he was. I saw nothing out of the way."

"You saw him again before dinner?"

"Yes."

"Did you notice any change in him?"

"Nothing I can remember."

"You were in the room during dinner. Did you see anything then that suggested a disagreement between Mr. Keith-Westerton and his wife?"

Again Ferrers considered carefully.

"No. I can't say I did," he admitted at last. "He seemed a bit absent-minded, perhaps; but it wasn't noticeable. When she spoke to him, he might have been thinking about something else; but he pulled himself up at once and answered her just in his usual

108

way. I saw no signs of the slightest friction, if that's what you want."

"After dinner, you went out with Miss Sandeau?"

"Yes."

Severn put some more questions with regard to the movements of the couple and the lights in the boat-house. Ferrers corroborated Louise's evidence. He had returned to the Dower House not long after the French girl, had gone straight to bed, and had learned of Mrs. Keith-Westerton's disappearance only in the morning.

"Do you know a man Horncastle, one of the keepers?" Severn demanded, when these points had been cleared up.

"I've had trouble with him," Ferrers volunteered curtly.

"You have? What sort of trouble?"

"I gave him a good hiding last Thursday," Ferrers explained, in a tone which betrayed his satisfaction. "He'd insulted Miss Sandeau the day before; and she complained to me about his manners, naturally enough. I had it out with him as soon as I could get hold of him; and I don't think he'll trouble her again after what he got."

Wendover, examining the spruce figure before him, was led to reflect that civilisation does not necessarily reach down to the core of a personality, even though the surface is presentable. Behind this rather vulgar little episode, the Squire could catch a glimpse of the caveman defending his mate from a rival and rejoicing in a victory. "He must be devilish fond of that French maid," Wendover concluded. "And that glad eye of hers will get him into a lot of trouble, if this is the way he goes about things."

"Thursday, this happened?" Severn demanded. "Have you seen Horncastle since then?"

"No. Has he been complaining about it?" Ferrers replied, in a faintly apprehensive tone. "I don't want any trouble over it. He was just asking for it and he got it; he's no cause to complain."

"He hasn't complained."

"Then what are you asking about it for?"

"Because he's been found dead this morning and I'm making inquiries about his death."

The tinge of apprehension faded out of Ferrers' voice.

"Oh, I see now," he said. "You got on to this scrap I had with him and you thought you had a clue? No, I'd squared the account with Horncastle over his rudeness on Thursday and I haven't come across him since then. He got enough then to make him keep out of my road."

"When did you enter Mr. Keith-Westerton's service?" Severn switched to a fresh line of inquiry.

"Just before Mr. Keith-Westerton got married. My predecessor preferred a bachelor; and he left on that account."

"You were with him through his honeymoon trip? Did you see anything that struck you?"

"They were like most honeymoon couples, very fond of each other, so far as I could see."

"And there's been no change in them since they came home again?"

"No, they've been just the same."

"H'm! You met nobody in the house when you came in last night?"

"No, I went straight to bed as soon as I came in."

Severn reflected for a moment, but seemed unable to think of any further questions. He glanced at the Chief Constable, but Sir Clinton obviously had no wish to make any inquiry.

"Well," said the Inspector, "that's all I want with you. Send the chauffeur here; I want to see him too."

Hyde turned out to be a heavily built, sullen-looking man of about thirty. As he came into the room, he glanced suspiciously at the Inspector.

"Your name's Hyde, isn't it? How long have you been in Mr. Keith-Westerton's service?"

"David Hyde. A couple of years."

"You spar with Mr. Keith-Westerton sometimes?"

"As little as possible. He hits too hard when he gets keen."

"I'm inquiring about a crime that's been committed. I want to know what you did yesterday evening."

Hyde was obviously taken aback by this.

"I've nothing to do with a crime."

"Then there's no harm in telling us what you were doing, is there?" Severn retorted.

"I suppose not," Hyde admitted reluctantly. "Well, what do you want to know?"

"Was the car out yesterday?"

Across Hyde's face there flitted for a moment an expression which Wendover could not interpret. Evidently the word "car" suggested something out-of-the-way to him; and for a moment it seemed as though he was about to volunteer something. Second thoughts

111

prevailed, apparently, for he confined himself to answering Severn's question.

"I took Mrs. Keith-Westerton into Ambledown to do some shopping yesterday morning."

"Anything else?"

"I was told in the afternoon that the car wouldn't be required for the rest of the day."

"What did you do with your spare time?"

"I took my motor bike and went into Ambledown in the afternoon. I'd some shopping of my own to do."

"You were back for dinner?"

"Yes."

Hyde seemed to have lost a certain amount of his earlier suspicion, Wendover noticed, though his answers were still curt.

"After dinner, what did you do?"

"I went for a walk with Miss Holland."

"The house-parlourmaid? Are you engaged to her?"

"Not likely," said Hyde, rather contemptuously.

"When did she come in?"

"About ten o'clock, I should think. She's an early bird."

"And you?"

"I strolled up the road a bit before turning in."

He reflected for a moment as though doubtful whether he ought to volunteer anything.

"I met a Salvation Army man on the road. He asked me the way to the Dower House, so I put him on his way and went on."

"What time was that?" Severn demanded sharply.

"How do I know? Round about ten o'clock. I didn't look at my watch."

"You didn't think it curious that he should be asking the road to the Dower House at that time of night?"

"No business of mine," Hyde retorted, rather surlily.

"How long was it before you came back here?"

"Half an hour or so. I don't really know. About that, I should think."

"And you went to bed when you came in?"

"Straight."

After answering the question, Hyde seemed to bethink himself of something. He made a gesture as though about to speak, then apparently refrained. Severn noticed his hesitation and put a further question.

"Did you wake up during the night?"

"Now you ask it, that's so," the chauffeur replied.

"About what time was that?"

This time Hyde had no difficulty.

"Just about half-past eleven. My bedroom's on the same side of the house as the garage. I'm a light sleeper. I woke up with the notion that some one was in the garage. I looked out of my window and I could see the garage lights on and the doors open. Thieves, I thinks, so I went downstairs. I looked out of the dining-room window. I could see the open door of the garage from there and I heard the car's engine running. I was just going to open the window and yell at them, whoever they were, when Mrs. Keith-Westerton drove the car out of the garage. I could see her plain enough when she got out of the car to switch off the lights and shut the garage doors. I knew it was all right, then, so I went back to bed."

"And what about the car?"

"What about it? It wasn't here this morning, of course. Mrs. Keith-Westerton hasn't come back."

"When you went upstairs again, after seeing the car go off, did you switch on the hall and stair lights to see your way?" Sir Clinton demanded.

"I did, of course. It's awkward finding your way about this place in the dark."

"There's a table in the hall beside the switch," Sir Clinton reminded him. "Did you see anything on it when you were turning on the light—anything that caught your eye?"

Hyde looked suspiciously at the Chief Constable.

"I didn't see anything out of the way," he answered. "A letter was lying there. It's the place where letters are put if they're to go to the post in the morning. I remember it because I usually take them down to the post office in the car; and when I looked for it this morning it wasn't there."

"You remember what it was like?"

"Just an ordinary squarish envelope, same as all the house letters are in."

"You didn't notice if it was stamped or not?"

"No. If an unstamped letter's left there, I stamp it at the post office when I'm posting it."

Sir Clinton had obviously no further questions, so Severn recommenced.

"Mr. Keith-Westerton borrowed your motorcycle this morning?"

Hyde nodded.

"You don't know where he went?"

"No."

"Have you a speedometer with a mileage dial on your motorcycle?" Sir Clinton inquired.

Hyde nodded again.

"Do you ever take readings of it?"

"I set the trip dial every time I come in, because I keep a note of my mileage and check my oil and petrol consumption by it."

"Did you reset it last night?"

"Of course."

"That's all I wanted to know," Sir Clinton said. "Don't reset it for the present."

Severn, seeing that the Chief Constable had no desire to put further questions, turned to Hyde.

"That'll do. Send the house-parlourmaid here."

Hyde's suspicions were evidently reawakened by this demand but he refrained from saying anything as he left the room. In a minute or two, Ida Holland entered, bringing with her Mrs. Keith-Westerton's paint box. Sir Clinton looked up as she came in.

"I think you were a little flustered, weren't you, when we saw you before?" he said soothingly. "There's nothing to be afraid of, but I want you to remember one or two things, if you can. I expect you were flurried at being questioned. Now, just think for a moment. Yesterday, do you remember a telegram or a telephone message coming for Mrs. Keith-Westerton?"

The maid thought hard for a moment or two before replying.

"No, sir. I'd have been sure to have known about it if it came when I was in. Nobody rang up and no wire came that I heard about. She got no letter by the post yesterday, either."

"Did anybody call that night?"

The maid's face showed more than a trace of confusion.

"Oh, yes, sir. I ought to have told you that, perhaps; but I was flustered, just as you said. A Salvationist in uniform came to the front door just after I came in—about ten o'clock at night."

"What did he want?"

"He asked for Mr. Keith-Westerton, sir. I went to look for Mr. Keith-Westerton, but I couldn't see him anywhere, and Mrs. Keith-Westerton wasn't there, either. I thought she'd gone to bed. I told the man that Mr. Keith-Westerton wasn't in. Then he asked for Mrs. Keith-Westerton and I said she was out. He seemed a lot taken aback at that and he was muttering to himself. I was quite glad to shut the door on him. He called again this morning, early; and I told him Mr. and Mrs. Keith-Westerton were out. He went away without leaving a message."

"You passed through the hall at that time. Did you see a letter—an envelope—lying there anywhere?"

"No, sir, I didn't see anything of that sort. Not on the table, at any rate."

"I thought not. Now, will you ask Mrs. Featherstone to come here for a moment?"

The cook was able to fill in the gap during which Ida Holland had been out of the house. No telegram, telephone call, or message of any kind had reached Mrs. Keith-Westerton, so far as could be ascertained.

"Now, Inspector," Sir Clinton suggested, when Mrs. Featherstone had left the room, "you'd better get all these people to sign your notes of the evidence, so as to have everything in proper form. And in doing that, you'll be able to get their fingerprints on the leaves of your notebook, if you go about it in the right way. I specially want Mr. Keith-Westerton's."

"Very good, sir."

"And now we'll get these ashes out of the grate as best we can without breaking them up too much. I think I can get some of them on to a soup plate; and if we cover them with the other soup plate, upside-down, I expect we'll be able to transport them without damage. You can cover our retreat to the car with our treasure; keep the household busy signing your stuff. And then you might have a look at that trip dial on the motorcycle and make a note of the figures."

"Yes, sir, I'll manage all that."

"Then there's another thing. Send some one at once up to town with these pearls and get them identified by the jewellers if possible. We must know definitely if they were from Mrs. Keith-Westerton's necklace."

"I'll see to that, sir."

"And, finally, when you've got Mr. Keith-Westerton's fingerprints—and Mrs. Keith-Westerton's from this paint box—you might develop the prints on this envelope addressed to 'COLIN' and see if it was handled by any one except those two people."

When all the witnesses had been dismissed, Severn's official mask relaxed, and now it was clear that he felt very perplexed.

"I don't see my way through this business at all, sir," he confessed frankly. "We seem to have dropped on a lot of weird goings-on here; and yet, when I come to think over it, I can't see much connection between them and Horncastle's death."

"On the surface, they haven't," Sir Clinton agreed, "but I'll be surprised if those pearls we found beside Horncastle's body didn't come from Mrs. Keith-Westerton's necklace. In which case, there's an obvious connection; and the weirder the doings round about here last night, the better chance we have of picking up something."

Severn made a sudden gesture of annoyance.

"I ought to have asked these people for the loan of a match," he said in a tone of vexation.

"To see if they carried Swan vestas? Quite right, but unfortunately there are no less than three match stands in this room, all of them filled with Swan vestas. I doubt if you would have got any of the men to take a box out of his pocket unless you'd asked for it point-blank. And, most likely, with all this supply of free Swans, you'd find each of them carrying a box."

He glanced round the room for a moment.

"I don't think there's anything further to be seen here. You'd better go off and attract these people's attention."

Under cover of the Inspector's doings, Sir Clinton had little difficulty in removing the ashes of the letter to the car which had been left outside. Severn returned soon afterwards with a slip of paper which he showed to Sir Clinton.

"These are the figures from the speedometer, sir."

The Chief Constable glanced at them.

"Rather more than twice the distance from here to Ambledown," he calculated. "That ought to simplify matters. Keith-Westerton didn't think of that."

Severn was evidently pondering on a different subject.

"She must have bolted in a hurry if she didn't take an evening dress and her jewels with her," he mused aloud, in evident reference to Mrs. Keith-Westerton.

"She may have gone to a place where they don't wear evening dresses or jewels either," Sir Clinton commented, in a curious tone. "Perhaps the Abbé Goron could give you a hint, Inspector. We'd better try him. You'll find him a tough nut, though, unless I'm much mistaken."

A sinister interpretation of Sir Clinton's phrase struck a chill into Wendover.

"Good God, Clinton! You don't mean she's dead?"

"We'll be fishing in deepish waters presently," was all that Sir Clinton would vouchsafe in reply. "Mark my words."

CHAPTER VII: THE SALVATIONIST

"I THINK we'll try Ambledown," Sir Clinton suggested.

Wendover obediently turned the car to the right as they left the Dower House grounds. A little beyond the gate, his eye was caught by the figure of the Salvationist who had appeared at the boathouse earlier in the morning; and at a sign from Sir Clinton the car drew up alongside the man.

"Stop a moment, Mr. Sawtry," the Chief Constable requested. "I want to ask you a question. Why did you call at the house up yonder, last night, and ask to see Mr. and Mrs. Keith-Westerton?"

A flash of suspicion crossed the Salvationist's face at the words. Then the light of fanaticism flamed up in his eye.

"If you saw a woman living in sin," he demanded, "would you let her go her way? Or would you stand up to Beelzebub like a man and send him howling?"

He paused, and then added, as though speaking to himself:

"He which is joined to a harlot is one body. St. Paul wrote that. It's true, like everything else in the Bible."

"Mind your language, when you're speaking of your betters," Wendover interrupted angrily, only to feel Sir Clinton's restraining hand on his arm under cover of the car's side.

The Salvationist seemed oblivious of the interruption. He had the look of a man absorbed in some deep problem for which he has found no solution; and, apparently he was musing aloud.

" 'A well-favoured harlot, the mistress of witch-crafts.' Nahum the prophet said that. 'Thou shalt not suffer a witch to live.' That's the Law. 'All things are lawful unto me, but all things are not expedient.' St. Paul wrote that."

To Wendover's surprise, Sir Clinton was listening intently while the Salvationist rambled on. In a few moments, however, Sawtry seemed to realise that he was speaking his thoughts aloud. He passed his hand over his brow and, turning towards the car, spoke in a different tone.

"You're Sir Clinton Driffield, the Chief Constable. I know you, now. Well, answer me this. When you set your men to get up a case against a man and hang him, do you mean to prevent him committing another murder, or do you want to deter other people from murder, or are you punishing him for what he's done? Why do you do it?"

"Because I'm paid to do it," said Sir Clinton prosaically. "It's part of my work."

Sawtry gave him an angry look.

"And meanwhile sin can stalk under your eyes in this very village and you would never lift a finger. A priest can receive a woman by stealth in the night, but that's no affair of yours? It's not part of your work. You aren't paid for that! So Satan gets a soul while you look on."

" 'All things are not expedient,' " Sir Clinton quoted. "One of them is to listen to cock-and-bull stories."

This stung the Salvationist on the raw. He dropped his semi-archaic phraseology and used plain English.

"Oh, you may sneer, but it's true enough. Last night, about half-past ten, I was coming along the road here near the house where that foreign priest lives, when a car passed me and stopped at the gate. A young woman got out of it, in evening dress. I saw her face quite plain in the light of a street lamp. And what's more, I saw her in a car on the wood road that leads up to that boathouse. She passed me there about ten o'clock last night. I'd know her again any day. She went up the path to the house. It was all dark except for one window on the ground floor—a sitting room. She went up and knocked on the window; the curtains were pulled back, and I saw the priest standing there. The woman pointed to the door and he went round and let her in quietly. She didn't come out again, for I waited there quite a while. What have you got to say to that, Mr. Chief Constable?"

"Would you swear to that yarn?" Sir Clinton asked in a sceptical tone.

"Of course I'd swear to it."

Sir Clinton thought for a moment, then he turned to Wendover.

"You've got those photographs in your pocket, haven't you? Let me have them for a moment."

Some days earlier, Wendover had entertained the

Keith-Westertons at tea on the boathouse balcony; and in the course of the afternoon he had taken several snapshots of groups. The prints had arrived that morning, and Wendover, without examining them, had thrust them into his pocket. Very reluctantly, he pulled the case out and handed it over to Sir Clinton.

"You didn't know this girl?" the Chief Constable asked Sawtry. "Well, then, was she like this?"

He picked out a print showing Mrs. Keith-Westerton lying back in a camp chair and passed it to the Salvationist.

"That's the woman," Sawtry admitted, evidently surprised by the Chief Constable's promptness.

"Are you sure? Look at this one," Sir Clinton handed over the picture of a group containing himself and the two Keith-Westertons. "How many people do you recognise there?"

"The girl for one. You for another. I don't know the other man." Sawtry seemed to consider for a moment. "What's this got to do with me? I was only chaffing you. It's no business of yours whether a priest keeps a fancy lady or not, is it? You can't raise trouble over that."

"The only trouble will be yours, if you spread that kind of story," Sir Clinton rejoined abruptly. "The Abbé Goron isn't that sort of man—very far from it, I believe. So I warn you to keep your tongue quiet—for your own good, you understand?"

He looked the Salvationist in the eye; and the man, after a second or two in hesitation, mumbled something which sounded apologetic.

"Turn round," Sir Clinton directed Wendover. "I want to go back for something."

Obediently Wendover reversed, leaving the Salvationist by the roadside. They drove back past the Dower House gate. A little beyond it, in the village, Sir Clinton signalled to Wendover to stop at the house in which the Abbé Goron had taken rooms.

"I'll do the talking," Sir Clinton said to Severn, as they went up the path. "We sha'n't get much."

They were shown into a sitting room on the ground floor, evidently the one of which Sawtry had spoken. As they entered, the Abbé Goron rose from his chair and stood confronting them with a small book in his hand, wherein his finger marked the place. In his other hand he held Sir Clinton's card.

"Well, gentlemen, what do you want?" he demanded, glancing at each of them in turn.

Wendover, despite his prejudices, could not help comparing the priest with the Salvationist and preferring the former. Sawtry he had disliked at first sight; and the second interview had merely confirmed him in his opinion. The Salvationist gave him the impression of an unbalanced mind, a fellow with a weak spot in him who would be prone to sudden impulses and equally sudden recoils after the impulses had carried him further than he intended. The Abbé Goron was of a different type. Scanning his clean-cut ascetic features, with the hard lines running from nostrils to the mouth corners, Wendover was impressed against his will. This was a man with a strong, even vivid personality, the kind of man who might be admired without being liked. And yet here too

Wendover sensed the fanatic, though of a different sort. This was the cold type, sure of itself and its mission, ready to drive weaker humanity with a whip, if persuasion failed. "That fellow would be equally ready to send a man to the stake or go to it himself," Wendover reflected. "He looks just what one would expect an inquisitor to be. He wouldn't flinch from anything."

"I see we have interrupted you," said Sir Clinton, with a pointed glance at the book in which the priest's finger still marked his place. "I am sorry, but we must plead urgency. We are investigating a murder which was done last night and I wish to ask you one or two questions."

"Murder?"

The priest's eyebrows rose very slightly at the word, but beyond that, his face betrayed nothing.

"Murder, Monsieur L'Abbé. One of Mr. Keith-Westerton's keepers has been shot."

Wendover, watching eagerly, thought he detected something like relief in the Abbé Goron's face; but the expression was so faint and fleeting that he could not feel sure.

"I know nothing of Mr. Keith-Westerton's keepers, not even their names."

"You had a visitor last night?" Sir Clinton asked, disregarding the Abbé's assertion.

"A penitent came to demand guidance," the priest admitted frankly, with a faint accentuation of the second word in his sentence.

He looked straight at the Chief Constable as he spoke. Sir Clinton nodded in understanding.

"And to confess to you?" he amplified. "I have nothing to do with that, Monsieur L'Abbé. Technically we recognise no secrets in English law; but in practice a priest is never asked to violate the secrecy of the confessional. I ask no questions on that point, you understand?"

The Abbé Goron bowed gravely in reply, as though acknowledging the courtesy of an adversary.

"At what time did Mrs. Keith-Westerton knock on the window here?" Sir Clinton asked.

The Abbé may have been surprised at the accuracy of Sir Clinton's information, but he showed no sign of this.

"That, of course, I can answer," he admitted. "She came at about half-past ten o'clock."

"She was in evening dress, I believe? And, after consulting you, she left again . . . ?"

"Shortly after eleven o'clock."

"Have you seen her since then, Monsieur L'Abbé?"

"No."

"Do you know where she is now?"

The priest made a gesture as though dismissing that subject.

"I cannot reply to that question."

Sir Clinton's answering gesture implied that he admitted this.

"I understand. It was part of her confession? Then, I think, we need not trouble you further just now, Monsieur L'Abbé. I must thank you for helping us so freely, so far as was possible."

With grave courtesy, the priest showed them to

the door. He did not linger, but returned at once to his interrupted reading.

"Not much change there," said Wendover ironically, as they walked down to the car.

"I got as much as I expected," Sir Clinton said cheerfully. "It's always nice to have one's preconceived notions confirmed, you know."

As they were getting into the car, a constable came hurrying up.

"Sir, they sent me after you from the station with a message. There's been a car found in the woods up behind here, near the lake. Empty, sir, and no one near it. Abandoned by the driver so far as can be seen, sir."

"Do you know where it's lying?" Sir Clinton demanded.

"Yes, sir, it's—"

"Then jump in behind, here, and tell us the road. We'll go up and have a look at it. Give Mr. Wendover directions as we go along."

As he got into the seat next Wendover, Sir Clinton repeated, with a quizzical intonation:

"As I was saying a moment ago, it's nice to have one's preconceived notions confirmed, Squire."

"You think it's the Keith-Westertons' car?" Wendover asked, in a tone of anxiety.

"I doubt if it is."

He turned around in his seat and questioned the constable.

"No, sir. Mr. Keith-Westerton's car is a blue saloon, almost new. This is a brown-painted saloon, a bit old-fashioned, by the look of it."

Just beyond the village they turned off the main road into a track leading up to the boathouse; and under the constable's direction Wendover ran his car cautiously along a little alley which branched off from the woodland trail near the boathouse. Around a bend, hardly twenty yards from the direct route, they found the abandoned car standing, well screened by some bushes.

"A London number," Severn pointed out, as they came up to it. "That doesn't mean much. Any one can register a car under a London number, no matter where they live."

"It means even less than that," Sir Clinton added, "for it happens to be a false number plate screwed on top of the real one. Just undo those thumbscrews, please, Inspector. H'm! The real number's GX.5749. We can find out something about that from the register—always assuming that it's a real number. It may be a fake also, for all one can tell."

Severn, notebook in hand, had begun an examination of the car.

"Brown Renault five-seater saloon," he noted. "Mr. Keith-Westerton's car's a dark-blue Sunbeam."

Sir Clinton had approached and examined the license card.

"GX.5749 seems the right number," he pointed out. "That saves some trouble. Ring up the licensing authority as soon as you can find time, Inspector, and find out what name the car was registered under."

Severn was pursuing his search of the car.

"There's a lady's coat here," he reported. "No initials on it, though," he added, in a disappointed tone. "I don't see anything more. The wheel might give some fingerprints, but I expect she was driving in gloves, if it was at night."

"You wait here in charge of this car until you're relieved," Sir Clinton said to the constable. "Meanwhile, we'd better be getting along to Ambledown. Stop at the police station as we pass," he added to Wendover. "We'll need to make arrangements for getting this car shifted into a place of safety."

When they reached Ambledown, Sir Clinton directed Wendover to stop at the post office.

"You go in, Inspector. They know you. Find out if any one put a trunk call through on the 'phone this morning and look up the address if you can get the number. If it was 'phoned from this office, ask what the person was like."

In a very short time the Inspector returned.

"There was only one trunk call this morning they say, sir. A man—his description corresponds roughly to Mr. Keith-Westerton—came in here and asked to be put through to a London number. They were able to get me the address. It's the Sisterhood of the Good Hope in Kensington. I warned the girl, of course, that she wasn't to mention my inquiries to any one. She seemed an intelligent girl; I don't think she'll talk."

"Quite right," Sir Clinton approved. He glanced at Wendover. "That relieves your mind, I hope? One doesn't need to look in the Hereafter for a place where a girl wears neither evening dress nor jewels, you see. A convent fits the bill just as well. Where else would a Roman Catholic girl go, if she were in trouble and had no friends in this country—especially after paying a visit to her confessor? It wasn't certain, but I was pretty safe in making the guess."

"Am I to get a warrant, sir?" Severn asked. "London's outside our jurisdiction, and I'll have to get our warrant countersigned by a London J.P. That'll take time."

Sir Clinton's eyebrows lifted slightly.

"Arrest her? On what charge, Inspector? You've got to prove the pearls were hers before you can even connect her with Horncastle's death."

"You've nothing against her at all, so far as I can see," Wendover put in. "She's left her home and gone into a convent. There's nothing criminal in that, surely. She saw her confessor before she went. That's not illegal, is it? She went off in her own car. What's wrong with that?"

"I'd rather put it this way, Mr. Wendover," said the Inspector gravely. "She left home hurriedly and unexpectedly just about the time that Horncastle was shot. Why did she do that?"

"If you could answer that question, you'd have the secret of the whole case," Sir Clinton volunteered. "But as things are, you haven't enough evidence to justify even detention, let alone arrest."

"But if we don't get hold of her now, she may slip through our fingers," Severn protested.

"We've got to risk it," said Sir Clinton, in a tone which showed that he disliked the hazard but could see no way to avoid it. "So long as she thinks she's got away unnoticed, I don't suppose she'll change her address. Besides, to judge from this business, she's hardly likely to baffle pursuit. Between them, they seem to have made every possible blunder."

He seemed to dismiss the subject.

"Now for the next port of call—the all-night garage nearest to the railway station. You'll go in, Inspector, and find out if the Keith-Westerton car was left there last night. If not, we'll try the other garages near by. Then we'll go on to the station and see if any one there can tell us whether Mrs. Keith-Westerton left by the midnight train for London. And that finishes the morning's work, unless something fresh turns up."

Severn did not take long over the first part of this programme. The nearest garage yielded nothing; but his second choice proved lucky. He was able to identify the Keith-Westerton saloon there; and he learned that a lady answering to Mrs. Keith-Westerton's description had left it late on the previous night with instructions that it was to be given up to a gentleman who would come to take it away later on.

The railway inquiries took rather longer, since the night porters were off duty and had to be hunted up at their homes. Fortunately one of them remembered that a lady had actually taken the 11.55 P.M. train; and from the photographs he was able to identify her as Mrs. Keith-Westerton. The booking office clerk also remembered a lady travelling first class; but he was unable to identify her definitely.

"When do you expect to hear about these pearls?" Sir Clinton asked, when they were once more on the road to Talgarth.

"Some time in the afternoon, sir," Severn explained. "When we stopped at the station to give orders about that derelict car, I gave a man instructions to go to London by the next train. He's to ring me up as soon as he's got the information."

"You'd better ring me up as soon as you hear from him," Sir Clinton suggested. "You've wasted no time," he added, in a tone which gave Severn as much pleasure as more direct praise might have done. "It seems you've got a busy afternoon before you, Inspector, what with fingerprints and so forth. I'm going fishing; but if anything special turns up, you can let me know."

CHAPTER VIII: DRAMATIS PERSONÆ

"I'M sorry for Severn," Sir Clinton admitted to Wendover, as they sat in the Grange smoking room after lunch. "He's got enough work on his hands to keep two men busy. He didn't blench, though. A sound man."

Though sparing in praise of subordinates to their faces, the Chief Constable never failed to give them full credit for good work.

"Not very brilliant," Wendover qualified, in a doubtful tone. "He didn't elicit much, after all."

"He didn't ask useless questions; and when he had a free hand he got at the relevant facts," Sir Clinton pointed out. "There's more in that than you'd think, Squire. Unfortunately, if this affair's to be cleared up, we'll need some imagination as well as the facts; and whether Severn will rise to that or not, one can't tell just yet."

"You mean: 'Has he enough wit to fill in the missing bits in the puzzle?'"

"The trouble with this case is that the most important desiderata aren't facts at all, in the dictionary sense of the word. We've unearthed a lot of *facts*. We've picked up a fair amount of evidence bearing on what happened last night—and a pretty jumble it makes. What's obviously missing is the whole psychology of the thing: the motives at work behind the façade."

"Admitted," said Wendover judicially.

"That's where I'm afraid Severn may fall down, through no fault of his own," Sir Clinton argued in defence of his subordinate. "He may be all right in his judgment of people like Horncastle. But he's a middle-class Protestant. What chance has he of fathoming the motives of a Roman Catholic like Mrs. Keith-Westerton, let alone those of my friend the Abbé Goron? He and Mrs. Keith-Westerton come from different social strata; their conventions are dissimilar; his moral views may be quite at variance with hers, for all one can tell. So far as the mere collecting of facts goes, Severn is all right; but when he tries to get behind the facts . . . well, he's likely to be badly handicapped, I'm afraid. I can understand his difficulty because I'm in much the same boat myself, in this case."

"How? You've met the Keith-Westertons more than once." Wendover pointed out. "You haven't Severn's handicap there."

"True," said Sir Clinton, taking a fresh cigarette, "but I didn't know the late Horncastle, for instance. You could help me out there, Squire."

Wendover leaned back in his chair, crossed his legs, and reflected for a moment or two before answering.

"*Nil nisi bonum,* and all that," he said at length, "but the plain truth is that I never liked Horncastle much. I suppose he must have been all right when Keith-Westerton's agent took him on; but he was an unlikeable fellow at the best. The village Don Juan is a nuisance, sometimes. And there were stories about him, too. If they were true, then some of the poulterers around about here were getting pheasants a good deal cheaper than they might have done. It was never proved, of course, but Horncastle wasn't quoted, locally, as an example of honesty. The impression I got of him, from one thing and another, was that he was a mean fellow, keen on the dibs and not minding much how he did it, so long as he got his paws on them. He got the name of being more than vindictive in some of his quarrels, too."

"Ah! Vindictive, you say? That's interesting," Sir Clinton commented in a serious tone.

He was interrupted by the arrival of a maid, bringing the telephone. The message was from Severn, and Sir Clinton's talk with the Inspector was a fairly long one. At last he hung up the receiver and turned to Wendover with an apology.

"Severn must have lunched on bread and cheese; he's been working like a Trojan while we've been taking our ease. Here's the stop press news. First of all, the police surgeon has found nothing on Horncastle's body except the shot wound in the skull, the bruise on the chin, and another bruise on the back of the head."

"The one you asked him to look for?"

Sir Clinton nodded, but added nothing further on that point.

"The next thing is the jewellers' report," he went on. "It seems that necklace was made up by them, partly from some family pearls of Keith-Westerton's and partly from new stuff which they supplied themselves. They've no doubt whatever that these pearls came from Mrs. Keith-Westerton's necklace."

Wendover discovered that all along he had been mentally discounting this possibility; and the facts gave him an unpleasant shock, now that they were indisputable. All through the morning he had clung to the idea that the murder and the flight of Mrs. Keith-Westerton were two entirely independent affairs, events which had no connection beyond the mere coincidence of time. But the identification of her pearls seemed to put that hypothesis out of the question. Ruefully he realised that the prestige of the country gentry in the neighbourhood was threatened with a grievous shock. His rather old-fashioned chivalry was roused also; for his mind conjured up the picture of a girl, isolated from her relatives, cut off from her husband in some mysterious manner, and now passing under the shadow of an accusation of complicity in a sordid crime.

Sir Clinton, guessing what was in his friend's mind, passed hastily to the next item in his bulletin.

"Severn's found no fingerprints of any value whatever on the oar handles and so forth, up at the boathouse."

"He must have found ours. We've been using the boats lately."

"So have the Keith-Westertons. Beyond these four sets he's spotted nothing."

"That's why I said he'd found no prints of any value," Sir Clinton explained. "These of ours don't help. The third item is another blank. Your gramophone motor and horn haven't turned up, though Severn's had a search party looking for them all through the wood."

"I can't think what a murderer would want with these things," Wendover grudgingly admitted, with a puzzled air.

"The thief evidently attached great weight to them," Sir Clinton pointed out, with almost owlish solemnity. "That must be so, surely, or they wouldn't be missing."

Wendover got the impression that the Chief Constable was as much at sea in the matter as he himself was, but was trying to disguise his ignorance by making statements of the obvious.

"Even Severn's imagination would rise to that level," he said ironically.

Sir Clinton brought him back to seriousness by the next item in his bulletin.

"That envelope addressed to 'COLIN' has no fingerprints on it except those of the two Keith-Westertons. Evidently it passed direct from her to him without any one else having tampered with it, so far as one can see."

"That proves nothing."

"It proves nothing," Sir Clinton said, and this time he was evidently more serious than he had yet been. "But it brings us to the kernel of the whole affair, if I'm not mistaken. If I had the text of that letter, I'd know definitely whether I'm on wholly wrong lines or not in this affair. You know these people better than I do. Can't you think of something to account for the girl decamping so suddenly?"

Wendover's mental hackles rose at the question. "It's hardly my business to pry into the private affairs of my friends," he said, with a touch of anger in his tone.

" 'I will do right to all manner of people after the laws and usages of the realm, without fear or favour, affection, or illwill,' " Sir Clinton quoted from the oath taken by Justices of the Peace.

Wendover, though he suspected that the Chief Constable was stretching the oath in making it cover his private conduct, was brought up sharply when the phraseology was invoked. He had a simple code, in which oath-breaking formed no part and which would hardly tolerate one standard of conduct on the Bench and another in a private capacity. Sir Clinton had gauged him accurately, and Wendover recognised that his friend would never have used this thumbscrew had he not been in deadly earnest.

The Chief Constable, scanning Wendover's expression, saw that he had gained his point; but he was not so tactless as to make a direct attack when a roundabout one would serve as well. Mrs. Keith-Westerton was the more dangerous subject, so he began with her husband.

"I remember you telling me something about young Keith-Westerton the day I arrived. Led a rackety life in town for a while, and then pulled up short, you said?"

Wendover, evidently relieved at the turn of Sir Clinton's inquiry, had no objection to confirming this.

"H'm!" the Chief Constable said thoughtfully. "That might mean either that he waked up suddenly to common sense or else that he got a fright. If it was the first, then one has to credit him with some backbone in cutting loose from the sharks. If it was the second, then perhaps there's a black mark in his record, somewhere. It's worth thinking over."

"You mean it might be something of that sort that led to her leaving him?"

Sir Clinton flicked the ash from his cigarette mechanically, as though his thoughts were concentrated on some problem. For a few moments he made no reply. When he did speak, it was evident that his mind had turned to a fresh aspect of the case.

"Just let's get the sequence of things clear. About six o'clock last night, young Keith-Westerton was sparring with his valet. At that time, according to Ferrers, Keith-Westerton seemed to have nothing on his mind; and later on the house-parlourmaid heard him whistling upstairs. Presumably that means he was in good spirits. Up to 7.15 P.M., then, it's fair to assume that nothing out of the common had happened."

Now that the line of inquiry seemed to be avoiding Mrs. Keith-Westerton, Wendover was off his guard. This was the kind of investigation which he enjoyed; and as he had no great liking for young Keith-Westerton, it left his withers unwrung.

"At 7.15 P.M.," Sir Clinton continued, "the maid Holland heard a lady's voice at the telephone, asking for Keith-Westerton. Keith-Westerton went to the 'phone. After that episode, we have the evidence of both the maid and the valet to prove that the whistling mood passed off."

"That's my recollection too," Wendover confirmed.

"It's plain sailing up to that point," Sir Clinton went on. "But at the next stage somebody must have been lying hard. On the one hand, the maid told us that at dinner Keith-Westerton mentioned the telephone call and said a friend wanted to see him later on in the evening. By the way, Squire, what did you make of that maid?"

Wendover assembled his recollections with some difficulty and was surprised to find how meagre a collection they made.

"Well, she seemed to me honest enough," he said, in a judicial tone. "She was flurried—or seemed so—when she was questioned. I don't think that means much, for I'd probably feel worried myself if I had to answer a lot of questions without knowing why they were asked. She has her head screwed on right, I think, for she managed to remember important points, although they weren't things which were out of the common when they happened."

"A credible witness, then?"

"I don't think she was lying."

"She saw no signs of friction between the Keith-Westertons at dinner. Keith-Westerton seemed absent-minded, that was all. The valet confirmed her evidence on that subject."

"I noticed that they both used the same word to describe it," Wendover pointed out.

"You think they may have been telling a tale they'd got up together beforehand?" asked Sir Clinton.

Wendover had not thought of this possibility and when it was presented to him he shook his head.

"No, I didn't get that impression," he admitted. "So far as I could see, the valet wasn't interested in Holland, not in the very slightest."

"What did you make of him?"

"Ferrers? Well, except when the French maid came into the question, he seemed to me a cool, collected sort of individual. He wasn't rattled by questions and he gave you straight answers to everything that was asked. I should say he was rather better class than the ordinary valet; and I'd be prepared to bet that he'd be efficient in his work, by the look of him. From the frank way he volunteered his tale about giving Horncastle a thrashing, it was pretty clear that he didn't know the keeper had come to a bad end, else he'd have kept his thumb on that subject, obviously. I should, I know, if I'd been in his shoes."

"Anything more about him?"

"The rest of it was obvious. He's fairly enamoured of that French girl. That stuck out all over him, even without the Horncastle shindy. He struck me as a cool-headed sort of fellow, and yet, when the girl came into question, he evidently flared up and lost his temper completely. I'm sorry for him, really, for he's not likely to have a happy time if he marries the woman."

"You don't seem to approve of her, Squire?"

"I don't. She's a forward piece, from what I saw of her; and she'll give trouble to any man she marries, I judge. Look at the way she ogled the lot of us when she was being questioned."

"She's got rather fine eyes," said Sir Clinton, with a faint smile.

"Yes, and she uses them on all and sundry, too. She's the sort of woman who doesn't give a damn how much trouble she raises so long as she can get admiration. Look at the Horncastle episode. Any one can see what happened. She led Horncastle on and then turned him down because he went too far, by her way of it. I expect she was just asking for that. Then she runs off to Ferrers and pours the whole yarn into his ears—poor little innocent insulted by brutal keeper, I suppose, with no provocation at all. She works Ferrers up to go and lay Horncastle out. That's a nice brand of female, isn't it? And then, instead of keeping quiet about it, she practically boasts about the affair to us, just to enhance her value."

"I don't say you're wrong, Squire. She's one of these women who have the luck to be sexually attractive and who simply can't help using their attraction on the first comer. And I should think you're right about Ferrers and her too. However, let's get back to the history of last night. After dinner, the Keith-Westertons went into Mrs. Keith-Westerton's sitting room. Keith-Westerton, by his own admission, was keeping his eye on the clock, obviously because he had made an appointment with the person who rang him up on the 'phone at 7.15 P.M. And yet he did his best to leave us with the impression that he went out for a mere aimless stroll."

"He's not a credible witness," Wendover admitted with a certain reluctance. "He did try to mislead us there."

"I had the impression that some parts of his tale

rang true, though," Sir Clinton conceded. "When he denied any disagreement with his wife, he sounded as if he were speaking the truth."

"The servants' evidence confirms that," Wendover pointed out.

"Yes, so far as the dinner table's concerned. They might have had dissensions after they went into her sitting room, which the servants wouldn't know about. But still, I'm inclined to think he was giving us the truth when he said there was none. He left her about 9 P.M., then, and she supposed that he was going to see a friend, some man or other in the neighbourhood, probably. And after that, he vanishes, so far as we're concerned, until 1 A.M. this morning, when he says he returned home. Did anything occur to you, Squire, when Severn was pressing him about a visit to the boathouse?"

"He denied it," Wendover admitted glumly, "but if ever I saw a man lying, it was then. I've no doubt whatever that he was at the boathouse sometime that night."

"Neither have I," Sir Clinton agreed quickly. "Now we come to the pearl necklace." Wendover shifted slightly in his chair as this ill-omened subject came up, but the Chief Constable took no notice. "Mrs. Keith-Westerton was wearing it at dinner, according to her maid; and Keith-Westerton confirmed that."

Wendover contented himself with a faint gesture admitting that this was beyond dispute.

"This morning, parts of it turned up in the boat-house and other bits of it were beside Horncastle's body. That's one of the few points in this case where we're not dependent on other people's statements."

Sir Clinton's tone hinted that he had no entire faith in the oral evidence which they had collected during the day.

"There seem to be only three possibilities to account for the pearls," Wendover argued, though with a certain reluctance. "She was in these places herself last night: that's one. Or she gave the necklace to some one who went to these places: that's the second possibility. Or else the pearls were stolen from her by some one who went, later on, to the boathouse and Friar's Point. That covers the whole business, and it must have been one of the three that happened."

Sir Clinton shook his head.

"One might just as well suppose that she gave her necklace to a second party from whom it was stolen by a third party who took the pearls to the places where we found them. And there are other possible explanations as well. Let's get back to the sequence of events last night. At 9 P.M., Mrs. Keith-Westerton was left alone in her sitting room. No message had reached her during the day, so far as we know. Yet she goes to the garage, takes out the car, and drives up to the boathouse. That Salvationist fellow saw her on the wood road at about 10 P.M.; and I'm inclined to believe his evidence, since he quite evidently didn't know who she was."

Wendover, in whose mind several motives were struggling grimly for the upper hand, refrained from making any comment on this.

144

"Half an hour later, she was at the door of the Abbé Goron," Sir Clinton pursued. "In the meantime, something happened—something so serious that she flew at once to her confessor for absolution and advice."

Wendover saw his opening and plunged.

"Horncastle wasn't shot until about midnight," he pointed out, with a certain triumph in his tone. "At 11.55 P.M. Mrs. Keith-Westerton was in the train at Ambledown."

Sir Clinton's gesture of surprise gave Wendover a thrill of honest satisfaction, but his delight was only momentary.

"You didn't suppose I'd overlooked *that?*" the Chief Constable inquired in mild astonishment. "Nobody could possibly suppose that Mrs. Keith-Westerton knocked Horncastle out and then carried his body neatly up to the bank, arranged it, and so forth."

"Then why are you concentrating your attention on her at all?"

Sir Clinton deliberately lit a fresh cigarette before answering. Wendover, who thought the pause was intended to give the Chief Constable time to furbish up a reply, fumed at the delay.

"Because," Sir Clinton explained frankly, "Mrs. Keith-Westerton seems to me to be the central point of the whole affair. If there had been no Mrs. Keith-Westerton, Horncastle might be alive this afternoon. That's what I think, not what I know, remember, Squire. This is one of these infernal cases where the accessories may be more important than the actual criminal, so far as the springs of action are concerned. So I judge, anyhow."

Without giving Wendover time to digest these statements, Sir Clinton returned to the chronology of the case.

"Mrs. Keith-Westerton left the Abbé Goron about 11 P.M. Most probably she went straight to the Dower House and packed a suit case with some necessaries. She also wrote that rather mysterious letter to her husband and left it on the table for him. Barring the name of the Abbé Goron, there's nothing to be made out of its ashes; but from that alone it's reasonable to suppose that she mentioned her visit to the Abbé in it. Probably, if we had that letter, we'd have the centre of the case quite clear."

"Then why not question young Keith-Westerton about its contents?" Wendover inquired.

"Because I'm sure he'd lie if we did. We'd gain nothing and we'd let him know that we've spotted the letter, which he doesn't realise at present," Sir Clinton pointed out. "Now the next bit of evidence came from the chauffeur, who saw Mrs. Keith-Westerton take her car out of the garage again at 11.30 P.M. By the way, what did you make of that chauffeur, Squire?"

"I didn't like the look of him much," Wendover said glumly. "He struck me as a coarse brute. And the way he laid himself out to sneer at that maid,—that rather annoyed me. He seemed to think he was too good for her. I'd have put it the other way around, myself."

Sir Clinton refrained from any criticism of this verdict.

"Mrs. Keith-Westerton drove off to Ambledown, left her car in the all-night garage where we found it, took the 11.55 to London, and evidently got to the convent to which the Abbé Goron recommended her to go. Now let's dispose of the other characters for that night. The housekeeper and the scullery maid didn't leave the house that evening and they were both in bed quite early. Holland, the parlourmaid, came in about 10 P.M., and her statement's checked by Hyde's. Hyde says he came in at 10.30 P.M. There's no support for that; but I should think he really was indoors at 11.30 when Mrs. Keith-Westerton went off in her car. He may have gone out later, for all I know, of course. The French maid was home at midnight, she told us; and her story's borne out by Ferrers. Ferrers himself says he came in shortly after twelve, but there's no confirmation of that. Keith-Westerton said he came home about one o'clock in the morning, but that's unsupported too."

"That seems to leave plenty of loose ends."

"We can pare it down a bit, on certain assumptions," Sir Clinton rejoined, in a speculative tone. "We don't know what Keith-Westerton did after nine o'clock; nor do we know what his wife was doing between nine and half-past ten. The other witnesses from the Dower House fall into pairs; and if one member of a pair was lying, the other would have to lie also to make the stories tally."

"You've left out that Salvationist fellow," Wendover pointed out.

"Severn's hunting up his record," Sir Clinton reassured him.

"He's a mysterious devil, it seems to me," said Wendover, in a disparaging tone. "He comes to the Dower House at ten o'clock at night and clamours urgently to see either of the Keith-Westertons; and he turns up again on much the same errand at the boathouse this morning. And yet, when you show him a photo with both of them in it, he doesn't recognise either of them. He actually saw Mrs. Keith-Westerton herself twice, last night, and didn't know who she was. Why all this urgency in the matter of a couple of total strangers? It beats me."

Sir Clinton made a vague gesture in reply.

"There are one or two loose ends yet; but Severn's trying to find them," he acknowledged. "There's the telephone call at a quarter past seven: we want to know where that came from. There's the ownership of that abandoned car that turned up in the wood too. Severn's going to ring me up later on, if he gets the information."

He seemed struck by a sudden idea.

"By the way, Squire, when did young Keith-Westerton grow that moustache of his?"

"About a year or so ago, I think."

"Did it alter his looks much?"

"To a fair extent. It made him look older, for one thing."

"H'm! That might fit in," Sir Clinton mused aloud.

CHAPTER IX: SIR CLINTON'S FISHING

BEFORE Wendover had time to realise the implication of Sir Clinton's last statement, a maid brought him a visiting card.

" '*Mr. Oliver Thewles,*' " Wendover read aloud, in a rather puzzled tone. "I seem to remember the name, but I can't place it. He's pencilled '*Urgent*' on his card. What does he want?"

"I think he wants to see Sir Clinton, sir. He asked for you; and then he asked if Sir Clinton was here just now."

Wendover consulted the Chief Constable with a glance.

"Very well. I'll see him here."

In a few moments, the maid showed the visitor into the room. The thin stooping figure in light tweeds was quite unfamiliar to the Squire, but Thewles' first words served to identify him.

"Mr. Wendover? Ah, perhaps you may remember my writing you a letter recently, asking permission to enter your grounds at night—for entomological purposes."

Wendover knew where he was now.

"Oh, yes. Very glad to be of any service to you in that way. I warned my keepers about it. I hope you haven't been troubled in any way?"

"Not at all, not at all," Thewles hastened to assure

him nervously. "Really, as a matter of fact, my mission is quite different. This is Sir Clinton Driffield, is it not? My business really lies in his province."

Tactful transitions were evidently not Thewles' strong suit; but Wendover could see that no offence was intended by this abrupt dismissal of himself from the affair.

"I am an entomologist, Sir Clinton, specialising in the nocturnal lepidoptera—moths, in fact. I have contributed several papers to various journals, among others to the Transactions of the Entomological Society, the Bulletin of the Italian Entomological Society, and the Entomologische Zeitschrift."

"An international reputation," Sir Clinton interjected politely.

He was perfectly well aware that in science an international reputation implies merely that an author's papers are read by a handful of specialists, half of whom probably disagree with the conclusions. He kept a grave face, however, and waited patiently for the lepidopterist to get to business.

"I mention these things merely to indicate that I am a reliable witness," Thewles pursued, quite unaware that this statement was not accepted at its face value by at least one of his hearers. "I now come to the real purpose of my visit,—I mean this deplorable murder of the poor man Horncastle."

Wendover had taken a dislike to his uninvited guest.

"Damned pedant," was his tacit verdict. "No manners. I wonder if he knows any way of beginning a sentence except with a capital I?"

"I presume you are unaware of the methods employed in securing specimens of the nocturnal lepidoptera?" Thewles continued, with a superior air which irritated the Squire to the point of breaking in on this purely rhetorical question.

"Mix up brown sugar with some beer and rum; and paint it on tree trunks during the day time to attract the moths when they come out at night. Isn't that it? Or else lure them with a lantern? I used to do it when I was a boy."

"That is, approximately, the proper procedure," Thewles agreed, a little taken aback to find his thunder stolen by Wendover. He turned rather pointedly to the Chief Constable. "I prepared certain tree trunks yesterday afternoon, though it is not an entirely propitious time at present, owing to the strong moonlight which weakens the effect of a flash lamp on the creatures. I selected for treatment trees near the edge of the little wood behind the boathouse, I may say, since these appeared to offer the most favourable chances, judging from my previous results."

Sir Clinton listened patiently. Apparently Thewles had something to tell, and probably would get to the point quickest if he were left to tell it in his own way.

"I am staying temporarily at the Talgarth Arms," Thewles continued, "and last night, with my appliances, I left the hotel about ten o'clock, intending to visit the various trees which I had prepared beforehand. I was delayed on the way by an attempt, fruitless I regret to say, to capture a very interesting specimen which came within range of my flash lamp. When I approached the edge of the wood, I was surprised—I think quite naturally—by discovering that the lights in the boathouse were switched on. I had a particular reason for noting this, you will observe; since obviously these lighted windows formed a counter-attraction for nocturnal insects and were liable to draw the creatures away from my flash lamp and my sugar lures. I felt that it was unfortunate that, on so propitious an evening—warm and calm—the boathouse should be in use for mere social purposes. I glanced at my watch to gauge if the boathouse would soon be vacated; and I noted that the time was then twenty-five minutes past ten. I am quite certain of that."

Sir Clinton made no comment, which seemed to vex Thewles slightly, since he had paused with the obvious intention of drawing one from the Chief Constable.

"As I emerged from the wood," he continued, "I observed a car standing on the road. I am not a motorist; in fact, I detest these vehicles: but I am familiar with this particular make because it is used by my next-door neighbour at home, who frequently wearies me with his descriptions of its so-called excellencies. I was therefore able to identify this car as being similar to that used by Mr. Keith-Westerton, a Sunbeam saloon, in fact."

Again he paused, as though expecting a compliment; but neither of his hearers rose to the occasion.

"I was standing under the trees," the entomologist

pursued, in a slightly disappointed tone, "when the door of the boathouse opened, and I saw a woman's figure come out. I did not see her face; but from her walk I have little hesitation in saying that it was Mrs. Keith-Westerton. She closed the boathouse door behind her, entered her car, and drove off towards the village. To my annoyance, however—as you can well understand—the boathouse lights still remained on.

"I moved along the edge of the wood in this direction, intending to examine first those of my lures which were most remote from these disturbing lights. In about three minutes, I was relieved to see the electric lights switched off in the boathouse; but I had hardly begun to congratulate myself on their disappearance when once again they were lit up. I was then surprised by a peculiar phenomenon, for the boathouse lights were switched on and off, several times in rapid succession; and were then left full on. My impression at the time was that some child must be entertaining itself with the switches. I have since come to the conclusion that this is unlikely."

"Very interesting," said Sir Clinton dryly.

His face showed no flicker of amusement, though Wendover knew that the naiveté of the entomologist's last two sentences must have tickled the Chief Constable's sense of humour.

"Much to my vexation," Thewles continued, "the illumination of the boathouse persisted; and naturally, from time to time, I glanced in that direction. At one time I observed two shadow figures on the lowered blind of a window; but owing to the distortion produced by the light being above them, as well as behind, I was not able to determine whether the figures in the room were male or female. To be perfectly explicit, I did not make a very careful observation of them, as they seemed to be no affair of mine."

Sir Clinton made a faint gesture, as though approving Thewles' caution.

"Shortly after eleven—I can estimate it no more accurately for I did not examine my watch—I was greatly relieved by the extinction of the lights in the boathouse; and thereafter I began to work backwards over my lures, in the direction of the building. As I approached it, I was somewhat surprised to observe that foreign ecclesiastic who frequents the village—I find that the local rustics have nicknamed him Father Go-Wrong, a curious and possibly prejudiced denomination—I observed, I say, this ecclesiastic walking up to the door of the boathouse and knocking on it as though he expected to find some one within. That was about half-past eleven, for I had occasion to examine my watch almost immediately after. At the moment, I was much engrossed in an attempt—which proved successful—to capture a specimen. When I chanced to glance again at the boathouse, the priest had evidently retired.

"I continued to work along the line of my lures and had got past the boathouse when, greatly to my annoyance, the lights were once more switched on in the boathouse. I retreated to the end of my line of lures farthest from the boathouse on the west side. Fortunately, at that period, clouds began to obscure the moon and I was able to utilise my flash lamp to some advantage."

"About what time did the lights go on again?" Sir Clinton inquired.

"That I cannot do more than estimate very approximately from my recollection. I should place it about half-past eleven at the earliest, but there must obviously be a large margin for error in such cases. The lights shone for ten or twelve minutes on this occasion and were then extinguished. I confess that although it was no concern of mine, I was somewhat intrigued by these curious phenomena to which my interest had been so vexatiously drawn. That is one reason why the sequence of them made so strong an impression on my memory.

"By this time, it was growing late. I glanced at my watch and found the hands within a few seconds of midnight. I had taken the precaution of promising the boots at the hotel a liberal *douceur* if he would sit up and let me in when I arrived back; but it seemed unnecessary to delay further. I was turning homeward when my attention was attracted by a dull sound from beyond the lake and on glancing across the water, I observed a figure rowing a boat towards the boathouse. The moon was obscured at the moment and I was unable to distinguish whether the rower was a man or a woman. Naturally, had I known then that I had heard the fatal shot, I should have made more careful investigation; but except for wondering why any one should choose that time of night to row on the lake, I admit that I paid no attention to the matter. I packed up my appliances and made my way home through the wood to my hotel, where I found the boots half-asleep, waiting for my arrival."

During Thewles' rather laboured narration, Wendover had collated the fresh facts with those which he already knew; and at the end of the story he had to admit to himself that this new evidence had an ugly look.

It left no doubt that Mrs. Keith-Westerton had been at the boathouse. Further, since the lights were left on after her departure, it was hardly possible to deny that some other person had met her there and had remained behind after she left. She and her husband could have discussed anything in their own house; they had no need to go independently to the lakeside for that purpose. Ergo, the second person in the boathouse was not Keith-Westerton. And from the boathouse, she had driven straight to the Abbé Goron for confession. Wendover, despite his prejudice, could not deny that this behaviour looked suspicious, when taken in conjunction with the rest of the night's doings.

The signalling by means of the boathouse lights could have only one meaning. Obviously the occupant of the boathouse had prearranged this code with yet another person, and the flashes were meant to indicate that the coast was clear after Mrs. Keith-Westerton's departure. Keith-Westerton, for all his denial, had probably been at the boathouse that night. Was he the person for whom the signals were intended? Apparently some one had come in answer to the call, for shortly after that Thewles had seen the shadows of two people on the blind.

Then there was the new fact of the Abbé Goron's appearance at the boathouse door. His behaviour there proved that he had no key to the Yale lock. Obviously his visit must have been a sequel to what he learned from Mrs. Keith-Westerton when she went to him to confess. And had he "retired", as Thewles supposed? The facts might just as easily be explained if, after knocking, he had been kept waiting for a time before being admitted into the boathouse, for Thewles had not seen him go away from the door. In that case, the boathouse must have been occupied even when the lights were out. It sounded improbable; but Wendover felt that he could not exclude this possibility entirely.

Then came the two final episodes, obviously interwoven with the murder of Horncastle. The lights went on at about 11.30 P.M. and remained so for ten or twelve minutes before they were again extinguished. Perhaps a boat left the dock at the moment when they were put out. Shortly before midnight, Thewles heard the fatal shot; but at that very moment he saw a boat on the lake moving back towards the boathouse. The rower could not be the actual murderer, since the shot had been fired at close quarters. This fitted in, Wendover remembered, with the single-way trail away from the body, and also with Sir Clinton's chaffing remark about the cleverness of the boat in bringing itself back to the dock after the murder.

To Wendover's mind, the whole problem seemed to centre in the identity of the person whom Mrs. Keith-Westerton had gone to meet at the boathouse. And with that, although he had no proof, he coupled the discovery of the abandoned car. Some one had come to the boathouse that night, somebody whose identity had still to be established. That lay at the root of the business. And, on the fact of the evidence, that character in the drama had not gone away again, though the car was waiting only a few dozen yards from the boathouse. An unpleasant suspicion shot through Wendover's mind. Suppose Mrs. Keith-Westerton had taken this unknown individual away in the Sunbeam saloon? Then, with relief, Wendover remembered that Thewles had seen Mrs. Keith-Westerton come out of the boathouse and drive away —alone. But then, on the other hand, she might have returned later, unnoticed by the entomologist.

"I naturally paid little attention to all these episodes at the time," Thewles continued, "for I had no idea, of course, that they were of public importance. It was only at lunch time to-day that the waiter at my table—a somewhat garrulous personage —insisted on giving me a *réchauffé* of the local gossip about the murder of this poor keeper; and one or two of his remarks set me thinking about the events of last night, so far as they concerned me. I devoted some thought to the matter after lunch, and finally I came to the conclusion that my evidence might fill a gap and might possibly assume more importance when collated with other material already in the hands of the police. I do not believe in dealing with underlings, and as I had heard your name mentioned, Sir Clinton, in connection with the case, I thought it best to come direct to you."

"That's very interesting, Mr. Thewles," said Sir Clinton thoughtfully. "A very reasonable attitude on your part. Now officially, of course, this evidence ought to go to Inspector Severn, who's in charge of the matter. Would it be too much if I asked you to repeat to him what you've told us? It's only a formality, you understand? but . . ."

His gesture suggested that red tape was abhorrent but still indispensable.

Thewles, evidently not ill-pleased to find that his tale had attracted attention, took his leave when he found that no one encouraged him to stay longer. When he had been shown out, Sir Clinton glanced at his watch.

"And now, Squire, what about the Simple Simon business?"

"Simple Simon?" Wendover repeated, in a puzzled tone.

"Never heard of him, Squire? Education neglected from the very cradle, evidently. Tut! Tut!

"Simple Simon went a-fishing,
For to catch a whale.

"My ideas are more modest than Simon's, but my purpose is similar. Care to join me?"

"You're not going to waste the afternoon on trout?" Wendover demanded, for he had not taken seriously Sir Clinton's earlier remarks about fishing.

"Did I mention trout? No, the fish I'm out to catch will need a grapnel for a hook, and some light rope for a line, if you have such tackle on hand."

"You're going to drag the lake?" cried Wendover,

suddenly enlightened. "Was that what you meant by all this talk about deep waters?"

"Well, I meant it both literally and metaphorically. And now, do I take you or the constable? I warn you that we may have Simple Simon's luck; and if we do catch anything, you may not like the look of it. Don't come unless you want to."

Wendover's mind swung back to the abandoned car. Its unknown owner was one of the missing pieces in the puzzle. Sir Clinton's project seemed to suggest where that owner might be found. Then Wendover recalled that Sir Clinton had spoken of fishing long before the information about the car had come to hand.

"Of course I'll come," he said. "We can get a small grapnel and a light line at the boathouse."

"And I think you'd better add some sandwiches, a flask, and a couple of flash lamps," Sir Clinton suggested. "And postpone dinner till we get back, whenever that happens to be. This may be a long business."

It turned out to be longer business than Wendover had anticipated. At the boathouse, Sir Clinton fitted the outboard motor to one of the larger boats and saw that the tank was full before starting. Then began a wearisome systematic cruise with the boat kept rigidly on bearings which were changed ever so slightly at each crossing of the lake. Sir Clinton began in the shallow water at the shore nearest the Grange and kept their craft moving on a series of almost parallel lines to and fro across the lake, so that practically every foot of the bottom was raked by the grapnel in its passage. It was a tedious business, and as time went by with no signs of success, Wendover's initial enthusiasm cooled until at last it was replaced by something akin to boredom and hopelessness. The sun sank lower and lower, and still the monotonous trips continued without an incident of any sort to break the rhythm. North; keep her in the bearings; stop; pull in the grapnel; throw it inshore; turn south; keep her in the fresh bearings. . . . It seemed to last for ages. The only breaks were when Sir Clinton surrendered the tiller or took it over again from Wendover.

"If we go on much longer, we sha'n't have light enough to see our marks," the Squire protested at length.

By this time they had reached a line rather to the west of Friar's Point. Sir Clinton glanced at the sky.

"Another half-dozen trips, then," he stipulated. "It's round about here that we're most likely to make a strike; but I wanted to be systematic instead of groping wildly all over the place. Besides, I'm not sorry that it's into the dusk. If we do catch anything, nobody will see what we're after very clearly now."

On the third trip, the grapnel caught something and the boat's way was suddenly checked.

"Gently, Squire," Sir Clinton recommended from the tiller, as Wendover caught at the line. "Don't be in too much of a hurry. We don't want to lose the catch, whatever it is."

At the feel of the line, Wendover's excitement rose, for it was clear that they had hooked some heavy mass. He pulled in carefully and the weight on the grapnel was so great that their boat moved slightly towards the point of attachment, until at last they were almost vertically above it. Then, exerting more strength, Wendover hauled in, while Sir Clinton trimmed the boat. Foot by foot the line came in, until at last Wendover knew that he had only a yard or so overboard.

"The flash lamp," he said, and when Sir Clinton passed it to him, he held the line with one hand while with the other he turned the flash-light beam down into the water. As he did so, a half-stifled exclamation escaped him. A couple of feet below the surface, clear as in a mirror, appeared a girl's face, set and marble-white under her chestnut hair. Wendover's involuntary movement of amazement disturbed the boat; its librations ruffled the water; and the vision dissolved into the lambent reflections of the flash light from the ripples.

"Good God, Clinton! It's a girl's body."

"Ah!"

Sir Clinton, at least, did not seem surprised. His tone suggested rather the feelings of a chess expert who has discovered the key move in a problem. Wendover, still under the emotion of the moment, resented this.

"It's damnable!" he exclaimed.

"We'd better get her into the boat," Sir Clinton suggested prosaically. "Don't let that grapnel lose its hold in your excitement, Squire. I've no wish to begin all over again."

Wendover, revolted by his friend's businesslike attitude in the face of the tragedy, sullenly gave his assistance. As they lifted the body, he noticed a band passing around the waist; and a moment later he found that this attached to the corpse the missing parts of his gramophone.

"I told you the thief attached great weight to that motor, Squire," was Sir Clinton's only comment, as they turned the boat's head towards the dock.

"Damn your funniments. They're too gruesome for my taste," said Wendover, whose feelings were jarred by Sir Clinton's rather macabre turn of humour at that moment.

Sir Clinton seemed in no way depressed by this rebuke; but he apparently decided to reserve further comment for a more suitable season. When they reached the boathouse, he summoned the constable who was on guard there; and the girl's body was carried up into the lounge. Sir Clinton, with more gentleness than his recent grim humour foreshadowed, had composed the dead face; and he now stood beside the body, intently studying the features and evidently striving to recall something which they suggested.

Wendover had felt few qualms when he was called to the scene of Horncastle's murder; but this fresh tragedy made a far deeper impression on him. He stood beside the Chief Constable and gazed down at the pitiful thing which lay at his feet.

Quite young, he saw, twenty-five or so. Wonderful chestnut hair and a transparent skin which must have flushed and paled: when she was alive, she must have been a beauty, he reflected sadly. Even in death, there was a slight droop at the corners of the mouth, not exactly plaintive and yet curiously appealing in some manner. If ever he had seen an innocent face, this was one; and his anger blazed up at the thought of something so young and fair being swept ruthlessly out of existence.

His eyes left her face and he noted mechanically that the young figure was as perfect as the features. Then, at the back of his mind, a vague feeling made itself apparent. Something seemed to be wrong somewhere in the *tout ensemble*. What was it? He began a more minute inspection of detail, hoping to trace the thing which jarred on him. Her shoes were expensive and showed her arched feet to advantage. It wasn't that. The stockings which covered her slim ankles were obviously real silk. Not that, either. Her clothes were evidently cut by a first-class tailor; they must have cost her a good deal. And yet, somehow, the effect was by no means all that it should have been.

Sir Clinton had given up his private problem and was now watching Wendover out of the corner of his eye.

"Expensively dressed and yet just a shade dowdy; is that what's puzzling you?" he demanded. "Well, think of the fashion of four years back. Wouldn't she have been just 'it' in those days?"

The words solved Wendover's problem for him. He had some difficulty in recalling the exact fashion to which Sir Clinton referred; but now that his eyes were opened, he could see that the girl's skirt was of no recent cut. An up-to-date shopgirl would have disdained to be seen in such a costume, expensive though it evidently was.

Sir Clinton knelt down beside the body, lifted one

of the hands, and inspected the fingers closely. Wendover, craning over his shoulder, was surprised to find that they were rough, with nails which obviously had not been manicured regularly.

The Chief Constable rose to his feet again and it was plain that he was still engrossed in an attempt at identification. Wendover had no such troubles. He was positive that he had never seen the girl alive.

Sir Clinton, with a gesture of vexation, put his problem aside for the moment.

"I'm almost certain I know the upper part of her face," he said mechanically. "I've seen her, or her portrait, at some time or another. But I can't place it. That doesn't matter. We'll have her identified in a few hours, without the slightest bother, I hope."

He stooped down and tried the fit of one of the dead girl's shoes.

"They took a risk there. One of these things might have loosened and drifted ashore. They're fairly tight-fitting though, and as things turned out, the risk didn't amount to anything."

"How do you think she was killed?" Wendover asked.

Sir Clinton shook his head.

"Ask me another," he said frankly. "There's no wound apparent. She may have been poisoned; or knocked on the head, perhaps; or there may be another explanation. We'll need to wait for the P.M. before we can say for certain."

He turned to the constable who was in the room with them.

"Inspector Severn and the police surgeon will be

here soon. I'm going to send for them when I get back to the Grange. Once this body's been removed, there's no need for you to wait here any longer. I don't want the place guarded after this. You understand?"

With a gesture to Wendover he left the boathouse. As they drove back to the Grange, Wendover had time to fathom this last move.

"You were afraid that the murderer might come back in the night, fish up the body from the lake, and dispose of it elsewhere?"

"Yes, there was always the chance of that happening last night, if we hadn't taken precautions."

"So you knew there was a body in the lake all the time?"

"No," Sir Clinton admitted with a smile; "I merely made a guess at that. Hence my thoughtfulness in leaving the Inspector out of the fishing expedition. I didn't care to take the risk of drawing a blank in his company. One must save one's face if one can, Squire."

Wendover passed to a fresh aspect of the question.

"These clothes puzzle me," he admitted in his turn. "That girl quite obviously could afford to dress perfectly—and yet, as you said, she was hopelessly behind the times. The impression I got was that the material was quite new, too, though it's hard to be sure after all that soaking in water."

"These are just the points I'm banking on for an identification," Sir Clinton confessed. "And now, here we are, Squire, and the first thing I want is the telephone."

In about ten minutes he came into the smoking

room where Wendover was impatiently awaiting him.

"I've rung up Severn. He's to get the police surgeon and go up to examine the body at once. The surgeon ought to be able to tell us, after his P.M., whether that girl was drowned or was dead before they put her into the water."

"What practical difference does that make?" Wendover demanded. "She's been killed, anyhow. That's the main point."

"It might make a difference in the charge," Sir Clinton pointed out, "especially in one case, which seems just within the bounds of possibility in this affair. There were no marks of violence on the body, so far as I could see: no throttling, or wounding, or anything of that sort. She may have been sandbagged, of course."

He did not pause to explain further, but continued the summary of his conversation with the Inspector.

"I've ordered Severn to take her fingerprints and see if they lead to anything. We'll know about that to-morrow, probably. Then Severn reported that he's traced the origin of the telephone call which wrought such a surprising change in young Keith-Westerton's habits last night. It came from an A.A. box on the London road, about ten miles from here."

"That leaves no clue to the person who rang up, then, except that that person had an A.A. key," Wendover commented. "It was a woman's voice, the maid said. Was it that poor girl, Clinton? She must have come here in the car we found derelict."

"I suppose you think that since she had old-fashioned clothes she would have an old-fashioned car to match?" Sir Clinton asked in a flippant tone. "Well, there might be something in it."

"Then . . ." Wendover found himself unable to formulate his charge. Instinct was against him. At the last moment he changed his sentence. "Then I'm sorry for Mrs. Keith-Westerton. It's going to be a bad business."

"I told you before," Sir Clinton said patiently, "that Mrs. Keith-Westerton is the centrepiece of the whole affair. If there had been no Mrs. Keith-Westerton, two people might have been alive to-day instead of dead."

He paused for a moment, as though to prepare Wendover for his final remark:

"I should think that girl's death may have been very opportune for young Keith-Westerton."

Despite the lightness of the tone, Wendover was impressed by the sinister suggestion behind the words.

"You mean . . . ?" he began.

"I mean just what I say, Squire, no more, no less. Think it out."

CHAPTER X: CINCINNATI JEAN

On the following morning, Wendover was impatient for the latest news of the fresh field of inquiry which had been opened up by the discovery of the second body. Sir Clinton, however, damped his zeal.

"I don't want to give Severn the impression that I'm standing over him the whole time and leaving him no initiative whatever, Squire. It's not fair to him. There's no shilly-shally about him, so we're losing nothing by being patient. He'll report in due course."

With this, Wendover had to be content throughout the day, for it was not until after dinner that the Inspector put in an appearance. When he arrived, Wendover saw at a glance that he was well pleased.

"I haven't been able to report before, sir," he explained, as he took the seat which Wendover pushed forward. "I've been in London since last night, and kept pretty busy too. It seemed best to go up myself; for there were one or two things I didn't care to put into the heads of a sergeant. I'd rather see things with my own eyes."

"Sound principle," Sir Clinton admitted. "Another good one is: get to business at once, even in a report," he added, with a twinkle in his eye.

Severn's gesture acknowledged the thrust which he saw was not meant to hurt his feelings.

"Well, sir, I took the girl's fingerprints as you told me; and in addition, since I happen to have a camera, I took one or two photographs of the body. I thought they might be useful for identification purposes."

"Very sound," Sir Clinton commended. "My congratulations on the idea. Yes?"

"The police surgeon and I examined the body, sir. There wasn't a trace of violence on it—nothing whatever to suggest how she came by her death. I'll come to that again later. I'm taking things in their order, if you don't mind."

"Quite right. Go on."

"While we were undressing the body, another pearl dropped on to the floor, sir. It must have slipped down inside her dress at the neck, I should think."

Sir Clinton made no comment, but Wendover saw from his expression that this fact evidently closed a gap in the chain.

"There were no names on her underclothing, no initials even on her handkerchief. There was a laundry mark; and I daresay we might have found that useful if we'd failed on the direct method."

He put up his finger to stop Wendover, who was pouring out whiskey for him.

"Thanks. I left the police surgeon to examine the body. I developed the photos, took bromide prints in a hurry, and caught the first train up to town."

"You didn't find a Yale key, the key of the boathouse door, anywhere among her belongings?" Sir Clinton interrupted.

"No, sir. Nothing of that sort. I found a Yale key, but you'll hear about it later."

"Sorry to interrupt. Go on."

"I went straight to the Fingerprint Department at Scotland Yard. It's a wonderful system they have there. I'd some general notions about it; but it looks next door to miraculous when you see them actually at work. Simply marvellous, the way they have these complicated affairs indexed. . . ."

"So they managed to identify her for you?" Sir Clinton demanded, cutting into the Inspector's flow of laudation.

"Yes, sir. Guess who she was."

"If I'd been able to do that, you wouldn't have had your trip to London. That face has been tantalising me for the last twenty-four hours."

"It's Cincinnati Jean, sir."

"Cincinnati Jean!" Sir Clinton's gesture betrayed his vexation. "That's what's been bothering me. The only portrait of her I ever saw was a blotchy production in one of the cheap newspapers, nothing like the real face except about the eyebrows and the nose. That accounts for my recognising her vaguely and yet not being able to place her."

To Wendover, the nickname suggested nothing.

"Who was Cincinnati Jean?" he queried.

"About the second most dangerous woman in England, sir," the Inspector said gravely.

"I'll tell you about her later on," Sir Clinton promised. "Business before pleasure. Go on, Inspector. This case is going to make you a notorious character, whether you like it or not."

"You, sir, you mean," Severn protested. "I didn't find the body. The credit's yours."

"My part comes under the head of 'Information received'," Sir Clinton said decisively, silencing any further discussion.

"Well, sir, after they'd got the fingerprints settled, I produced my photographs of the body and they hunted out a portrait of Cincinnati Jean that they had. No mistake about it; they were as like as two peas."

"After that, it seems they couldn't do too much for me, sir. Very decent indeed, they were. One of them stood me supper. They got me a room at an hotel. And meanwhile they set the wires buzzing, it seems, and fairly got to work. Cincinnati Jean's been a lot of trouble to them, one way and another; and they seemed to be on to the business from the word Go."

He paused and and took an appreciative sip of Wendover's whiskey.

"This morning, they had a lot of the business cut and dried for me. This is how that part of it figures out. Cincinnati Jean slipped a cog in one of her deals: the usual thing, a nasty case, but the man stood up to her and that finished the business so far as she was concerned. She got five years, though it was her first conviction over here; and she was sent to Aylesbury. She was a model prisoner, so of course she got her remission and came out on licence after forty months. She was liberated from Aylesbury the day before the Horncastle murder."

Severn paused, as though to indicate the end of a chapter in his narrative. When he resumed, his tone showed that he expected to surprise his audience.

"She was a notorious character, so naturally they

172

took more interest in her than they would do in a common-or-garden convict. That's made it easier to pick up information. Now at the gate at Aylesbury, she was met by a man. Who do you think it was, sir?" the Inspector asked, with a tinge of triumph in his voice.

"Is this a report or a guessing competition?" Sir Clinton inquired testily.

"It was a fellow in Salvation Army rig-out, sir; and from the description, there's not a shadow of doubt that it was this Save-your-soul Sawtry man who turned up here on the night of the Horncastle murder."

"Do you know what's become of him since then?" Sir Clinton demanded.

"No, sir," Severn admitted, with a rather crestfallen air. "He's cut his stick while I was in London."

"H'm! Well, if I wanted him, I ought to have asked for him, I suppose," the Chief Constable said curtly, taking his share of the blame. "What happened next?"

"They seemed to be old friends, it appears. I've learned since then that this Save-your-soul person was one of her gang in earlier days, so there was nothing in that. It seems he talked to her a bit excitedly and she seemed a bit cold in her replies—got impatient in a very short time. Then they walked off together towards the station and took the train up to town."

Another pause marked the termination of a fresh section in the narrative, and Severn used it to apply himself again to his glass.

"She's got a flat in town, in Gray Mare Street, off Piccadilly. It's been shut up during her holiday, of course, but the rent's been paid regularly by some cheap lawyer she employed to attend to that sort of thing. He paid the garage rent too, for the storage of her car, and things like that. She must have known she'd get pinched—arrested sooner or later, and she had everything cut and dried, so it seems.

"Being such a notorious character, naturally the man on the beat was curious to see her. I expect he hung about a bit. Anyhow, he had the luck to spot her going up to the door when she arrived *and there was Mr. Save-your-soul Sawtry in tow still,* with a little bag in his hand. And no tearful farewells on the mat, it appears; he walked right in with her and upstairs to her flat. And he didn't come out again."

Sir Clinton flicked some cigarette ash from his sleeve. Wendover, completely taken aback by this fresh piece of puzzle, made no concealment of his eagerness for the rest of the Inspector's narrative.

"By-and-by Cincinnati Jean came out again, alone. She went straight off to the police officer in charge of her district and reported her arrival, according to the terms of her licence. That was just as it should be, of course. Then—it was easy enough to follow up her trail, they said—she took out a motor licence and a driving licence. Then she went to one or two shops and bought a few things, mostly food, soap, and affairs of that sort to start housekeeping on. And she gave standing orders for the delivery of milk and some other things. In fact, it looked as though she'd come back to settle down for a while. She made no big purchases. I gathered she was about broke when she came out of Aylesbury. Her defence had cost her a lot and she wasn't the kind that saves money much, since it was so easy come by in her line."

"You're sure of that?" Sir Clinton demanded, as though he attached some importance to the point.

"Well, sir, I can only give you what was told me. I think they had their information, partly from the lawyer fellow and partly from putting two and two together. But they seemed fairly sure of their ground."

"There's other evidence for it, as well," Sir Clinton confirmed. "Well, go on."

"This morning I went down to her flat. One of the C.I.D. men came with me to make things easy with the man on the beat, in case there was trouble. We went up to the flat, and I found that the Yale key I'd picked up here fitted the lock; so we got in without any bother. There was no maid there. The place was empty. Two people had been having a scratch meal and the dishes were standing about, unwashed. A very stylish flat, sir, though some of the things in it made you think a bit. The only thing I need trouble you with is a sheet of burnt paper in the grate. The C.I.D. man didn't make much of it, naturally; but it was as plain as print to me, all curled up as it was. I could see some lines and a cross on the ashes clear enough; and when I looked at them, plain enough there was a rough map of this district and the boathouse marked with a cross. The rest of the ash looked like burnt notepaper —a letter, most likely—but it had been crushed up so that there was nothing to be made of it."

"You couldn't get even a word or two intact?" Sir Clinton asked.

"No, sir. We did our best, but the stuff was in flinders. As we were coming away from the flat, the C.I.D. man rang the bell of the flat opposite and made some excuse to talk to the maid when she came to the door. That was a lucky shot. It seems that on the morning of the Horncastle murder, she was out on the landing when the door of Cincinnati Jean's flat opened and that Holy Joe, the Salvationist fellow, leaned out in his pyjamas and took in a bottle of milk that was on the mat. What do you think of that for a canting humbug, sir? Goes about with his mouth full of texts and spends the night with her in her flat! I'd like to meet him again, just for the pleasure of letting him know that I know what sort of character he is."

This piece of information seemed to impress Wendover much more than it did Sir Clinton, so far as obvious effect went.

"I'd no notion the Salvation Army sheltered things like that," Wendover exclaimed. "He ought to be turned out of it at once."

"I shouldn't write to headquarters about it, though, if I were you," Sir Clinton counselled smoothly. "There's such a thing as a law of libel, you know. The Salvation Army's a sound concern and a huge affair like that might well have a weak brother or two in it through no fault of its own. Though what a weak brother would want to be in it for is a bit of problem. From all I've seen of the rank and file, they're remarkably good people."

Severn took no notice of this interlude.

"We went on to the garage where she kept her car," he pursued, "and I made inquiries about that. It seems she took it out on the afternoon of the Horncastle murder, got the garage people to look over it and see that it was all right, filled up with oil and petrol, and drove off. That was the last they saw of her."

"Friend Sawtry wasn't with her, was he?"

"No, she was alone, they said. After that, we went to the post office and made inquiries about any recent deliveries of letters."

Sir Clinton did not interrupt, but it was clear that he had given the Inspector a good mark for this precaution.

"It was easy enough," Severn went on, "because the flat had been shut up for so long that the postman was struck by the fact that letters were starting again. He'd delivered two: one on the morning when she got out of Aylesbury, the other one a day or so earlier. That would be the stuff we found in the grate, most likely; for the ashes were fairly fresh."

The Inspector paused again and took a fresh sip from his glass.

"That covers the London side of things," he pursued. "When I got back here again, I looked up the police surgeon at once. He'd done a P.M. on Cincinnati Jean's body. He could find no external wounds, not even a bruise which might have been caused in a struggle. There were no signs of poisoning, either, so far as he could see. He couldn't estimate exactly how long the body had been in the water; the indications were too rough to be any use."

"Her wrist watch had stopped with the hands close to twelve o'clock," Sir Clinton commented, "but that's not altogether a good criterion. Was there any water in the lungs?"

"No, it seems there wasn't; nor in the stomach, either."

"So she was dead before she got into the water?"

"That's what he believes. He laid stress on the fact that he found no mud particles or anything of that sort in the stomach. From some food that he found there, he gauged that she must have had a meal—dinner—about four hours before her death. That checks fairly well with evidence from another side, sir. I've ascertained that after telephoning from the A.A. box, she stopped at The Brown Stag Hotel in Lamfield and had dinner there about half-past seven. The waiter remembered her perfectly well, partly because of her looks and partly because of her clothes. That puts her death about midnight, just about the same time as Horncastle's."

He took another drink and Wendover pushed the decanter across the table.

"The only other thing that the P.M. brought out was a rather funny one and the police surgeon appears to attach some importance to it. It seems some gland or other—I have a note of it here . . . Yes, the thymus gland—was considerably enlarged."

Sir Clinton made no effort to conceal his interest.

"Ah! I expected something of that sort. *Status lymphaticus*?"

"That's what he called it, I remember," the Inspector admitted. "It was a new name to me. Well, sir, it seems this gland was what he called a persistent thymus gland and it was about two inches wide and it weighed close on two ounces. It lies at the base of the heart and according to him an enlarged gland like that would be very dangerous, although the person having it would show no symptoms of anything wrong. Is that so?"

Sir Clinton nodded.

"It's a condition known as *status lymphaticus,*" he explained. "A man I knew was in that state, but nobody, least of all himself, had a notion that there was anything wrong with him. It doesn't betray itself. This poor chap had to undergo a very minor operation, hardly more serious than having a tooth drawn. They put him on the operating table, started to anæsthetise him . . . and, he was dead. They hadn't even begun to operate. Cardiac inhibition was what they called it. His heart just stopped short. Anæsthetics may have that effect in a case of *status lymphaticus,* or fright, or strong emotion of some sort, or even, in some cases, a very slight mechanical injury, such as a blow on the arm."

"And you can't tell whether you've got it or not?" the Inspector inquired uneasily.

"Apparently not, in most cases," Sir Clinton said, with a hardly suppressed smile. "I shouldn't worry, Inspector. You're like the man who opens a medical book and immediately suspects that he suffers from seven fatal diseases. Cases of enlarged thymus aren't so common as all that."

The Inspector grinned sheepishly at finding his thoughts read so accurately.

"Lucky I've got good teeth, sir," he admitted. "Tales like that are enough to put you off having gas when you go to the dentist's. There's just one thing more, sir. I hope you won't mind, but I'm afraid the whole Cincinnati Jean business will be in the papers. Some of these reporter fellows got hold of it."

"All the better," Sir Clinton said amiably, to the obvious relief of the Inspector. "No harm in that. Quite the opposite, in fact. Think what a weight it will take off the shoulders of a lot of poor devils whom she'd got into her clutches, when they read the glad tidings at breakfast time. It'll give them an appetite. And now, have you anything more to report?"

Severn had come to the end of his budget, it appeared; so, after finishing his glass of whiskey and soda, he took his leave.

"You see you underrated him, Squire," said Sir Clinton, when the Inspector had gone. "You can't say that he isn't a good man within his limits. He's worked like a horse since yesterday morning; and when it's been a case of collecting evidence, I don't think I'd ask for anything better. That's not where he'll fall down in this case, at any rate."

Wendover had little interest in the Inspector, since that individual was obviously becoming a mere tool in the hands of the Chief Constable.

"Who was this woman, Cincinnati Jean?" he asked. "I gather she was a bad lot, though one wouldn't have thought so from her face."

"Her face was her fortune, to some extent," Sir Clinton explained. "That particular type appeals to a certain brand of men. I suppose they think they've got hold of some gentle little thing. In practice, they'd be safer in kissing a wildcat."

He lit a fresh cigarette and put the match into his ash tray before continuing.

"Ever hear of Chicago May, Squire?"

"I've got some vague recollection about her—an American crook, wasn't she?"

"No, Irish by birth, really. America doesn't produce all that it gets credit for. She'd been over there at one time, of course. When she was convicted here, the papers starred her as The Most Dangerous Woman in the World or something like that—journalistic licence, really, because she was only a nasty little specimen of our baser social vermin. Her line was simple enough. Get hold of some wealthy man; lead him on; get him photographed on the sly by some of her gang, in a compromising position; block out her own face in the print; and bleed him for all she could get, on the strength of that."

"And this Cincinnati Jean was the same kind, you mean?" Wendover asked, in a tone which even yet betrayed some remaining traces of incredulity. "I can hardly believe it, you know, when I think of her face, Clinton. She looked such a gentle little thing."

"Nice soft peach," Sir Clinton said grimly; "but if you'd been led into nibbling at it, you'd have found a very hard stone in the middle. She was another of our home products—born in Bradford, if I remember. She went to the States before she was twenty and apparently made herself notorious over there, to judge by her nickname. She was back in London just after the War. You were talking, a while ago, about the weird mix-up in our social classes just after the Armistice. That period was Cincinnati Jean's heyday; it gave her just the chance she wanted. The night clubs and dance halls were the very places to scrape acquaintance with people; and no one asked too many awkward questions about who you really were, then. There were plenty of old fools who had made easy money in the War—just the sort of people that Chicago May battened on. Cincinnati Jean played the same game; but she had a second line in human material as well."

"What were they?" Wendover inquired.

"Youngsters with no money but good prospects, or youngsters with money who might get married later on. Chicago May was rather like the smash-and-grab window thief. She'd spend some time in netting her bird; but once she'd got him, she wanted quick returns. Cincinnati Jean was a more dangerous type. She looked ahead farther; and if there was a chance of bleeding a man better by waiting, she was quite prepared to do so.

"For instance, suppose she got hold of a youngster with a certain amount of money but with bigger expectations. She 'got him where she wanted him', as the phrase went, procured her compromising pictures, and then . . . sat tight. He never supposed he'd been landed. But in a year or two, when he was worth perhaps ten times as much through the death of relations, then Jean presented her little bill. It paid to delay, you see, in a case like that. Or a young fellow with cash might fall into her clutches. As things were, she could have milked him for a fair sum, no doubt. But she'd get more if she postponed her demands until he got engaged. Surprise is half the battle in these affairs; and a man's not half himself when he's suddenly faced with the evidence of something that he thought was all over and forgotten. She did it once too often and got sent to Aylesbury; but no one except Scotland Yard is likely to guess how many of these promising transactions got nipped in the bud when her thymus gland got to work the other night. She must have had quite a number of victims still in hand, I should think."

"What a damnable trade!" Wendover exclaimed. "And you think young Keith-Westerton was one of her victims?"

"I'd rather like to see the counterfoils of his checkbook," Sir Clinton admitted. "One of the most recent of them might be highly suggestive."

CHAPTER XI: THE ABBÉ GORON OFFICIATES

"THESE cases of yours seem to be hanging fire in the last few days," Wendover observed, with a faint touch of malice, as he and the Chief Constable entered the smoking room after dinner.

"Well, don't you think your Sleepy Hollow here has had enough sensations to keep it going?" Sir Clinton inquired lazily. "First of all, you have the Horncastle murder. Then the hurried departure of Mrs. Keith-Westerton gave them a lot to talk about. Then we fished up Cincinnati Jean—and, by the way, she got full obituaries in the press, portrait and all; more than most honest folk achieve. Then you had the inquest on Horncastle, with the usual verdict against some person or persons unknown. And after that there was the inquest on Cincinnati Jean, when they very wisely confined themselves to giving the enlarged thymus and shock as the cause of death, without committing themselves any further. It seems to me that Talgarth has supped on sensations lately, without even including the latest one."

"And what's that?" Wendover asked suspiciously.

"Why, the happy reunion of the Keith-Westerton family. Your charming young friend is back again at the Dower House, you'll be pleased to learn."

"Oh, is she?" said Wendover, rather blankly.

"Starting a second honeymoon," Sir Clinton volunteered in a neutral tone.

"Second honeymoon? What d' you mean?"

"Well, isn't the first month after a marriage generally called a honeymoon? She was married in the Catholic chapel here this morning. The Abbé Goron officiated, Severn tells me. A very quiet affair."

Wendover seemed puzzled by this news.

"But . . ."

"It's quite all right, Squire," Sir Clinton explained blandly. "They were married under the Registrar's certificate and licence. Two days ago, Keith-Westerton gave notice to the Registrar. There was no publication of the names—it's not required with that particular procedure. One clear day elapsed—that was yesterday. This morning, Mrs. Keith-Westerton arrived from London, went straight to the Catholic chapel, was married in due form by my friend the Abbé Goron, and she and her husband went back to the Dower House to enjoy what I think must be described as a honeymoon. As I said, the whole affair was very quiet—almost clandestine, one might say; but it's quite sound legally. And as that rather rigid ecclesiastic, the Abbé Goron, presided over the nuptials, I think I'm safe in saying that it's morally all square and aboveboard."

"Well, I'm damned," Wendover ejaculated.

"You say that so often and so assuredly that I begin to think you must have a straight tip on the subject, Squire."

But Wendover refused to be drawn. He hunched himself up in his chair, instead of answering, and very obviously plunged into consideration of the case in the light of this fresh evidence. At one point, his face lighted up as though he had seen a fresh aspect on the face of things; but immediately it clouded again, as though his new ideas had furnished merely a partial illumination of the affair. When at length he broke silence, his tone showed clearly that he found himself still befogged on the main issue.

"If you *are* married, you don't get married again— not to the same girl, at any rate."

"There's nothing legally against it, if you want to make a hobby of it," Sir Clinton commented.

Wendover disregarded this.

"Then if they got married this morning, they weren't married before," he pursued. "But they *were* married before, unless . . ."

"Unless they weren't?" Sir Clinton interjected to fill the gap which Wendover's perplexity had left in the sentence. "You can go through a form of marriage without getting married, you know, Squire."

"Yes, yes, I see what you're driving at," Wendover retorted testily. "I'm not such a fool that I can't spot an obvious thing like that. But it doesn't seem to clear up much, even when one does see it. Where does Horncastle come in?"

" 'How now! A rat?' 'Hamlet', Act III, Scene 4," Sir Clinton quoted, instructively.

"What's Polonius got to do with it?" Wendover demanded indignantly.

"Well, he blundered in where he wasn't wanted, Squire. And my impression is that if you could recall Horncastle from the Beyond, he wouldn't be able to

give you much information about the real complications in this case."

Wendover digested this suggestion for a few moments before speaking again.

"You mean that he saw Cincinnati Jean's body being sunk in the lake? Of course it was dropped in
quite near to where Horncastle's own body was found.
That's true. And he had to be silenced? Is that it?"

"That's somewhere near the truth, I expect," Sir
Clinton confirmed. "But I doubt if Horncastle even
knew whose body was being put out of the way."

"Just a pawn in the game, you mean?"

"Some pawns have a trick of turning into queens,"
Sir Clinton reminded him. "They're more important
potentially than actually, at times. Horncastle may
be a pawn of that sort."

"Oh, indeed," Wendover observed cautiously, in
an attempt to conceal the fact that Sir Clinton's remark had not proved very enlightening.

The Chief Constable evidently decided to put his
cards on the table.

"Here's the trouble, Squire," he admitted frankly.
"I'm not bluffing when I say that I believe I can see
my way through this case fairly well. I've a pretty
clear idea of all that happened on that night at the
boathouse. It's not so very difficult to fit together,
after all; for we seem to have got most of the really
necessary evidence. *But,* you've got to convince a
jury, finally; and some jurymen are not bright. I
could give a prosecuting barrister a very pretty tale
to work on; but—well, the jury might not swallow it.
And where would we be, then? Short of screwing a

confession out of somebody, I don't see how we can go into court with a cast-iron case. The only problem is: what lever can we use to extract that confession? I've got a notion about that; but these psychological factors are the very devil to handle properly. That's what's giving me trouble just now."

"You mean the motive?" Wendover asked.

"No, I don't mean the motive," Sir Clinton dissented, rather to Wendover's surprise. "The motive has nothing whatever to do with it."

He seemed to regret his momentary indiscretion, and Wendover could see from his expression that further revelations were not to be expected.

"My friend, the Abbé Goron, seems to be in charge of the moral affairs of the Keith-Westerton family," Sir Clinton said, after a pause. "You'll be interested to hear, Squire, that he has been visiting the Sisterhood of the Good Hope; and, as a result of that, I suspect, Mrs. Keith-Westerton was persuaded to come back here and go through a form of marriage this morning."

"A form of marriage?" Wendover demanded, pricking up his ears at the wording.

"Well, I can only guess," Sir Clinton said, with a pretence of caution. "I wasn't there, you know. But that's what I think it was."

"You're an infernal mystery monger, Clinton," Wendover protested plaintively, when he found that he was to get no further enlightenment.

"I don't know, you see," the Chief Constable retorted. "I make a guess, and I tell you it's a guess, and now you want more. What more can you get?"

Before Wendover had time to pursue the subject, a maid came into the room with a message.

"Oh, send her in here," Wendover ordered. And when the maid had gone out, he turned to Sir Clinton.

"This is an old woman from the village. She 'wants to know something about the law.' Half the country-side seems to think that since I'm a J.P. I ought to give them legal advice. They get my opinion for nothing and probably they get just what they pay for. She's quite a decent old soul, Mrs. Tetbury. Does a bit of cheap dressmaking and runs a sort of second-hand clothes exchange in the village."

The maid showed into the room a rather shabbily dressed old woman, obviously slightly perturbed at the sight of Sir Clinton. In her hand she carried a neat brown paper parcel.

"Well, Mrs. Tetbury, what's the trouble?" Wend-over inquired, as he placed a chair for her. "This is Sir Clinton Driffield. He'll give you his advice. It's better worth having than mine."

Mrs. Tetbury evidently found it difficult to get to grips with her subject. She fumbled with her parcel, fidgeted in her chair, and then, as the two men sat silent, she was at last driven into an ex-planation.

"Well, sir, really I'm sorry to bother you, I am really; but I don't quite know what I ought to do, really, and I thought most likely you'd be able to give me a bit of advice that I'm in need of, for I don't want to be doing anything without knowing just what I ought to do, you see? It's this coat. . . ."

She attacked the parcel feverishly, got confused

with the knots, and at last wrenched the string off and opened out the paper.

"It's about this raincoat, sir, that I wanted to ask you."

She disengaged it from its wrappings and held it up for them to examine. Wendover had no difficulty in seeing that it was of good material and well cut.

"Well, what about it?" Wendover asked, without impatience. "It seems a good enough coat, nearly new."

"Yes, sir, it is nearly new, a very good bargain indeed, really. Once I've put some stitches into it, it'll make a really nice coat for somebody."

"Then what's the trouble?"

Wendover knew Mrs. Tetbury quite well enough to remember that little would be gained by hustling her.

"Well, you see, sir, I bought this coat about a week ago from Mr. Ferrers, him that's Mr. Keith-Westerton's valet. It's Mr. Keith-Westerton's coat, really; but Mr. Ferrers had orders to get rid of it."

"What day did you buy it from him?" Sir Clinton asked in a casual tone.

Mrs. Tetbury named the day, two days after the Horncastle murder. Sir Clinton seemed to pay no special attention to this answer, but his glance encouraged the old woman to continue her tale.

"Well, you see, sir, it has a tear in it—here."

She opened out the coat again and showed a cut in the fabric near the shoulder at the back.

"Mr. Ferrers told me that Mr. Keith-Westerton found he'd ripped his coat on some barbed wire and it was no use to him any more after that, of course, so he'd given instructions to Mr. Ferrers to dispose of it. It's not stolen goods, sir, really; I'm quite sure of that, for I'd never dream of doing anything of that sort at all, as I'm sure Mr. Wendover would tell you at once. I've bought one or two things from Mr. Ferrers before, and I'm quite sure he wouldn't sell me anything he hadn't a right to sell."

"That seems all right," Wendover confirmed. "But I don't see what your trouble is, Mrs. Tetbury."

"Well, you see, sir, when I got this coat, I was busy with other things; so I just put it aside amongst some other old garments I've got, meaning to look over it again by and by and see if I would put a few stitches into the tear and make it look all right again, which would be easy enough, as you can see, sir. And what with one thing and another, I've never had a minute to look at it until to-day. But this afternoon I found I'd more time on my hands, and as it's just a few minutes' job to put a tear like that to rights, I went and got out the coat from amongst the rest of the things."

She fumbled for a moment or two in a battered old handbag and produced from it a small screw of paper which she held as though she feared she might lose it even at this stage.

"Well, sir," she continued, addressing herself to the more familiar of her two listeners, "I never like to take advantage of people; and before I sell anything, I like to go through the pockets and see that the last owner hasn't overlooked anything when he parted with the garment. You'd be surprised how careless some people are, really. So when I got out this coat, I thought to myself, 'Now, I just wonder if Mr. Keith-Westerton hasn't left something in the pockets. I'll have a look.' So I felt in the pockets—not really expecting to find anything, you understand? but just by way of precaution, because I like to be sure of things. And, lo and behold! When I put my hand into one pocket I felt something like a couple of peas. And when I pulled them out, this was what they were."

Steadying the coat on her knee with her elbow, she unrolled the paper screw and held it out towards Wendover.

"What are these, sir?"

Wendover suppressed a movement of astonishment, for there before him were two more pearls which might easily have come from Mrs. Keith-Westerton's necklace.

"May I look at them?" Sir Clinton demanded, putting out his hand for the paper.

A very short scrutiny sufficed.

"These are two pearls, I believe, Mrs. Tetbury. And fairly valuable ones too."

"Now are they, really, sir? That's one thing I wanted to know, and I'm glad to hear it, for all along I've been afraid I've been coming here on a bit of a wild-goose chase and taking up your time with nonsense. I was afraid they might be just these Woolworth things, the sixpenny stuff; and yet, I thought to myself, what would Mr. Keith-Westerton be doing with rubbish like that in his pocket. And then, besides, there's been some talk in the village about pearls and I just wondered . . . And then Mrs. Napton dropped in. She's an old friend of mine, sir, and lives next door, and often she pops in to tea with me, or I go around to have a cup with her. So when she came in, I showed them to her and asked her what she thought about it. And we talked it over and talked it over, and at first she was all for thinking they were just rubbish and I'd be making a fool of myself if I went to Mr. Ferrers with them; and then she swung around and began to think they might be real. 'And if they are,' these were her very words, 'you've got something there, Nancy, that'll add a bit on to your Old Age Pension when you come to draw it.' Then we talked it up and down for a bit longer, and at last Mrs. Napton says: 'This is the way of it, Nancy. You bought that coat in the open market, including anything anybody was fool enough to leave in the pockets. So if these pearls *are* pearls, then they're yours at this very moment. And if you don't believe me, then you take my advice and go up and see Mr. Wendover this very night, after his dinner when he won't be busy, and he'll tell you the ins and outs of the thing and he'll see you get your rights.' And, really, sir, that seemed to be the best thing to do, though I'm sorry to trouble you about it. I don't want to be doing anything I oughtn't to do. So I just tied up the coat straight away in a parcel and put it aside to bring with me, just to let you see it so that you'd understand everything; and as soon as I thought you'd be quite finished with your dinner, I came up to the Grange to ask you what you thought about it, for really I don't know what's the best thing to do."

Sir Clinton glanced down at the pearls in his hand.

"Will you take my advice, Mrs. Tetbury?" he asked kindly.

"Oh, yes, sir, I would, really. You ought to know about these things, if any one does, I'm sure."

"Well, if these are Mr. Keith-Westerton's pearls, I think I could arrange the matter on terms more favourable than you might be able to get if you handled the matter yourself."

"I'm sure you could, sir."

"That's settled, then. I'll take charge of the pearls. Got an envelope, Wendover? Thanks. Now I'll seal up the pearls in this envelope and you'll write your name on it."

Mrs. Tetbury did so, evidently much impressed by this formality, and Sir Clinton slipped the envelope into his note case.

"Oh, that reminds me," he said, as he returned his note case to his pocket. "I think I'd better have the coat too. By the way, what price were you thinking of putting on it?"

Mrs. Tetbury named a very moderate figure.

"Well, I may have to keep it for a while, so the easiest way will be to take it off your hands for good. I'll give you ten shillings more than you thought of asking for it, just to cover the chance that you might have made a good bargain with some one for it. That do? By the way, did you go through all the pockets?"

Mrs. Tetbury seemed almost overwhelmed by this generosity.

"Well, really, sir, it's very good of you indeed. I don't know what to say about it, really. No, sir, I didn't go through all the pockets. When I was going through them and came on these pearls, I was all taken aback, you know, at thinking what I'd come across if they really were real pearls, you understand? And when Mrs. Napton came in, we talked the thing up and down so much that we never thought of going through the rest of the pockets, though it seems funny that we didn't, now I come to think of it. But I was bringing the coat up to Mr. Wendover anyhow, and I never thought of looking to see if there was anything else in the pockets."

"I think that's everything, then, Mrs. Tetbury," Sir Clinton said, as he rose to his feet. "I'll let you know how I get on with Mr. Keith-Westerton about the pearls. It may take a day or two, you understand? But I'm sure you won't be the loser."

Mrs. Tetbury expressed her relief at coming so well out of the affair and took her leave with many protestations of thankfulness to them both.

"And what do you make of that, Squire?" Sir Clinton demanded, when the old woman had gone.

Wendover's face betrayed both perplexity and apprehension.

"I don't much like it," he admitted frankly. "These pearls look suspiciously like another fragment of that infernal necklace; and . . ."

He left his sentence unfinished; but it was plain enough that he saw the pointer of suspicion swinging around once more toward the Keith-Westerton ménage. The necklace was Mrs. Keith-Westerton's. Part of it had been found beside Horncastle's body. Another pearl had actually been discovered on the corpse of Cincinnati Jean. Further fragments had been brought to light in the lounge of the boathouse. And finally, another pair of pearls had turned up in the pocket of Keith-Westerton's raincoat, the coat which he had apparently been wearing when he went out on the mysterious errand. On that fatal night, at dinner, Mrs. Keith-Westerton wore the necklace; and now its jewels ran like the trail of a paper chase throughout the case, until the chain ended in Keith-Westerton's pocket. And yet, if the evidence was to be believed, Keith-Westerton had never seen his wife again on that evening, after he had left her at the Dower House.

Sir Clinton paid no attention to Wendover's aposiopesis. He picked up the raincoat and began methodically to go through the pockets. In the right-hand pocket his fingers encountered a small piece of paper which he drew out and examined.

"Here's something interesting, Squire," he said. "It's a cutting from an American newspaper. Just listen:

"DEATHS: KEITH–WESTERTON. — On January 3, 1925, at Sunnybank Hospital, Ormidale O., Ellen Amy Keith-Westerton, wife of Colin Keith-Westerton of Silver Grove, Talgarth, England. English papers please copy."

"That seems very illuminating."

"That's something I never guessed," said Wendover, after a moment or two. "So the young beggar was married before? He kept his thumb on that pretty tightly. I never heard a whisper of it."

He reflected for a moment before adding:

"But I don't see much in it. His first wife was dead long before he got engaged to his present one. The only queer thing is that he should be carrying the cutting about in his overcoat pocket at this time of day."

Sir Clinton stared at the cutting for a few moments.

"Yes, that's very curious," he said in a dry tone, as he stowed it away in his pocketbook.

"You think it's got some bearing on this affair?" Wendover questioned.

"It confirms a couple of suspicions that I had, certainly," Sir Clinton admitted. "But I was pretty sure I was right on these points, even without this. It doesn't get me much nearer a plan of campaign, though; and that's what's on hand at present. It's a question of how much one should stake on a bluff; and I don't want to hurt people who are really innocent and yet have got dragged into the affair."

He considered for a moment or two, then added:

"I must ring up Severn and let him see this bit of paper. If there's something on it, then I'm all at sea; but if the thing isn't on it, then I think the way's clear and we may be able to put some one under lock and key within twenty-four hours, if I can steer things right."

"Fingerprints?" asked Wendover.

"Or the lack of them," Sir Clinton corrected.

CHAPTER XII: THE PEARL NECKLACE

SEVERN and I are going to the Dower House again this morning," Sir Clinton announced after breakfast on the following day. "Care to come along, Squire? I think it would be a sound idea. No one could suspect you of having an axe to grind in the affair, which is more than can be said for any of the rest of us. Besides, you'd be a guarantee to young Keith-Westerton that his evidence won't be distorted for police purposes."

Wendover knew that Sir Clinton had not the slightest intention of twisting any evidence he might elicit; but still, a friendly face might serve as a moral backing to Keith-Westerton. There was something to be said in favour of his going with the officials; yet the position was an awkward one. He hesitated for a few seconds before making up his mind.

Sir Clinton saw that he was undecided.

"You'd better come," he urged. "My friend, the Abbé Goron, will be there too, I believe; so you won't be the only disinterested spectator."

"Oh, if it's to be a general meeting," Wendover said, in a faintly sarcastic tone, "then there's no harm in my attending."

At the gate of the Dower House they picked up Severn, who was waiting for them.

"You've had a look at that advertisement?" Sir Clinton inquired.

"They're not there," the Inspector answered tersely. "It seems rum."

Sir Clinton made no comment and Wendover was left to puzzle over these cryptic remarks.

When they reached the Dower House, the maid, evidently forewarned, showed them at once into a room where the Keith-Westertons and the Abbé Goron were waiting for them. Wendover began to wish that he had acted on his first thoughts and refrained from coming. Now that he was actually on the spot, he felt acutely that his intrusion was tactless; and inwardly he cursed Sir Clinton for having, in mistaken kindness, insisted on his seeing this particular move in the game.

Keith-Westerton stiffly introduced Sir Clinton to his wife. Wendover, to distract his mind from uncomfortable thoughts, forced himself to examine the three people. Keith-Westerton had the look of a man who sees himself being driven into a corner. It was plain that he had something to conceal and that he was more than doubtful if he could avoid detection. The same shadow lay on the girl's face; but from a glance which she threw at her husband, Wendover imagined that her anxiety was less on her own account than on his. She looked as though she had spent sleepless nights, for her whole carriage seemed to have lost its spring; and when the introduction was over, she sank back into a chair as if she could face things better with its support. And still, under her physical weariness, she was evidently gathering up her resources to

face this new ordeal. The Abbé Goron, frigidly courteous, seemed to have cast himself for the rôle of a
pure spectator; and Wendover noticed that when he
sat down, he chose a chair from which he could get a
clear view of both Sir Clinton and Mrs. Keith-Westerton. Keith-Westerton fidgeted for a moment or two
and then seated himself in such a position as to range
the two opposing sides opposite to each other: the officials and Wendover in one group, the Dower House
trio facing them.

Sir Clinton seemed determined to ignore the obvious strain of the situation. To Wendover's surprise,
he opened his campaign in what seemed a friendly
tone; and he addressed himself to Mrs. Keith-Westerton instead of to her husband.

"I know you've had a distressing time, these last
few days; and, if I could avoid it, I shouldn't trouble
you now. Unfortunately, there's no way out of it. We
need certain information which only you can give us,
and which I hope you'll give us. You can refuse it,
of course, if you choose. There's no compulsion to
give evidence at this stage."

The Chief Constable's sympathetic manner obviously surprised Mrs. Keith-Westerton as much as
it did Wendover. Apparently she had braced herself
for the interview, expecting to be handled roughly;
and Sir Clinton's kindly tone seemed a relief to her.
Almost imperceptibly she relaxed the tenseness of
her attitude.

"I merely want you to check some points for us,"
Sir Clinton explained. "If you don't care to say anything on some specific details, then you needn't do so."

His glance swung for a moment towards Keith-Westerton's face as he added:

"We'd prefer to have no evidence rather than misleading statements."

Wendover could see that this shot went home. Keith-Westerton's face betrayed his feelings only too plainly; but he evidently thought that it was unsafe to notice the innuendo.

"I'm going to ask as few questions as possible, Mrs. Keith-Westerton," Sir Clinton pursued. "I don't want to worry you more than we can help. You quite understand that? Good."

Wendover could not quite follow the line which Sir Clinton had taken. Was this sympathetic manner genuine, or was it assumed merely in order to entrap the girl into some incautious statement? If it was meant to put her more at her ease, it was certainly succeeding. Her eyes, though still betraying her nervousness, had lost something of the acute mistrust they had carried at the opening of the interview. She leaned her chin on her hand and awaited Sir Clinton's next move.

Without giving her time to speak, the Chief Constable went on:

"On the night when you left home, you had dinner with your husband as usual; and after that, you and he went into your sitting room, I think. You were wearing a pearl necklace that evening."

Mrs. Keith-Westerton gave a slight involuntary nod in confirmation of this.

"About nine o'clock, your husband left the house," Sir Clinton continued. "Some time after that, you found you had mislaid your bag, I believe; and you discovered that you needed it for some reason or other."

Mrs. Keith-Westerton seemed surprised.

"I don't know how you learned that," she said, with a faint misgiving in her tone.

Then she glanced across at the Abbé Goron, as though in search of guidance.

"It's quite true, though," she went on. "I meant to write a letter—to order something—and I found I'd left my note of the address in my bag. A friend gave me the address a day or two before that, and I wrote it down on a scrap of paper and slipped it into my bag at the time. And when I came to look for it, I couldn't find it—my bag, I mean."

"I thought so," Sir Clinton continued. "And then, I think, you remembered that you'd been out on the lake in the afternoon and had perhaps left your bag behind then by mistake. That was how it was?"

Mrs. Keith-Westerton's confirmatory nod was delayed for a moment or two, but when it came at last it was quite decided.

"You wanted that address immediately, I gather; and the boathouse is not far away. Your car was in the garage. The chauffeur was not on the premises, but you drive yourself; so you decided to run up to the boathouse and see if you could find your bag. It was only a matter of five minutes in the car."

Wendover, with a certain sardonic satisfaction, noted how at the word "boathouse" the whole attitude of the girl altered. Sir Clinton's finely woven structure of mutual confidence dissolved away, as though at the touch of a magician. They were back at the very start again, as the girl's face showed only too clearly. She half-turned in her chair and shot a glance towards the Abbé Goron, as though she were accusing him of some breach of faith. But the priest, his eyes intent on Sir Clinton's face at the moment, failed to catch her glance. Young Keith-Westerton was equally perturbed and it was only with a strong effort, evidently, that he restrained himself from interrupting.

"When you reached the boathouse," Sir Clinton continued, taking no direct notice of the byplay, "I suppose you were surprised to see it lit up. But as no one has a key of the boathouse except yourselves and Mr. Wendover, you probably assumed that he had gone across there for some purpose; and, of course, you had no hesitation in going up to the door. You had your key with you."

There was no question of confidence now, Wendover could see. Panic was written clear on the girl's pale face, on her parted lips and startled eyes. Keith-Westerton moved sharply as though to rise from his chair and go to his wife's side; but a gesture from Sir Clinton arrested him. The Abbé Goron, with an inscrutable face, seemed to wait philosophically on the turn of events. Severn, a side glance of Wendover showed, was intent on the unfolding of Sir Clinton's narrative of the night's doings; and it was plain that he was fitting the tale to the evidence which he had.

When Sir Clinton broke the silence, it was in an unexpectedly soft tone.

"I know how distressing this must be to you, Mrs. Keith-Westerton. I've a fair idea of what you went through; and unless it were absolutely necessary, I shouldn't remind you of it. Frankly, I'd rather get it over and done with. I merely want you to check what I say and tell me if I'm right or wrong at any point."

Keith-Westerton half rose from his chair.

"I can tell you that myself," he said heatedly.

Sir Clinton's voice lost all its kindliness and took on an incisive tone as he replied.

"You weren't at the boathouse *at that time*. We must have first-hand evidence, and only Mrs. Keith-Westerton can give us it. I prefer a reliable witness, such as she is. I'll have some questions to put to you later on, when I hope you'll be perfectly frank."

Wendover had no difficulty in seeing the double-edged thrust here. Without emphasising it, Sir Clinton had shown he knew that Keith-Westerton himself had been at the boathouse and he also made clear that he had not believed his previous statements about his movements on the fatal night.

"You went into the boathouse," the Chief Constable continued, turning again to the girl, "and in the lounge you found a woman whom you had never seen before, I think. She was about your own height, handsome, with chestnut hair, and she was dressed in unfashionable clothes which must have struck you at the first glance. She asked who you were, or you asked her who she was and volunteered your own name. In any case, she learned that you were Mrs. Keith-Westerton; and probably when she heard your name she betrayed some feeling or other, surprise and possibly an unpleasant satisfaction."

Mrs. Keith-Westerton made a gesture of repulsion which confirmed Sir Clinton's tale more conclusively than any verbal statement could have done. Quite clearly, the mere recollection of her interview with the stranger was sufficient to horrify her.

"You needn't be afraid," Sir Clinton put in hastily. "I'll not say more than I need to do. We know all about her. She was a notorious criminal. She knew something which affected you intimately and she sprang it on you brutally. She blackmailed you, in fact. That's all I need say. She demanded money—a large sum."

Mrs. Keith-Westerton seemed almost grateful to find that Sir Clinton had passed so lightly over this point. Her manner changed, as though this had been the thing which she was afraid would come to light.

"That's exactly what happened," she admitted, in a shaky voice. "You . . . you might have been there yourself, from the way you tell it. She was a horrible woman."

Sir Clinton showed clearly that he had no intention of dwelling on that particular matter at any length.

"She demanded money, as I said. Of course you had no money in hand at the moment. She looked you up and down and her eye caught the necklace you were wearing. She was a good enough judge to know that it was worth something—perhaps she asked you its value—and she proposed to take it as security for the money she demanded."

Mrs. Keith-Westerton seemed to realise for the first time the surprising accuracy of Sir Clinton's story of the affair; and Wendover, from this, got the impression that, so far as she was concerned, the worst part of the evidence was over.

"I don't know how you guessed that," she said, in a wondering tone. "It's perfectly true, though. She insisted on my giving her the necklace. I was . . . It had come as such a shock to me, the whole thing, like a thunderbolt, you know; and I was ready to do almost anything to keep her quiet. You've no idea what sort of woman she was. I felt quite sick with the surprise of it all, and I was ready to do anything to shut her mouth at the moment. I took off the necklace and she smiled—maliciously, you know, for I don't think she'd quite expected me to give in so easily. And then she put the necklace on herself with some remark about that being the safest way to carry it. And then she ordered me out of the place. She was . . . oh, she was contemptuous, as if I were a mere child who had to do as I was told. And she warned me that I would have to raise the money somehow without telling Colin. 'And now you can go,' she said. 'I've got you where I want you, Mrs. Keith-Westerton.' I was glad to get away from her. I think I must have been nearly hysterical, for the whole thing was so unexpected and so dreadful, I hardly knew what I was doing."

"We needn't dwell on it," Sir Clinton said soothingly. "I don't want to bring it back to your mind. Let's go on. You got into your car and drove straight to your confessor."

A tinge of distrust crept into the girl's face and she threw a troubled glance at the Abbé.

"You made your confession," Sir Clinton went on

hastily, as though to avoid any misunderstanding. "I've nothing to do with that."

Obviously Mrs. Keith-Westerton had been afraid of questions on this point, for relief showed on her face at Sir Clinton's words.

"He gave you some good advice," Sir Clinton continued, with a side glance at the Abbé's imperturbable face. "You drove back to the Dower House, packed a suit case with a few necessaries, wrote a letter to your husband, telling him that you had been to your confessor and that you were going away at once. And then you drove to Ambledown and caught the last train up to London where you went to the convent which, I suppose, the Abbé recommended to you. That, I think, is a fairly accurate account of your doings on that night?"

Now that the ordeal was obviously at an end, Mrs. Keith-Westerton seeemed to recover her balance.

"That was almost exactly what happened," she admitted frankly. "I don't see how you know these things; but you've described everything I did, just as if you'd been watching me."

The major part of Sir Clinton's reconstruction was plain sailing to Wendover, who already knew the evidence on which it was based. Two of the Chief Constable's points, however, gave him qualms of conscience: the incident of the vanity bag and the matter of the pearl necklace. All along, he had insisted on his belief in Mrs. Keith-Westerton's complete innocence. And yet, deep down in his thoughts, he had been more than uncomfortable about the part she had played in the affair. Try as he would, he had not been able to get the vanity bag and the pearls out of his mind. With all his prejudice in favour of Mrs. Keith-Westerton, these things had looked very black to him. And now Sir Clinton, who had never made any show of sympathy with the girl, produced a simple explanation of both items, an explanation which made the whole transaction appear innocuous. Now that they were banished, Wendover realised how deep his suspicions had been; and he cursed himself for having allowed them to take root in his mind.

Sir Clinton rose and moved towards the door.

"That's all I wanted to know," he said pleasantly. "I'm sorry we had to trouble you, Mrs. Keith-Westerton; but it was essential to have the facts clear. I know it's been very irksome for you, but I'm sure you realise that we needed your help."

He opened the door and stood aside for her to go out. As she seemed to hesitate, he added in a casual tone:

"I'd like to have a few moments' talk with your husband and Monsieur L'Abbé, here; but there's no need for you to stay. You've helped us very considerably and we mustn't keep you on the strain any longer."

The dismissal was perfectly courteous in tone, but plain enough in substance. For a moment longer, Mrs. Keith-Westerton hesitated; then, with a brave attempt to appear at ease, she passed out of the room.

CHAPTER XIII: PROLOGUE AT THE
BOATHOUSE

As Sir Clinton closed the door behind Mrs. Keith-Westerton, all the friendliness vanished from his expression and when he turned towards the little group, his face was hard.

"And now, Mr. Keith-Westerton," he said grimly, "I want the true story of your doings on the night of the Horncastle murder. Your last account was a lie from start to finish."

The directness of the attack evidently took young Keith-Westerton by surprise; but he attempted to cover this by bluster.

"I don't know what you're talking about. I never heard such a thing. Isn't my word good enough for you?"

"No, it isn't," Sir Clinton replied brutally.

"I sha'n't say anything. You've no right to question me. I can refuse to answer, if it suits me. Are you charging me with murder? You must be mad."

"I'm not charging you with anything, so far. If I were, I couldn't put questions to you. But murder isn't the only crime in the calendar, Mr. Keith-Westerton, remember."

"I don't know what you're talking about," Keith-Westerton repeated, but his tone showed that Sir Clinton's thrust had gone home.

The Chief Constable made a weary gesture.

"At about seven o'clock on the night of the Horn-castle murder, a woman rang you up on the 'phone. You arranged to meet her at the boathouse. At nine o'clock you went out to meet her. Her Christian name was Ellen. . . . Ellen Amy, I believe. I see you remember it."

"I know nothing about her," young Keith-Westerton protested, but it was clear that he hardly hoped to convince his hearers.

Wendover, glancing at the Abbé's face, noticed the faintest expression of contempt pass across it.

"Perhaps this will refresh your memory," Sir Clinton said dryly.

He pulled out his pocketbook, extracted a newspaper cutting which Wendover recognized, and held it in front of Keith-Westerton.

"No, don't touch it," he said sharply, as Keith-Westerton put out his hand. "It's plain enough, isn't it? *'Ellen Amy Keith-Westerton, wife of Colin Keith-Westerton, of Silver Grove, Talgarth, England.'* The game seems to be up, Mr. Keith-Westerton."

Young Keith-Westerton buried his face in his hands.

"Oh, God," he groaned at last. "Now it'll all come out. I thought I was safe, and you've got me, after all."

"Looks pretty black, doesn't it?" Sir Clinton commented unsympathetically.

"You've got me. You needn't sneer at me. I never meant to do it, I'll swear that. It just happened. . . . That infernal newspaper cutting. . . . I thought it was all right. . . . I never meant any harm. . . . It just happened. . . . Everything seemed all right; and I thought. . . . Well, she's dead now."

Wendover was overwhelmed by this incoherent outburst, and especially by the tone of the last phrase. Young Keith-Westerton seemed to be actually rejoicing over the woman's death.

But his amazement was doubled by Sir Clinton's next speech.

"If I arrange to hush this up, will you promise to tell us exactly what happened, that night?"

Wendover felt that the world was upside down. He had known the Chief Constable for years and had never found him to swerve a hair's breadth from the line of duty. Always he had acted as a mere machine, regardless of any personal factors in a case upon which he was engaged. And now, with his own ears, Wendover had heard him propose to compound a felony, as if it were a matter of no importance. A glance at Severn's face showed the Squire that the Inspector was as much dumbfounded as he himself was.

"You can't do that," young Keith-Westerton said, as though he could hardly believe his ears. "You couldn't, could you? Could you really? D' you mean it?"

"Tell us the truth," said Sir Clinton unhesitatingly, "and I'll see you through. I've enough influence for that. But you'll have to make a clean breast of the whole business, from the very start, remember that. Otherwise, the bargain's off. And no lies this time," he added sternly.

Wendover thought he saw light. From the post-mortem evidence, Cincinnati Jean was in such a state of health that very little would be enough to kill her. Slight overexertion *or strong emotion* might have led to her death. In that last event, young Keith-Westerton might have a fair case if he were put on his defence. The charge would be one of manslaughter at the worst; and in cases of manslaughter the police have a large discretion. A case might well be dropped on the ground that no conviction could be expected on the evidence. If there had been a stormy interview between her and young Keith-Westerton, her thymus gland might have stopped her heart's action, and no one could say that Keith-Westerton had a hand in her death. But he might have thought himself in-volved beyond hope and might, on the spur of the moment, have taken steps to get rid of the body.

"Where do you want me to start?" Keith-Westerton asked Sir Clinton.

"Tell us how you met this woman in the first instance."

"It was after the War. I'd come of age and got my income into my own hands. I went up to London. I'd no friends to speak of. Everybody seemed to be having a good time. I wanted to have a good time too. There wasn't much difficulty in getting to know people. Lots of them seemed very friendly, took me up, you know, and introduced me to other people, and so on. I liked it. I'd lived a pretty dull life, before that; and I liked the excitement and the night clubs, and all the rest of it. I'd enough money to play about with.

"I told you how it was. Somebody introduced me to somebody else and they passed me on further. Amongst the lot, I came across Ellen and her father and mother. He was a rather pompous old devil, just a shade strait-laced in some ways. The mother was good-looking for her age, but nothing out of the common and not a bit like her daughter."

"The real mother died long before the War," Sir Clinton put in, "and the real father is a spinner in one of the Lancashire mills—a decent working man, by all accounts. What you met were a couple of the gang—no relation to each other or to the girl."

"Well, I didn't know that, of course. One took people as one found them, in those days. And I was pretty green. I just accepted their story. Things went pretty fast in those days in scraping acquaintance with strangers. These people didn't strike me as being out for anything. They didn't sponge on me, like some of the others. In fact, they seemed rather decent, on the whole. The girl seemed to take to me. I wasn't in love with her or anything of that sort, you know. But she was uncommonly good-looking; and I liked taking her about. She didn't lead me on. We just seemed to be pretty good friends. She was . . . amusing; but there was no hanky-panky of any sort.

"Then one night, they asked me to dinner at their flat. I'd taken her about a good deal and this was the first time I'd been to dinner with them. When I arrived, the two old people apologised. They'd forgotten an engagement, had to go out. But it would be all right. I could stay and keep Ellen company at dinner. Well, I saw nothing amiss in that. I stayed.

"I don't really know quite what happened. I've never been able to remember. But next morning I woke up in the girl's room with the father and mother raising Cain."

"She drugged you, no doubt," Sir Clinton interjected.

"I expect she did. Certainly I couldn't remember much about the end of that dinner, though I tried hard enough afterwards. But just at the moment they didn't give me much time to think about that. The mother was weeping over her daughter; and the old man was talking to me like a polite bargee. And there I was, only half-awake, and absolutely unable to say anything for myself. You couldn't explain away a situation of that sort very easily. And the girl herself was in a dreadful state, too, which made it all the worse.

"Well, there it was. I suppose any cub with the least knowledge of the world would have smelt a rat. But I'd been brought up by two old aunts. They'd dinned a lot into me about chivalry and not letting a girl down. And that came up and hit me just at the wrong moment. Besides, I was a bit at a disadvantage, even if I'd known what was what.

"The end of it was that they came over me completely. The girl's reputation had to be patched up, and quick too. Now I wasn't fond of the girl in that way; but from all I'd seen of her she was a good sort. I'd never been in love—didn't know what it meant, even. I was just a kid, really. So what with one thing and another, they got me to agree to marry her at once. It sounds a bit incredible, I expect; but then you haven't been through that sort of thing, and . . . well, I knew nothing about the world and I thought I'd pretty well committed an unpardonable sin and ruined a decent girl. It was up to me to repair the damage. And although I wasn't fond of the girl in that way, still, I'd liked her, liked going about with her, and all that sort of thing. It wasn't such a dreadful prospect, getting married to her, for we'd got on so well together.

"That was how it was. They kept me in hand at the flat until they got a licence. The old man never let me out of his sight. He was a terror, I found, when one came to scrape the top layer off his character. He and his wife managed to give me the impression that I was deuced lucky to get off so easily. And they never mentioned money from start to finish. Their whole idea was to see that their daughter wasn't landed—quite natural, I thought.

"We got married almost before I'd time to sit down and think about the thing at all. They didn't leave me much to myself in the interval, you see. And then they suggested that I'd better go back to my rooms and pack up for my honeymoon while she did the same at their flat. I was absolutely dazed by the whole affair. I did as I was told. I packed up some stuff, got a taxi, and drove round to their flat. And when I got there, they'd gone.

"The girl had left a letter for me. Quite a nice letter, you know, and it struck me as just the kind of letter a nice girl might have written in the circumstances. She'd been shocked by the whole business. Her parents had persuaded her to marry me to put things straight. But she felt she didn't care for me in just that way, though she liked me—just my own feelings about her, which made it sound genuine—and she felt she couldn't face me just then, as things were. She was going away with her parents, and by and by, perhaps, when she'd had time to think things over, she'd write to me and give me her address. That would mean that she'd got to care for me, really; and then it would be all right.

"The whole business left me completely stunned. Looking back, with the letter in my hand, it seemed like one of these things that one wakes up out of in the night—damnably vivid and yet growing more and more incredible as one thinks it over. And yet, incredible and all, it had actually happened to me. There were my suit cases in the taxi outside, real enough. I went back to my rooms. I'd nobody I cared to consult about the affair. The less said, the better, until the whole business got shaken down. If they'd even so much as hinted at money, I'd have guessed where I was. But they hadn't come anywhere near that.

"You can guess that the thing pulled me up with a round turn. I hadn't much heart for amusement, just then. And there was no way of getting into touch with them. It dawned on me that I knew absolutely nothing about them except their names. I inquired at the flat—no good. Nobody knew anything about them. I advertised cautiously in the papers. Nothing.

"And nothing more turned up until some years

later. Then an envelope came, with an American post-mark, and inside it was that cutting you showed me— the one that advertised her death. Well, in a way, it was a relief. I'd never been really fond of the girl. I was sorry she was dead, of course; but there it was. The whole thing was over and done with, once and for all. By that time I knew a bit more about the world than when I was twenty-one; but this final bit of information wasn't the kind that would suggest anything wrong. Even if I'd been suspecting anything, that newspaper cutting would have taken away my doubts. From start to finish, remember, money had never come into the affair."

"Most ingenious," Sir Clinton admitted, with the air of a connoisseur examining some rare work of art.

"There I was," Keith-Westerton went on, in a rather less nervous tone. "My hands were free again. The whole business was wiped out. And a while after that, I met my wife. I want to be clear about this. As soon as I fell in love with her, I felt I ought to be sure about the other thing. I got some inquiries made in America. It seemed all right. A woman had really died in that hospital and her name had been given as Ellen Amy Keith-Westerton. It was an old story by then and nobody had much recollection of her. Besides, you know, I didn't care to advertise the real story. I didn't want it to be blazoned in the American papers: 'Aristocrat's Romance. Strange Story of Marriage That Didn't Come Off' and all that sort of thing. But I got enough information to satisfy my mind, and that was all that mattered to me. I'm telling you the plain truth and keeping back nothing."

"You had a copy of that advertisement," Sir Clinton interrupted. "Have you got it still?"

"Yes, I have. It's in one of the compartments of my desk."

"You might let me see it."

Rather puzzled, Keith-Westerton left the room and returned in a few minutes with the slip of paper.

"That's all right," Sir Clinton said, after a glance at it. "Now will you go on with your story?"

"Well, all that matters is that I got married. We came back here to settle down while Silver Grove was being put in order for us. You know that. Everything seemed all right. I never gave a thought to the old affair. It was closed.

"And then, one evening, just before dinner, some one rang me up on the 'phone. At first I didn't recognise the voice, but she soon let me know who she was. It was my first wife."

"Now I want you to be careful," Sir Clinton cautioned him, though not unkindly. "This is the point where details begin to be important. Don't omit anything."

Keith-Westerton nodded.

"You needn't be afraid of my forgetting anything," he said bitterly. "It made a big enough impression on me, I can tell you. When I heard that voice, I was completely knocked out. Just put yourself in my place. What would you have felt like? I hardly knew what I was doing."

"What I want is the gist of that telephone conversation," Sir Clinton interposed. "Give us an exact account, if you can."

"Well, she let me know that she was alive. She told me she knew I'd married again. She pointed out what a hole I'd got myself into by marrying while she was still alive. Then she began to threaten me. She'd see she got her rights, and she'd have my wife turned out and exposed to the world for what she was. It was all so sneering and malicious, just a common little shrew letting off a lot of accumulated venom. I didn't know what to say to her. I didn't care to say much at my end of the wire. Somebody might have come in and overheard something. So then she told me to meet her at the boathouse at a quarter past nine. And she rang off with a jeer about hoping I'd enjoy my dinner as much as she'd enjoy hers."

"Is that the plain truth?" Sir Clinton demanded.

"It is. It is, really," Keith-Westerton assured him with obvious earnestness.

"Very interesting," Sir Clinton commented, though without seeming to pay much attention. "Go on."

"I dressed for dinner, somehow. I was so clean knocked out that I hardly knew what I was doing. I tried to keep it under and behave as if nothing had happened. I wasn't thinking of myself, you know, honestly."

He glanced at Sir Clinton as though to assure himself that this statement, at any rate, was credited.

"I got through dinner somehow. About nine o'clock I made an excuse and went out."

"You didn't go wandering about the roads in a dinner jacket without a coat?"

"No, I put on a light raincoat. I walked up to the boathouse. When I got there, the lights were on.

I went in and she was there, waiting for me in the lounge. She looked older, of course. And she seemed dowdy. It made her look common, somehow. And at the first glance, she seemed coarsened. She'd been a nice, smart youngster when I married her; and I couldn't help noticing the change. She saw I noticed it and that made her angry, straight off. She was like a wildcat one moment, and then she turned into a jeering harridan. And I remember I stood there, saying to myself, "Good God! I married this creature." She was so different from my recollection of her, you know.

"Well, she made no bones about it. She wanted money to keep her mouth shut. If I paid her, nobody need know anything about my marriage to her. If not, then the whole thing would come out. She'd claim her rights and make such a scandal that my wife would be hurt as badly as could be managed. That was the gist of it all. You can guess what a jar it gave me. I didn't stop to think. She didn't give me time for that. My whole idea was to silence her temporarily, at any rate, until I had a chance to think things out. She'd told me over the 'phone to bring my checkbook to the boathouse; and I wrote out a check to bearer for Five Hundred Pounds. 'That'll do as a start,' she said. And she made it pretty clear that she had ways of cashing checks which would be quite safe for her, even if I tried to stop the check. 'And if you try that game, you'll be sorry,' she warned me. As soon as she got her hands on the check, she told me to get out. She'd arrange another meeting later on, she said. So I went away."

"What time was that?" Sir Clinton demanded.

"I can't say exactly. I didn't look at my watch, naturally. I should think it would be sometime before ten o'clock—say a quarter to ten. But that's just a guess, you know."

"And after you left the boathouse, what did you do?"

Keith-Westerton made a little gesture indicating despair.

"I just walked about, thinking. It had been a fearful jar, and I wanted to see if I could think of some road out. I wandered about at random without caring where I was going. I was thinking all the time."

Sir Clinton seemed dissatisfied with this vague reply.

"I daresay you were in a brown study, Mr. Keith-Westerton, but you must have some idea of where you went. No matter how hard one's thinking, there are some things that force themselves on one's attention. You wouldn't have walked through a stream without noticing it, would you?"

"I was almost worked up to that point," Keith-Westerton confessed half-ashamedly, "but I admit that if I'd done that, it might have waked me up."

"And as you didn't wake up . . . ?"

"I didn't walk through any stream. But you're quite right. I did notice one thing. I got into the fields, and in trying to get through a gap, I ripped my coat on some barbed wire."

"You've got that coat?"

"No," Keith-Westerton shook his head. "It was rather badly torn. I told my man Ferrers to give it away."

"Well, go on with your story," Sir Clinton ordered.

"I got back home at last. It must have been some-time in the small hours. I hadn't been able to think of any way of getting out of the mess."

"Now be careful," Sir Clinton warned him. "I want every detail, remember."

"I'm not keeping anything back. When I came in, I found a note from my wife on the table in the hall. I took it into the smoking room and opened it. It wasn't very clear. Something had happened, she wrote, and she'd gone to see the Abbé here about it. She'd gone to London, and I was to ring up the Sisterhood of the Good Hope the next morning—that morning, it was, by then. My mind was full of this trouble I was in, and naturally I jumped to the conclusion that my wife had got wind of it somehow—I couldn't think how. She's a Catholic, you know; and they're stricter than we might be in matters of that sort. That put the lid on the business.

"I didn't sleep that night. Next morning, I bor-rowed my chauffeur's motor-bike and went off to Ambledown on it. My wife had taken our car when she went away. From Ambledown, I rang up the convent and spoke to my wife. She knew all about the affair, as she told you."

"You haven't got that note your wife left for you?"

Keith-Westerton shook his head.

"No, I burned it. It wasn't the kind of thing I'd care to leave about, with things as they were."

"And what was your next move?"

"The next thing was that you came down on me. Naturally I thought that woman had given the whole show away and that you were after me for bigamy.

I didn't know she was dead, then. And when it turned out to be the Horncastle affair, I was quite relieved, though it sounds rather beastly to put it that way. I knew nothing about Horncastle. It was a load off my mind when I found you'd nothing against me on the real thing. And then these pearls came into the business, and I didn't know where I was. I couldn't make head or tail of the thing. So I played for safety and gave as little away as I could. My wife hadn't mentioned the pearls to me on the 'phone, and I was completely muddled up over them."

"You didn't consult a solicitor?"

"Good Lord, no! The less said the better, so far as I could see."

"And after that?"

"Well, the next thing was the discovery of the woman's body. I recognised the portrait of her that was in some of the papers. That seemed to clear things up to some extent. She was dead. The whole affair was done with. I consulted the Abbé, here, and he advised me to put things straight at once. I was a free man again, and there was nothing to hinder me marrying. So he went up to see my wife in London, brought her down with him, and married us quite legally. That made my wife's position quite regular."

Sir Clinton turned to the Inspector.

"I think you might 'phone down to the station and get them to bring that fellow up, now."

Severn left the room and returned again in a few moments.

"That's all right, sir."

Sir Clinton turned to Keith-Westerton.

"I promised that, if you'd be frank with me, I'd see you through; and by that, I think we both meant that there would be no charge of bigamy. You can make your mind easy. There won't be one. If you'd consulted a solicitor, he'd have told you it was unlikely that any such charge could be substantiated. Your first wife hadn't been continually absent from you for the statutory seven years. True enough, so you had no defence on that score. But undoubtedly you had a 'bona fide belief on reasonable grounds' that your wife was dead. That's been held to be a good defence. There was a case, Rex v. Tolson, about forty years ago, which turned on that point. I don't think there would be the slightest chance of a conviction in your case, even if a charge were brought; and nobody would think it worth while to bring a charge in these conditions. That ought to relieve your mind."

"It does," said Keith-Westerton, with all the emphasis of relief. "You've no notion how this affair has weighed on my mind."

"One can guess," Sir Clinton dryly suggested.

He turned to the Abbé Goron.

"Now I'd like to hear what part you played in the affair. As I understand it, Mrs. Keith-Westerton, after her meeting with the woman at the boathouse, went directly to you. You obviously advised her—quite soundly, if I may say so—to go into the convent until things had cleared up a little. You also promised her to interview this woman if possible. And you went up to the boathouse for that purpose, after Mrs. Keith-Westerton had left your house."

The Abbé, seeing that Sir Clinton had not attempted

to violate the secret of the confessional, contented himself with a nod which might have been taken as confirming the Chief Constable's statement either in whole or in part.

"Perhaps you can tell us what happened after Mrs. Keith-Westerton left you?"

"I see no harm in that. There is very little to tell. I left my house a few minutes after eleven o'clock and walked up to the boathouse, hoping to find this woman still there. When I arrived at the boathouse, it was all dark. Evidently the woman had gone away. I knocked at the door without effect. As I came away, I saw a man at the edge of the wood, who seemed to be lurking among the trees. It was no affair of mine, naturally, and I paid no attention. Failing to meet the woman at the boathouse, I returned home. That is all."

Sir Clinton seeemed inclined to dispute this last statement.

"But not all you know about the case," he said shrewdly.

The Abbé apparently had his reasons for declining this challenge, for he made no answer.

Sir Clinton turned back to young Keith-Westerton.

"I hope your mind's quite easy now."

"About the bigamy business? Are you dead sure about it? It's a tremendous weight off my mind, if you're right."

"You can consult your solicitor if you've any doubts. But in any case, I think there's some more evidence available."

As he spoke, the figure of the Salvationist, accompanied by a constable, passed the window; and in a moment or two Sawtry was ushered into the room. He seemed to have lost a good deal of his assurance, Wendover noticed.

"Now, Mr. Sawtry," Sir Clinton began, "your movements, lately, have attracted our notice; and there are one or two points which need clearing up. I've had your record looked up. No convictions against you, I admit; but once or twice your escape was like Mr. Wendover's salvation—a deuced narrow squeak. I tell you that to save you the trouble of protesting too much."

"That was all before I found grace," Sawtry said, in a sullen tone. "Since the Army got me, I've run straight."

"I have a great respect for the Salvation Army. They often make a success in cases that look quite hopeless. What I'm interested in at present is whether they scored a success in your case."

"I can give you my word that they did."

"I'm not much interested in your words; it's your deeds that matter. To the uninitiated, some of them seem rum companions for your professions."

"I've done nothing I'm ashamed of."

"That hardly gets us much further," Sir Clinton pointed out cynically. "But assuming your conversion's genuine, I take it that you prefer truth to lies, nowadays. Very well, I want the truth. What took you to Aylesbury Prison, the morning before the Horncastle murder?"

For a moment, Sawtry seemed completely taken aback to find that his trip to Aylesbury was known to the police. He pulled himself together almost immediately, however, and with a faint return of his fanatical manner he declared:

"I went there to save a soul."

"The soul of Cincinnati Jean, I take it. And were you successful?"

A cloud passed over the Salvationist's face.

"No," he admitted morosely. "That soul went straight to hell with sin fresh on it. Satan won the stake."

"Pursuing your mission," Sir Clinton went on, "you accompanied her up to town. You went with her to her flat, didn't you? And you spent the night with her there, I believe."

He paused almost imperceptibly and then added sharply:

"Were you married to her?"

Sawtry's tone was almost triumphant as he retorted:

"Yes, I was. A man can spend a night in his wife's flat, can't he? There's no sin in that."

Sir Clinton seemed not a bit surprised by the answer.

"When did you marry her?" he asked, as though in mere curiosity.

"During the War."

Young Keith-Westerton started in his chair as he realised the implication of this statement.

"You can prove that?" he demanded. "You really did marry her then? Legally?"

"I married her at a registry office," Sawtry replied, with obvious frankness. "It was in 1918."

"I told you I expected to get further evidence,"

Sir Clinton reminded Keith-Westerton. Then, turning back to Sawtry, he continued his interrogation.

"Between her coming out of prison and your arrival at her flat, had Cincinnati Jean any communication with any one except yourself?"

Sawtry shook his head decidedly.

"Not a soul. She never spoke a word to any one except me."

Sir Clinton seemed satisfied with this answer.

"I take it that in your attempt to dissuade her from her criminal courses you must have discussed her plans for the immediate future. Did she tell you anything about them?"

Sawtry hesitated for a moment and then appeared ready to answer.

"She was nearly broke, she told me; and she needed money at once. I had none to give her. She had some plan afoot for blackmailing Mr. Keith-Westerton over an affair that had been framed up in the old days. I had no hand in that job at all," he added, hastily. "She ran it with old Tommy Rigg and Cocoa Fanny as her partners."

"Now, be careful," Sir Clinton advised sternly. "When did she first mention this scheme for blackmailing Mr. Keith-Westerton?"

Sawtry considered for a few seconds.

"It was shortly after we got to her flat. She had a look around the place to see if everything was in order. Then she came back into the sitting room where I was, and I began to try to persuade her to turn her back on all that kind of thing, let her see what sort of work it really was, and how much better she'd be if she turned over a new leaf and went straight. She just sneered at me; and then she told me I might spare my wind, for she'd got this Keith-Westerton affair up her sleeve. I strove hard with Satan," he declared, with a faint return of his professional manner. "I wrought with her in every way I could. But you could never shift Jean a hair's breadth when her mind was made up. She was stone broke and didn't know where to raise cash; and Keith-Westerton would pay up like a lamb, she said."

Sir Clinton, apparently, seemed disinclined to accept Sawtry's statements.

"She was in Aylesbury Prison when Mr. Keith-Westerton's marriage took place. She must have got the news of that after she came out of gaol. You're sure you didn't give it to her?"

"No, I didn't," the Salvationist protested loudly. "Why, I didn't even know he had got married at all, till she told me about her scheme. I'd no interest in him at all. I'd had nothing to do with the original frame-up; it was Jean, and Fanny and old Tommy who ran the business. I only heard about it by chance. I knew nothing about it."

Sir Clinton did not carry the subject further.

"Well, let's get back to what you do know," he continued. "You tried to persuade her to drop this scheme, you say? And you failed. What happened after that?"

Sawtry reflected for a moment as though not very sure of his ground.

"This is the truth, anyhow, believe it or not," he said. "I saw Satan had been too much for me; he'd got Jean firm in his hands and there was nothing to be done with her. But I wasn't going to give in. I thought that perhaps if I stuck to it, I could wear her down; so I stayed the night at the flat with her. I've great faith in continual persuasion in cases of that sort; it's only the faint-hearted ones that give in to Satan after the first bout doesn't go in their favour."

"Keep to the point," Sir Clinton interrupted testily.

"What I'm trying to explain," said Sawtry, in an aggrieved tone, "is that I'd no notion she meant to get off the mark so quick. I thought she wouldn't be able to do anything for a week or two. She'd have to get her information about the lie of the land, find out Keith-Westerton's whereabouts and how she could get in touch with him. And all that time I meant to spend in dissuading her from going back to that line of business. I've been very successful in some obstinate cases, just by keeping at them all the time; and I had just a faint hope that it might come off, even with Jean, if I had long enough to do it.

"She didn't give me a chance, though. The afternoon after she got out of Aylesbury, she gave me the slip. She'd been talking about her clothes, and how the fashions had changed since she was sentenced, and how dowdy she looked in the clothes she'd had when she went to prison. Finally she said she'd have to buy herself a new rig-out at once. That seemed natural enough; and I let her go off without thinking twice about it. After all, I could hardly tag on to her when she was buying some of the things she wanted. She clean took me in, there. She went off in the afternoon,—to shop, she said. Well, I waited for her to come back; but she didn't turn up. And at last I tumbled to her game. She'd gone off to Talgarth to get her stroke in at once.

"When I spotted that, it was no good thinking about giving her a change of heart. She was back at the old trade again and I'd wasted my wind in trying to persuade her to chuck it. I was a bit cast down. It was a real failure. But I made up my mind that Satan wasn't going to get away with it so easy as all that. I mightn't be able to persuade her; but I could draw her teeth, anyhow, and score over the Evil One that way."

"So you followed her by train?"

"Yes, I landed here in the late evening. She'd made a slip and told me too much. I meant to see Mr. Keith-Westerton and tell him—well, warn him, anyhow. But when I got to his house, he wasn't in. Well, what about it? I've had enough experience to keep me from putting anything of that sort on paper; word-of-mouth's the right way to pass that kind of thing on. So I got a bed for the night and tried again next morning. Just the same luck then, though. I didn't get hold of him.

"And then there was the Horncastle murder; and you began taking an interest in me; and what with one thing and another, I lost my head a bit and made myself scarce. I'd done my best; no one could say I hadn't: but I wasn't over-eager to have my affairs raked over. I judged it best to clear out. Later on, when things had quieted down a bit, I could put Keith-Westerton wise to things. And then, I saw in the papers that Jean was dead. That seemed to close my side of the affair. If she was dead, she couldn't do any more blackmailing. There was no need for me to stir a finger."

"You don't seem to waste much emotion over the loss of your spouse," Sir Clinton said in an ironic tone.

"Why should I?" Sawtry queried in obvious surprise. "You don't suppose I was over-keen on her, even when I married her? It was a pure business deal. It paid, sometimes, to be able to produce a real marriage certificate in a frame-up. A genuine husband can call any man's bluff in that kind of case, so it suited Jean to have me handy with proper marriage lines when it came to putting the screw on or bullying some damn fool or other? See?"

Sawtry suddenly perceived that his reminiscences were carrying him on to dangerous ground.

"And by your story, you never were at the boathouse at all on the night of the Horncastle murder?" Sir Clinton asked in a purely formal tone.

"No, I never saw the place till next morning, when I came up against you there."

"I may need you later on, perhaps," Sir Clinton said, in a noncommittal way. "You're not objecting to being detained, I take it? Just as well. If you insist on consorting with notorious criminals engaged in illegal practices, you can't complain if we keep an eye on you. That'll do for the present."

Severn summoned the constable and Sawtry left the room.

CHAPTER XIV: PRINCIPAL AND
ACCESSORY

"AND now, Inspector, I think we're ready to inter-view Miss Louise Sandeau," Sir Clinton suggested.

As Severn rose, Wendover chanced to let his eyes fall on the priest's face and he was puzzled by the expression which flashed across that usually impassive countenance. It was only momentary; but the Squire got the impression that the Abbé was surprised by Sir Clinton's move and that he was now more than ever on his guard. Almost immediately Goron's mouth settled itself once more into its normal firm lines.

When the French maid entered the room, it was evident that the presence of the priest had its effect on her. "Not so much of the glad eye about her, this time," was Wendover's unspoken comment. "She seems a deuced sight less sure of herself than she was last time."

Sir Clinton, with a gesture, invited the maid to take a seat opposite him and the Inspector; then for a moment or two he remained silent, as though to give the girl time to recover.

"I have invited Monsieur L'Abbé to be present, so that you may not feel yourself alone among foreign-ers," Sir Clinton began slowly, so that she might have no difficulty in following him. "Besides, he already knows more about the matter than I do, I am sure."

For a moment Wendover failed to grasp the implication of the last sentence; then it flashed across his mind that the girl was probably a Catholic and that naturally she would choose a French priest for her confessor rather than the local man. Of course the Abbé must have the strings of the whole case in his hands, if this girl were mixed up in it as well as Mrs. Keith-Westerton. He stole a glance at the priest; but the Abbé Goron seemed completely aloof from the whole proceedings, so far as could be gauged from his expression.

"You were in the boathouse on the night of the murder of Horncastle."

Sir Clinton's tone made the sentence a statement and not a question. The girl started and made a faint gesture as though pushing something away from her. Her dilated eyes proved beyond a doubt that Sir Clinton had got under her guard by this sudden thrust. She was quite clearly in a state bordering on panic; but she mastered herself with an effort.

"No! No! I was not there!"

Sir Clinton dropped his hand into his pocket and brought out a little leather-bound volume which he held out to her.

"Will you swear that that is the truth?" he demanded harshly.

As she put out her hand for the Testament, the Chief Constable caught her eye and with an almost imperceptible gesture he led her glance around to the Abbé. Wendover, unconsciously following the byplay, was amazed to see the pitilessness of the expression on the face of the priest. The Abbé Goron might have sat for the portrait of an implacable avenger, stayed in the very act of launching his bolt. His fierce eyes fastened upon the girl's, held them for a moment or two, and then beat down her glance as swiftly and contemptuously as though he had struck an actual blow. "A sort of cold fanatic. He'd go to any length to stamp out sin." Wendover, impressed despite himself by the dynamic personality before him, owned inwardly that Sir Clinton seemed to have read Goron aright, even at their first encounter. This man would have no scruples in dealing out retribution to a wilful worker of iniquity.

The girl snatched back her hand as though the Testament had been white-hot.

"No! I will not swear that!" she cried, almost cringing under the Abbé's unspoken menace.

"Ah! Then you *were* at the boathouse that night?" said Sir Clinton quietly. "I was sure of it."

He paused for a moment, and when he continued, Wendover was surprised at both the subject and the tone.

"It's important that you should understand how we do things in this country, Miss Sandeau. You are a foreigner and cannot be expected to know about our English laws. If I do not make myself quite clear, Monsieur L'Abbé will be able to translate what I say into language which you can clearly understand. I am sure that he will not mind doing us that favour."

He glanced at Goron, who bowed slightly to show his acquiescence in this.

"In English law," Sir Clinton went on, "we recognise three ways in which a person may come to a

235

violent death: murder, manslaughter, and accident. You understand me?"

A glance at the girl's face showed Wendover that she was obviously afraid. Guilt and terror were clearly written on her features. She moistened her lips nervously, tried to pull herself together, and at last managed to say faintly:

"I think I understand, sir, but I am not sure of the words."

"I'll try to make it clear," Sir Clinton pursued. "When one person deliberately plans the death of another, we call it murder. You understand that? The punishment for murder is death, in most cases. Manslaughter is much less serious. If one person, *without intending to kill,* causes the death of another, he may be found guilty of manslaughter. For example, if I drive a car recklessly and run over somebody, and my victim dies, I may be put on my trial for manslaughter. If I am convicted, the sentence may be merely a comparatively short imprisonment. There is no question of the death penalty when the charge is merely one of manslaughter. And, even when a charge is brought, it many quite frequently fail, if there are any circumstances which tell in favour of the accused. You understand that, I hope?"

Louise nodded doubtfully.

"If you intend to kill, then it's murder; if you kill, but did not mean to kill, then it's manslaughter. Will you make that quite clear to her, Monsieur L'Abbé? It is important that she should understand exactly the difference between the two things and also the fact that in the case of manslaughter the punishment is light, and may even be escaped, whereas murder means a death sentence."

The Abbé Goron turned to the girl and explained curtly in French. For all the feeling he betrayed, he might have been an interpreter in a court.

"She understands," he reported, turning to Sir Clinton.

The Chief Constable seemed to take pity on the tense figure before him, with its anguished eyes.

"I am not a *juge d'instruction*," he pointed out. "My impression is that the woman at the boathouse was not murdered, and I am not trying to fasten an accusation of murder on you. But unless I know what actually happened at the boathouse, it may be very difficult to avoid charging you with murder. If things happened as I think they happened, then I do not believe you could be convicted of even manslaughter. But you are the only person who can give the evidence which would clear you of the charge. If you refuse to tell what happened, then the law will take its course. You may refuse if you wish. No one can compel you to speak, now or at any future time."

He turned again to the Abbé.

"Will you be so good as to make that quite clear to her? It is most important. I think you understand what I mean—knowing what you *do* know—when I say that it is entirely in her own interest to tell her story fully and truthfully."

Again there was a rapid interchange in French. The girl's face seemed to relax slightly and she looked doubtfully at Sir Clinton as the Abbé proceeded. At one point the Chief Constable broke in on the dialogue and emphasised something which the Abbé had said. Wendover, who was no French scholar, could see on the maid's features a dawning hopefulness as Goron urged something.

"She will tell her story," the Abbé said, at last.

"There's no pressure," Sir Clinton said formally. "It must be an entirely voluntary statement, remember."

The Abbé's slight inclination of the head confirmed this.

"Then tell us, if you wish, exactly what happened between yourself and the dead woman," Sir Clinton suggested. "Or, better, begin at the time when you left the house after dinner."

All the maid's assurance had fallen from her now. She looked like a caged animal which thinks it sees a door of escape falling slightly ajar and which gathers itself for a supreme effort to attain freedom, cost what it may. Quite evidently there would be no reticences, once she began her tale. She leaned forward, her hands clasped between her knees, and in a shaky voice she gave her story.

"This is the truth about it, as Monsieur L'Abbé well knows," she commenced. "On that night, my fiancé and I, we left the house about half-past eight, just as I told you before. We walked up through the woods to the side of the lake. As we passed the boat-house, my fiancé left me for a moment on some slight excuse. Then we went on and we sat down there. The time passed, I do not know how long but perhaps an hour."

"Did you see any lights in the boathouse?" Severn demanded.

Louise nodded.

"Yes, certainly. I saw the lights switched on in that dreadful place, perhaps half an hour, perhaps longer than that, after we left this house. Longer, perhaps. I cannot say precisely—you understand?—for I did not look at my watch."

"And they stayed on for a while?"

"They stayed on all the time we were there, I think. Yes, I think I remember that they were lit up all the time. Then all at once, they began to vacillate —go on and off once or twice; and I wondered if the fuse . . . well, I did not quite know what to make of it, but it looked as though something had failed for a few moments and had come right again. You understand what I mean? Now very soon after that— just a minute or two—my fiancé got up and said it was half-past ten and time we went home again. I was looking tired, he said, and I ought to go to bed. I was not tired, but he seemed anxious about it, so I consented and we walked back into the woods towards this house. All that is very clear in my mind, I can assure you. I make no mistakes."

She glanced at the Abbé Goron, as though for confirmation. Wendover suddenly appreciated Sir Clinton's motive in bringing the Abbé there. It was not merely that he might have an interpreter; it was because the woman had probably made her confession and the priest's presence would keep her to the path of accuracy when she told her tale. The Abbé Goron was not the sort of man to play tricks with, if you happened to be one of his flock.

"My fiancé"—she gulped as though she began to find some difficulty here—"my fiancé did not go all the way home with me. He made an excuse, said he wanted to smoke a pipe before coming in. He did not say it very well, but I let it pass. He turned back and I went on. But as I walked, I felt sure that there was something, something I did not like. It was not his usual way, when we went out together. I grew mistrustful. And at last I turned back towards the boathouse, for I had begun to wonder about those lights and how just after they flickered he had wanted me to go home. I did not understand and I wanted to have no misunderstandings of that sort. If he was playing double with me, I am not the sort of girl who would stand that for a moment. So I went up through the wood till I came to the boathouse, and there, among the trees, I watched. For a time I saw nothing except the blank windows with the drawn blinds and the lights behind them. Then one shadow crossed the blind, and then I recognised my fiancé's figure. And then a second shadow appeared for a moment—a woman's shadow. So then I was angry—oh, so angry. That he should dismiss me and go off at the very instant to meet this woman; I was furious and what girl would not feel the same?

"I thought of going up and confronting them together; but I could not bring myself to do it. Two to one is too many. I would wait till they parted. I would find out who this woman was that he had left me for. I was determined to find out that, at least. By and by, my fiancé comes out of the boathouse. From among the trees I watch him as he goes past, his hands in his pockets, whistling softly to himself as though well pleased. I let him go. I can deal with him any time. I wait for a few moments, so that he may be well away. The church clock in Talgarth strikes eleven. He has been with her for nearly half an hour, it seems. When I am sure he is quite gone, I come out from the trees and go up to the door of the boathouse, where the lights are still burning. No one has come out; the woman is still there. The door is open when I arrive at it."

"Had you ever been in the boathouse before?" Sir Clinton demanded.

"Yes, I had. Quite often. On rainy nights it was not pleasant to sit in the open air, you understand? My fiancé had procured a key of the boathouse—that was a secret of our own—and when it rained we could go up there and sit comfortably. We did not need the lights; no one knew we went there; and no one ever came to the boathouse after dark, so it was quite safe."

Sir Clinton's eye sought Wendover's at this naive confession. The Squire evidently was annoyed by learning the use to which his boathouse had been put by his neighbours' staff. Quite visibly he stiffened with disapproval as the revelation came home to him.

"I entered the boathouse," Louise continued. "The door of the lounge was wide open, and within the room I saw this woman standing with her back to me, as though she were thinking. She was dressed—it struck me at once, naturally—in old-fashioned clothes. But it was not her clothes I looked at, as I came forward; it was her neck. For around her neck she was wearing a pearl necklace and I had handled that necklace too often not to know it. The clasp is of a peculiar form, one which could not be mistaken by me. It was the necklace of Madame Keith-Westerton, beyond the possibility of a doubt."

She paused and glanced from face to face, as though fearing that she might not be believed; but her revelation missed fire, to her obvious surprise.

"I did not know what I should think," she continued. "At first I believed that this woman had seduced my fiancé into stealing that necklace. What else could I suppose? But then I remembered that Madame Keith-Westerton had worn the necklace at dinner that very night. It could not have been stolen from her unless she herself had been assaulted and the necklace taken by force. I did not know what to think. All this —you see?—passed like a flash through my mind almost as I caught sight of the necklace.

"The woman heard my step and turned round. It was this woman whose portrait has been in the papers, this Cincinnati Jean. I forget exactly what I said, and what she replied; but then I cried 'What are you doing with that necklace? It belongs to Madame Keith-Westerton!' And at that she seemed to know who I was. 'Oh, you're the French maid?' she said, with scorn. 'You're Danny Ferrers' fancy.' And then she said some things about me which I would wish not to repeat."

"You needn't," Sir Clinton assured her. "But I suppose they made you angry?"

"They made me rage," Louise admitted frankly. "I was in a fury with what she said. I stepped up to her and called her 'Thief!' and I demanded that she give me the necklace, to which she had no right. And she struck me with her open hand across the cheek. I am not patient. I caught her and struggled with her and I put my hand on the necklace at her throat. And then, suddenly—imagine my surprise!—she seemed to slip and fall backward into a chair; the necklace broke in my hand; the pearls scattered; and I stood over her, ready, you understand? But when I looked at her, I saw something was wrong—You know how they look? I have seen death once or twice. . . .

"Imagine what it was like, to be alone there with this woman who had died there—flick!—as though one killed her by an electric shock! I was dazed. I did not know what to do. I had at first a hope that I might be mistaken, and I tried to feel her wrist and then I listened for her heart. Nothing! Dead! I had killed her, it would seem, though I had no wish to do so. I was almost beside myself. I knew not what I should do. Then I remembered my fiancé. I could get him, if I ran fast after him before he reached here. I ran through the wood in terror; and I caught him before he reached home.

"I was all quivering and I could tell him nothing clear. 'I have killed that woman in the boathouse! She's dead!' That, over and over again, was all I could find to say. He asked questions, but I was in so nervous a state that I could give him no clear replies. I repeated again and again that I had killed her, as we hurried back to the boathouse.

"When we reached there and he saw she was dead, he looked very dark. He is so fond of me, and he seemed to think that it was going to be a bad affair, very bad for me. He said very little, but I could see what he thought from his face. And I was in a crisis of nerves, you understand? I had no control over myself to explain what had happened. But he is very cool. He said, half to himself: 'We've got to get rid of this somehow.' And he began to search about for the fallen pearls which had scattered themselves on the floor. While he was picking them up and putting them in his pocket, he was thinking, I could see; and when he had finished, he had his plan.

"He worked very swiftly. First he looked about for some weight to tie to the woman's body. But that was difficult, as he explained to me afterwards. Mr. Wendover, it seems, is very methodical, and he would have noticed if any heavy weight, like one of the anchors or the chains, had been missing; and he would have made inquiry. My fiancé went into the little workshop and got a screwdriver with which he dismantled the gramophone, taking out the motor and the horn, both of which were heavy. These he tied to the woman's body; and together we carried it down to the boat. He planned to sink it in the lake. It was the best hiding place he could think of, on the spur of the moment, you understand? He threw the screwdriver in with it.

"I did not understand, at the moment, what he meant. He told me, later, that the woman was not from the neighbourhood, that she would not be missed, if once we could rid ourselves of the body. No one knew her here. No one would look for her. It was the best plan, he said. We should hear no more about it and I would be safe. We took the body out on the water and sent it overboard."

"He wore gloves, all this while?" Sir Clinton asked.

"Yes, he put on a pair as we came up through the wood. And he gave them to me to wear when I was bringing the boat back . . ."

"Stop!" Sir Clinton ordered sharply. "I don't want to hear any more, just now."

"But . . ."

Sir Clinton seemed determined not to listen to any further revelations.

"That's enough for the present," he said firmly, though with no unkindness in his tone. "Now I want you to listen carefully. I'm quite sure you're telling the truth this time, for I can check your story. And if your tale is true, there's no ground for a charge against you. The surgeon who examined Cincinnati Jean's body found something which accounts for her death while she was struggling with you. No jury would convict you of even manslaughter, in the circumstances. You can make your mind quite easy—*so far as the death of the woman is concerned.*"

For an instant, relief shone in the girl's eyes. Then, as Sir Clinton's reservation penetrated her mind, she broke into reproaches.

"Ah! Now I see," she cried, in a tone of despair. "You are just torturing me, holding out a little hope while you are getting ready to accuse me. You are playing with me, cat and mouse. It is the Horn-castle. . . ."

"Stop!" Sir Clinton advised her. "I'm not trying

to trap you, as you ought to see from this. The less you say, the better, at this moment. But whether you're cleared or not will depend on your accomplice. If he tells the whole truth, we'll know where we stand. If not . . ." He shrugged his shoulders as though suggesting worse possibilities. "And now, would you go across and sit beside Monsieur L'Abbé? It will be more convenient."

As she did so, Sir Clinton turned to the Inspector. "Bring Ferrers here."

In a minute or two, Severn returned and ushered the valet into the room. Ferrers seemed momentarily surprised to see the number of people present; but he did not lose his coolness and came forward as though he were almost at his ease. Wendover noticed, however, that he threw a quick glance at the girl, as though to gauge what had been happening.

"Sit down, Ferrers," Sir Clinton said, pointing to the chair in front of him. "I'm going to put my cards on the table. You're a clever fellow—I'm not ironical —and we'll get on quickest, that way."

The valet gave a noncommittal nod, but made no vocal answer. It was evident that he was desperately puzzled to know what had taken place before he came into the room. He glanced again at the maid, as though hoping to read on her face some indication of what evidence she had given.

"Unless I'm mistaken," Sir Clinton pursued in an even tone, as though merely stating facts of common knowledge, "you were one of Cincinnati Jean's gang before she went to prison. We're going to look into your record and I've no doubt we'll find that. You were not directly concerned in the frame-up by which she proposed to victimise Mr. Keith-Westerton; but you were in her confidence about that scheme. I gather that from the fact that you had a copy of the American advertisement purporting to announce her death. When Mr. Keith-Westerton's engagement was made public, Jean was in Aylesbury. You saw it might be convenient to have some one on the spot, since Jean's plans were coming near the climax as soon as the engagement took place. You saw a chance of getting your finger into the pie, which was bound to be a juicy one if things went without a hitch. So you managed to secure the post as valet—forged references, I suppose."

Ferrers listened intently to Sir Clinton's statement, without betraying anything by his expression until the newspaper cutting was mentioned. At that point, he glanced up sharply, as though taken by surprise; but almost instantly the mask fell again into place.

"You knew, of course, all about Jean's affairs," Sir Clinton went on. "She had kept on her flat, and you could send letters there if necessary; though that was of no use till she came out of Aylesbury. Meanwhile, you had met Miss Sandeau here and had got engaged to her. In order to spend evenings in her company even when it was wet, you had taken an impression of Mr. Keith-Westerton's key of the boathouse and had got a similar key cut for your own use."

Ferrers seemed slightly disturbed by this stroke. He threw a swift glance at the maid; but Wendover, watching keenly, judged it to be a look of inquiry rather than of reproach.

"You knew the date of Cincinnati Jean's release

from Aylesbury," Sir Clinton continued, as though narrating something so commonplace that it interested him only slightly. "You wrote a letter, addressed to her flat so that it would reach her immediately on her release on licence. That letter informed her of the state of affairs and explained that Mr. Keith-Westerton was ripe for plucking. It contained also, I think, some topographical details: a sketch map of the district with the boathouse marked. You had decided that the boathouse was the most suitable place for an interview between the blackmailer and his victim. To cut a long story short, you planned the whole affair and you gave Jean full directions what to do. In fact, you made yourself indispensable, so as to make sure of a good share of the loot.

"Things worked out just as you planned. Jean arrived, rang up Mr. Keith-Westerton, arranged the meeting at the boathouse, and managed the whole affair with her usual adroitness. In fact, by accident, she bettered your plan, for she had the luck to run across Mrs. Keith-Westerton also and blackmail her as well as her husband.

"Meanwhile, you had gone out for a walk with Miss Sandeau. I suppose your object was twofold. You wanted an alibi for the time when the blackmailing interview was fixed, just in case trouble arose; and you had to open the boathouse door so that Jean could get in there and wait for Mr. Keith-Westerton.

"You had arranged a signal with Jean—the boathouse lights— so that you would know when the coast was clear. Naturally you wanted to know how the interview had gone. When you saw the signal, you got rid of Miss Sandeau rather clumsily. If it interests you, I may tell you that your lapse from finesse there led to the real trouble. But probably you know that already, since you're an intelligent person.

"You went up to the boathouse, where Jean was waiting for you; and probably both of you were in high glee at the way things had worked out. Another home threatened; another poor devil under the harrow; another girl's happiness wrecked; and some very dirty money on its way to your pocket. Excellent! You went off through the woods, whistling to yourself in pure contentment. Naturally you and Jean would not leave the boathouse together. You might have been seen in company and that would never have done."

Wendover had no difficulty in seeing that under the mask the valet's coolness was ebbing away. This succession of accurate details was evidently more than he had expected; and he was clearly deeply perturbed as to how much Sir Clinton was holding in reserve.

"Your simple enjoyment was disturbed," Sir Clinton went on, with the irony in his tone very slightly enhanced, "for Miss Sandeau overtook you with the news that your confederate was dead. An awkward business, especially as your hands were not quite clean. I'm not analysing your motives, but possibly your affection for Miss Sandeau had something to do with your subsequent actions. She said that she had killed Cincinnati Jean, and she was quite unable to explain the situation—which is hardly surprising.

"You are a clever man, Ferrers, and you seem to be a quick thinker. By the time you got to the boathouse, you had your plan cut and dried. The only people who knew of Jean's presence at the boathouse were yourself, Miss Sandeau, Mr. and Mrs. Keith-Westerton. You and Miss Sandeau could be trusted to keep quiet. Mr. and Mrs. Keith-Westerton would not publish the news; and if Jean simply disappeared, they could be trusted to make no awkward inquiries about her. Ergo, if you could dispose of the body, even temporarily, the whole business would be covered up. That was how it struck you, I think?"

Sir Clinton paused as though he expected to draw a reply from the valet, but Ferrers stared sullenly at the carpet and gave no indication that he had heard. Quite obviously, he was thinking hard.

"How to get rid of the body: that's always a troublesome problem for any one left with a corpse on their hands. In your case, it was simplified considerably. You had the lake. All you needed was a weight to tie to the body so that it would sink. But you knew Mr. Wendover's orderly habits. It wouldn't do to take the first heavy object that came to hand, for he would be almost certain to notice its absence when he visited the boathouse—and that might be on the following morning, for all you could tell. Then the gramophone caught your eye. The motor and horn were heavy enough to act as a temporary sinker. Unless the instrument was actually used, no one would spot that they were missing. So you got a screwdriver from the workshop and unshipped them. You overreached yourself when you pitched the screwdriver into the lake. You ought to have cleaned off any fingerprints and replaced it on its clip. Then you'd have left no trace.

"You picked up the pearls which had scattered themselves over the floor, and you put them in your breast pocket, I should think. You missed one of them. And that was your second mistake. You didn't stuff them well down into your pocket—Mistake Number 3. Then you got the body into the boat and rowed out towards Friar's Point, where you meant to sink the thing in deep water. Most unfortunately, Horncastle happened to be on the shore there and saw fairly well what you were doing. He waited till you were finished and then he shouted to you, I expect. Well, you knew Horncastle. He was a vindictive person. He had good cause to hate both you and Miss Sandeau. There was no chance of persuading him to shut his mouth about what he had seen. But his mouth had to be closed somehow. So over went the boat to the shingle where he was standing."

Sir Clinton's voice dropped as though he were bored by this tale. Then, in a fresh key, he recommenced.

"I'm just going to recall a point of law to you, Ferrers," he said in a businesslike tone. "There are four ways in which a person can be concerned in a felony. The principal in the first degree is a person who commits the actual felony. That's your case in the Horncastle murder. Miss Sandeau is quite free from that charge, you'll be glad to hear. Then there's an accessory before the fact, who procures, advises or aids some one else to commit a felony, but who is not actually present when the crime is done. That's obviously not Miss Sandeau's case—she did not plan this Horncastle affair with you beforehand, obviously. Then there's a principal in the second degree, who helps at the actual moment when the felony was committed. That person is liable to the same penalty as the principal in the first degree. And, finally, there's an accessory after the fact, who, knowing that a felony has been committed, helps or succours the felon in such a way as to assist him to escape from justice. The penalty for that is a light one, and in certain circumstances the accused may get off scot-free."

Sir Clinton paused and glanced for a moment at Louise Sandeau, who was listening intently to what he said. She seemed to be making an intense effort to follow the bearing which these statements had upon her own case.

"Now," continued Sir Clinton, "so far as the death of Cincinnati Jean is concerned, I don't think there's a case against Miss Sandeau. No jury would look at it. You understand that, Ferrers?"

The valet looked up for a moment and nodded.

"The Horncastle murder is in a different class," Sir Clinton pointed out. "As things stand, I don't see how Miss Sandeau can escape being treated as a principal in the second degree. She was on the spot with you in the boat when you went over to Horncastle. It's a question whether she helped or not. I'm using 'helped' in its widest sense, of course; I don't mean that she actually pulled a trigger, or anything of that kind."

He paused to let this sink well home.

"There's only one person who can clear her: yourself. She hasn't given you away. I've been careful not to question her on the Horncastle murder. You've nothing to gain or lose in the affair; for I may as well tell you that I've enough evidence now to convict you out of hand. You're done for, Ferrers. But there's no use in dragging the girl down with you if she's innocent. You can clear her easily enough if you'll make a plain statement. Think it over. I won't hurry you."

But Louise had grasped Sir Clinton's meaning clearly enough. Suddenly she threw herself on the ground at Ferrers' knees.

"Oh, Danny! Please tell them the truth; please, please tell them. You know I wasn't there when you shot him. You know I was taking the boat back across the lake, then. Tell them I'd no idea you were going to kill him. Tell them! Tell them, Danny! I can't bear to die. I'd nothing to do with it, nothing, nothing. I never said anything against you. They had it all ready before they questioned me at all. Please, Danny! Oh, I'm so terrified!"

Ferrers lifted his face and looked across at Sir Clinton over the girl's head.

"That's torn it!" he said. "But anyhow, I wouldn't have let her suffer."

His hand went out in a caress to the girl's shoulder. She had dropped her head on his knee and was sobbing hysterically.

"It's all right, Louie. I won't let you down."

He soothed her for a moment or two, but she showed no signs of mastering her emotion.

"Here," said Ferrers, at last, turning to the priest, "you take her away. I can't stand much more of this. I can trust you to look after her; she thinks a lot of you. And you know just how it was. She told me she'd confessed it all to you."

For a moment, Wendover caught a glimpse of a new Abbé Goron, as the priest gently led the weeping girl from the room.

"And now," Ferrers said, with a fair attempt at coolness, "you've jockied me fairly. If you don't mind my saying so, you must be a damned smart man, for I thought I'd got away with it. I can take my gruel, so long as you leave Louie alone. She'd no share in it. I'll make a statement that'll put that clear enough. Where do you want me to begin?"

"You can give us the whole story from the time you left the house, if you like; or, if you'd prefer it, the Inspector will write out the gist of what I told you, up to the point when you pushed off in the boat, and you can sign that as a voluntary statement, after you've read it over. If you do that, then you can start afresh at that stage now."

"All right," Ferrers agreed. "I'll do anything to keep the girl out of it. The time we got into the boat, you say. We pushed out on to the lake with the body. I thought she'd killed Jean in a fit of passion, you know. I hope that's right, and that you really aren't going to touch her for that business."

Sir Clinton's nod reassured him.

"That's a relief, anyway. Well, we pushed out towards what I knew was deepish water and we put the body overside. It was bright moonlight, and I was a bit nervous about being seen, at the last moment, of course. Then, just as we'd got rid of the thing, Horncastle came out on to the shingle and called over to know what we were playing at. I hoped he hadn't really seen what we were after; but in any case, he was dangerous. He'd only got to mention what he'd seen, and somebody would have wanted to drag the lake, just to see what we'd been sinking.

"I rowed ashore. I hadn't got any clear idea in my mind except that Horncastle's mouth had to be shut somehow and shut for good. As soon as the boat grounded, I jumped ashore, passed my gloves to Louie, and told her to take the boat back. I didn't want her mixed up with Horncastle. We'd had trouble enough with him before. She took the oars and I pushed the boat off, with Horncastle standing grinning beside me. He was a malicious devil, and as soon as I turned round and saw his face clearly, I knew it was him or us—nothing else would do.

"I wanted Louie to get well away, so I held him in talk for a minute or two. He just stood and jeered. He'd seen the whole affair and he meant to go off to the police, straight, and give the whole show away. I was thinking hard; in my line you have to have quick wits and keep them handy. He had his gun. If I gave him half a chance, he'd have me at a disadvantage. I'd Louie to think about. I took him when he wasn't expecting it, got him fair on the point of the jaw, and down he went on his back on the shingle, a devil of a smash. He lay there, clean knocked out, and I expect he hit his head as he went down. I'd got him where I wanted him. I've never done quicker thinking than I did then. The whole thing seemed to jump into my mind.

"I lifted him up; I expect it was when I was stooping over him that these damned pearls slipped out of my pocket, for when I counted them afterwards, some of them were missing and I hadn't the full number. I hoisted him up the bank, after I'd made a scrape on the earth so that it would look as if he'd slipped and shot himself. By that time a cloud had come over the moon and I had to strike matches to make sure of what I was doing. I shot him with his own gun. Then I cleaned my fingerprints off it. After that I walked over to the road and on the way I tramped clean through a water splash in the dark and soaked my shoes through and through. Then I went home through the Grange grounds."

He paused, as though thinking that this was sufficient.

"Go on," Sir Clinton suggested. "You haven't told us how you tried to cover up your trail."

"Oh, you mean Mr. Keith-Westerton's shoes and so on? Well, next morning you can guess how I was taken aback when you dropped straight in here. That was a bit too close a shot; but luckily I'd got in first. I didn't know what track I might have left in the dark; and I thought it would be just as well to confuse things a bit. So I suppressed my own wet shoes, put Mr. Keith-Westerton's pair under the tap till they were soaked, inside and out, and then handed them over to be dried. That was before you came.

"Then the pearls began to look important. I'd hidden the balance of the string; I'll show you the place, so that Mr. Keith-Westerton won't lose by that. Of course, I knew pretty well what was behind Mrs. Keith-Westerton's trip to town. Jean had told me all about the interview, and the rest was easy. Then you put a guard on the boathouse and prevented me fishing up Jean's body at night. I'd meant to do that and then take it away in the car, and dump it in some field, far enough away. If I'd managed that, there'd have been no detectable motive in the Horncastle affair and you'd have been side-tracked. But you did me there, by putting on the guard and then by fishing up the body yourself. Once Jean turned up again, the trouble was doubled; because, you see, Louie was mixed up in the affair directly. She'd killed Jean, she said.

"Well, on thinking it out, it seemed to me the best thing to do was to give you a fresh tree to bark up; and only two other people could be dragged into the business on that side. If the bigamy affair could be disclosed somehow, then there would be a fine trail straight to Mr. Keith-Westerton. So I put a couple of the pearls into his coat pocket—you seemed keen on the pearls and I knew they'd attract attention if they were found, for the whole village was buzzing with talk about them. And old Mrs. Tetbury always cleared the pockets of any clothes she bought, for she told me she did. So along with the pearls, I put in that newspaper cutting about the supposed death of Mr. Keith-Westerton's wife. That was a bit of evidence that Jean faked herself, and she gave me a copy. It was a real advertisement. She'd sent a dying woman into hospital under the name of Keith-Westerton, all right. Very thorough, Jean."

"You forgot one thing, though," Sir Clinton pointed out. "Mr. Keith-Westerton's fingerprints weren't on that cutting, as they would have been if he'd handled it recently."

Ferrers had recovered his coolness.

"That was damned smart, if you don't mind my saying it," he said, with no malice in his tone. "I didn't expect to be up against you, or I'd have been more careful, I guess. All I wanted was to bring out the bigamy affair and make it look as if Mr. Keith-Westerton had a motive for getting rid of Jean. I didn't expect you'd be able to prove it; but I thought it would put you clean off the scent of Louie and me. And that's the whole story."

CHAPTER XV: THE FOCUS OF SUSPICION

"A TRICKY business?" Sir Clinton echoed Wendover's description as they sat with the Inspector on the boat-house balcony, later in the day. "Yes, you might fairly call it that, in both senses of the phrase. Unofficially, I needn't keep up the George Washington pose. In dealing with a smart lad like Ferrers, it's worse than useless to be overscrupulous."

He took out a cigarette, tapped it to settle the tobacco, and then turned to Severn.

"You want to know how we groped our way through the affair? I'm not using the editorial 'we'. You contributed as much as I did, in the way of gathering information."

"Yes, but you put me on the road to most of it, sir," the Inspector amplified, honestly.

Sir Clinton waved that aside.

"You know what we got out of the Horncastle affair at the very start," he continued, giving the Inspector no time for further discussion of relative credits. "The man who killed the keeper was socially a cut above a farm labourer; he was a bit of a boxer; and his shoes must have been soaked with water. And in addition, we had the pearls, which seemed to mark the case out from some ordinary village affair.

"The murderer came on the scene either in a boat

259

or via the shingle along the shore. It was a toss-up between the two routes so far as evidence went; but the boathouse seemed likely to yield results quickest, so we went there."

He glanced at Wendover.

"Your fad for tidiness served us in good stead, then, over the missing screwdriver. A man doesn't steal a screwdriver unless he has a use for it; so clearly enough something had been unscrewed somewhere. It might have been somewhere outside the boathouse, of course; but the chances were that the unscrewed article had been on the premises. So far as visible things went, there wasn't anything that fitted the case. Then I began to think of screws that weren't directly visible; and the gramophone seemed to fill the bill. One could unscrew parts of it, inside the case, without betraying anything at the first glance. So I looked under the lid and found the horn and motor missing. And then we ran across the pearl on the chair, which showed we were on the right track.

"A gramophone motor and horn can't be used in conjunction with each other for any ordinary purpose. The only thing that's common to them is their weight. It seemed a fair guess that what the thief wanted was some heavy article. But he could have found heavy articles lying about: anchors, spare lengths of chain, and things like that. Why didn't he take them instead of bothering to unscrew the inside of the gramophone? Obviously because they'd have been missed at once by an owner with a fad for tidiness. So I inferred that quite possibly the thief had some knowledge of Mr. Wendover's love of order; and if this were so, then that thief must be somebody who knew Mr. Wend-over or knew about his methods."

Sir Clinton glanced rather impishly at the Squire as he explained this.

"The thief wanted something heavy. What for? Well, there was the lake right under the windows. One couldn't help thinking of a sinker, of some sort. It didn't seem pushing things too far to assume that the gramophone works had been tied to some object or other and the whole contraption sunk in the lake. And that led on to the reason for taking out a boat, that night; and so one gets a glimmering of the connection between the boathouse and Horncastle's body. I put that aside for the moment, but I made up my mind I'd have a shot at dragging the lake on spec, just to see if I was right.

"Then we found that vanity bag in the boat; and in the same boat another pearl turned up. But because two things turn up in the same place, it doesn't mean they have much connection with each other. I've got a driving licence and a five-pound note in my pocket-book; but that doesn't show that they're related to each other to any marked extent. What the pearl did show was that we were on the right track; pearls in the boathouse, pearls in the boat, pearls beside Horncastle's body: all from the same string. But Mrs. Keith-Westerton's bag might have been left in the boat by accident, for all one could tell. It had to be taken into account, but it proved nothing by itself.

"But one thing *was* certain. Whoever murdered Horncastle had a key of the boathouse. Well, who had a key, or who had the opportunity of forging a key? Mr. Wendover's servants are above suspicion. The only other keys were in the hands of the Keith-Westertons. A call at the Dower House was obviously necessary; and Mrs. Keith-Westerton's bag gave us the excuse for going there. By hook or crook, we had to find out something about the Keith-Westerton *ménage;* for somewhere in that group lay the only chance of a boathouse key, authorised or unauthorised.

"Before we got there, that Salvationist fellow bobbed up. A rum cove on a peculiar errand at that hour of the morning. My impression was that he was a genuine fanatic. There was no clear connection between him and the murder. Barring the fact that he had been a wrong 'un in earlier days, there was nothing of interest in him; and he let out his previous character himself, which did not look suspicious, to say the least of it.

"We went to the Dower House, and there we picked up a good deal more than I'd expected, I admit. Mrs. Keith-Westerton's hurried flight . . . I don't suppose you made any more of it than I did myself, and that was exactly nothing at the moment when we got the news.

"Then we interviewed Keith-Westerton. What struck me at once was that he seemed to think we'd got something against him; and yet when the Horncastle murder was mentioned as the reason for our visit, he was obviously relieved. A good actor might have carried off a thing like that; but Keith-Westerton's one of the poorest actors I've seen. The inference is obvious. Keith-Westerton was guilty of something or other, but it most certainly wasn't the Horncastle murder. In fact, I'd have been prepared to stake a fair amount that he'd never heard of the Horncastle affair when we dropped on him out of the clouds. But when you put his hang-dog looks in relation with his wife's flight, it gave something worth thinking over.

"What that something might be, came out very shortly. We heard about that telephone call in a woman's voice, and the effect it produced on Keith-Westerton. Happy family; incursion of strange woman; sudden departure of wife: there's no great difficulty in fitting that together, normally. But in this case, at first, it seemed that Mrs. Keith-Westerton had no obvious means of learning anything about the lady of the telephone. She hadn't seen her husband after he went out; she'd received no message; and yet she decamped before her husband got home again.

"The necklace suggested something, there. She had it on at dinner. In the course of the evening, its fragments got distributed between the boathouse, the boat, and the shingle beside Horncastle. On the face of it, she might have been at the boathouse—her bag had been left there, either at night or in the afternoon.

"Then came that little scullery maid's evidence—that Keith-Westerton's shoes were soaked. We saw them; they were soaked in a way that was quite beyond any mere wetting on dewy grass. But if Keith-Westerton's manner went for anything, he was not the murderer of Horncastle; and therefore he was

not the man who trudged through the water splash.
Now you can soak a pair of shoes under a domestic
tap, if you happen to have access to the shoes. Who
had access to Keith-Westerton's shoes? His man
Ferrers, or perhaps some one else on the domestic
staff. But no valet or any other servant would play
that sort of joke idly. Who knew that it was an important point that Keith-Westerton's shoes were
soaked? Only one person besides ourselves—the actual murderer. Therefore, if Keith-Westerton himself wasn't the murderer—which was neither proved
nor disproved at that point—then the murderer was
either Ferrers or the chauffeur.

"Any one of the three—Keith-Westerton, Ferrers,
and the chauffeur—would have fitted the character-
istics of the murderer as we knew them: good physique, some knowledge of boxing, and middle class at
least in the social scale. I didn't let myself be swayed
much, one way or the other, by this kind of reasoning; but obviously it made me try to see how things
fitted together with regard to the three men.

"Keith-Westerton's tale of his night's doings was
obviously a pack of lies. That was a pity from his
point of view. As to the chauffeur, if he was lying
about the earlier part of the evening, then the house-
parlourmaid was lying also. Again, if Ferrers was lying about his movements, then the French maid was
lying also. Altogether, it looked as though truth might
be hard to find amongst the taradiddles.

"The chauffeur came out of it best, for his story
about Mrs. Keith-Westerton's departure from the
garage rang true enough—the more so since we might

obviously be able to check it sooner or later. That fixed him as being at the Dower House up to half-past eleven—if we could check his yarn; and if he were the murderer, he'd have had to move fairly quick before midnight. Also, it was hard to see how he could have got hold of the necklace. If Mrs. Keith-Westerton left it behind in her room and he stole it from there after she had gone, that meant a few minutes occupied. Even by the short cut, it's ten minutes' walk from the Dower House to the boathouse. Add that to the time it would take to unscrew the gramophone parts, and you run the thing very fine indeed, if Hyde was the man who shot Horncastle at midnight.

"Finally, there was Ferrers. He could have soaked those shoes easily enough; and the scullery maid vouched that she got them from him, so they'd passed through his hands. Keith-Westerton is a careless type, so there was an obvious possibility that Ferrers had more than one opportunity of taking a wax impression of the boathouse key, from which he could get another one filed. In fact, in that line a valet has chances which no other person could have. Ferrers might very easily have picked up information about Mr. Wendover's orderly habits.

"Then, again, Ferrers had to admit that he was out very late on the night of the murder; but he relied on Louise Sandeau for his alibi. He was quite frank about his row with Horncastle; but that was a thing which might have come to light anyhow, and his openness might have been forced on him as the best policy, if he were the criminal. Better to admit it voluntarily than have it cropping up from an independent source, later on. As to his relations with the Sandeau girl, any one could see at a glance that he was enamoured of her; his whole behaviour pointed to that. He and she had far more motive for supporting each other's stories than the other pair, the chauffeur and the parlourmaid, had. But if Ferrers was lying, then the French maid's evidence was suspect immediately. At that stage in the affair, if I'd been asked what I thought about the chance of Ferrers' guilt, I'd have taken refuge in the Scots verdict: 'Not Proven.' It wasn't certain that he was the man; but it was quite certain that he wasn't cleared.

"Then friend Sawtry bobbed up again and supplied us with a fresh link in the chain. After we had done with him, we knew Mrs. Keith-Westerton had been at the boathouse and had gone straight from there to the Abbé Goron's house. And with that in hand, it didn't take much finesse to discover that she'd gone to the Abbé to make a confession. Obviously something had happened at the boathouse to give her a bad jar: either she'd committed a sin there, or else she'd discovered something which made it impossible—with her Catholic principles—to go on living with her husband.

"The facts we collected at Ambledown showed plainly that she wasn't on the spot when the murder was done. Further, the Abbé's evidence about her movements fitted neatly with the chauffeur's story about seeing her drive away from the garage at 11.30. That cleared her in the matter of the actual murder and it also established Hyde as a credible witness.

"Why had she gone off in such a hurry? Well, there was no definite evidence; but when you put her doings into relationship with the woman's voice on the 'phone, and Keith-Westerton's behaviour, it didn't seem stretching things much to assume that there was a woman in the business. Further, Mrs. Keith-Westerton's a Catholic, therefore she wasn't going to bring a divorce action, no matter what information had fallen into her hands at the boathouse. And my rigid friend the Abbé aproved of what she had done. One couldn't help feeling that, somewhere, there was a screw loose in the Keith-Westerton matrimonial affairs, and that Mrs. Keith-Westerton had just discovered it—at the boathouse. But she didn't learn it from her husband, or she wouldn't have needed to write him that note. Whence I inferred that probably at the boathouse she met the woman in the case. And that made me quite determined to drag the lake and see what was tied to the gramophone motor. The abandoned car in the wood made it practically certain that some person had come on the scene from outside, that night, and had not gone away again.

"Then you had the evidence of that amusing person, Mr. Oliver Thewles. It built up the picture a bit further, but the really important point, to me at least, was the fact that there was a boat on the lake at the very moment when the fatal shot was fired.

"Of course, we saw at the very start that there were two people mixed up in the proceedings which ended in Horncastle's death: one of them—the actual murderer—made the track over the grass, whilst the other party took the boat back to the boathouse.

The point of the boat incident was this: it seemed to offer a chance of driving a wedge in between the two confederates, if one of them was an innocent accomplice.

"Immediately after that, we fished up the body of Cincinnati Jean; and thanks to you, Inspector, we got all the facts about her very quickly indeed. When these were filled in, the main outline of the whole business was clear enough, so far as the Keith-Westertons were concerned. Further, somebody had supplied Jean with the topography of the district and had written to her suggesting the boathouse as a suitable rendezvous with Keith-Westerton. The only person who would do that was a confederate who had his own key of the boathouse. Put the whole data together, and suspicion lights pretty hard on Ferrers, with Louise Sandeau as his accomplice.

"The reappearance of Mrs. Keith-Westerton and the marriage ceremony both dropped neatly into place in the scheme. It was obvious that Keith-Westerton had been trapped into going through a form of marriage with Cincinnati Jean in earlier times, and that once she was out of the way, the thing had to be regularised. Take the pearl we found on Jean's body, and it was obvious that she and Mrs. Keith-Westerton had met at the boathouse, where Jean had scored double by blackmailing the wife as well as the husband, and had taken the pearl necklace as an advance or as a pledge of payment. A child could have fitted in the missing bits in that part of the puzzle.

"Every criminal makes one bad mistake, at least, if you're going to have a chance of catching him. Up to that point, in this case, there was only one mistake —the nonreplacement of the screwdriver on its clip. But Ferrers was finding that we were too slow for his liking, so he decided to spur us up a bit and the way he chose to do it was to plant some pearls and the newspaper cutting in the pocket of the torn coat and sell it to Mrs. Tetbury. The cutting was to supply clear evidence of a motive involving Keith-Westerton in the murder of Cincinnati Jean. But where Ferrers slipped a cog was in forgetting that Keith-Westerton's fingerprints weren't on that cutting and that therefore Keith-Westerton hadn't handled it.

"That move made it practically certain that Ferrers was a party to the blackmailing scheme; and if he was in that, his general character wasn't good enough to make his evidence reliable. The bother was to get definite proof that he had killed Horncastle. And the only way around that difficulty was to drive a wedge between him and Louise Sandeau, who evidently had been the person who brought back the boat at the time of the murder. I gauged that he was fond of her, very fond. The question was, how fond was he? To what lengths would he go to save the girl?

"The P.M. evidence showed that Jean's death wasn't a sure case of murder. In her state of health, it might quite well have been accidental entirely. It wasn't likely that Ferrers would quarrel with Jean: their interests ran together in the affair. But suppose the interview with Mrs. Keith-Westerton and the other one with Keith-Westerton had strained Jean's emotions a bit, she would hardly be in a fit state to stand a third scene with some one who would be less restrained than the Keith-Westertons. If that person were Louise Sandeau, then one could see at once why Ferrers would take a risk to hush the whole affair up. And no other explanation seemed to fit the facts, so far as I could see.

"In that case, there was a very fair chance of driving a wedge in between the two accomplices, provided that Ferrers was really deeply in love with the girl. And he must have been, on the face of it, or he wouldn't have murdered Horncastle merely to shield her—which was how I read the facts. I made up my mind to stake everything on that. If it failed, we were no worse off than before. If it came off, then we had him beyond any dispute.

"The first thing was to get the pearl necklace connected definitely with Jean. The only person who could prove that was Mrs. Keith-Westerton, so we tackled her and got what was wanted. Then came the problem of the other two. Louise Sandeau's a Catholic, and I guessed that she would make her confession to the Abbé Goron. He'd been attached to the family and he was one of her own people, to whom she could confess in her native language— a much easier business than trying to make things clear to an English priest. I've a considerable respect for the Abbé's force of character. I was pretty sure that with his eye on her that girl would be more likely to tell the truth—since he already knew the whole story and could check her statements, though he couldn't give us his information. So I invited him to be there when I examined her; naturally it was easy enough to plead that she ought to have a fellow countryman to watch over her interests.

"I stopped her before she got to the Horncastle episode for two reasons. First, it wasn't fair to let her incriminate herself if she was guilty. It might have had a bad effect at a trial—poor girl, foreigner, bullied by brutal police in a strange land, didn't know the language and made mistakes . . . you can guess what a sharp lawyer might have made of that. And, secondly, I wanted to leave her free to tell Ferrers that she hadn't given him away. I didn't want to risk his feeling that she'd let him down. That might just have tipped the scale in his mind. But when she was able to protest her loyalty . . . well, what could he do? He'd been prepared to kill a man to shield her, as he thought; he had to go through with it, if he was going to save her. That was made pretty clear. We'd have got him in any case, I think; but it was surer to get him to tell his story."

THE END

>>> If you've enjoyed this book and would like to discover more great vintage crime and thriller titles, as well as the most exciting crime and thriller authors writing today, visit: >>>

The Murder Room
Where Criminal Minds Meet

themurderroom.com